# HUNDRED PERCENT

## by Karen Romano Young

chronicle books · san francisco

Library of Congress Cataloging-in-Publication Data:

Names: Young, Karen Romano, author.

Title: Hundred percent / by Karen Romano Young.

Description: San Francisco : Chronicle Books, [2016] |

Summary: Christine Gouda, called Tink, and her best friend Jackie are entering sixth grade, and suddenly everything seems awkward and just plain wrong—boys are behaving differently, clothes do not fit the way they should, long term friendships suddenly seem tenuous, and most of all she needs a new nickname because "Tink" just does not fit anymore.

LCCN 2015047481 | ISBN 9781452138909 (alk. paper)

LCSH: Sixth grade (Education)—Juvenile fiction. | Best Friends—Juvenile fiction. Friendship—Juvenile fiction. | Nicknames—Juvenile fiction. | Families—Juvenile fiction. | CYAC: Schools—Fiction. | Best friends—Fiction. | Friendship—Fiction. Nicknames—Fiction. | Family life—Fiction.

LCC PZ7.Y8665 Hu 2016 | DDC [Fic]—dc23 LC record available at
http://lccn.loc.gov/2015047481

Manufactured in China.

Illustrations by Natalie Andrewson.
Design by Kayla Ferriera.
Typeset in Scala.

"Never Die Young" (James Taylor). © 1988 Country Road Music.
Used By Permission. All Rights Reserved.

10 9 8 7 6 5 4 3 2 1

Chronicle Books LLC
680 Second Street
San Francisco, California 94107

Chronicle Books—we see things differently.
Become part of our community at www.chroniclekids.com.

for Barbara

*We were ring-around-the-rosy children,*
*they were circles around the sun.*
*Never give up, never slow down,*
*never grow old, never ever die young.*
*Synchronized with the rising moon,*
*even with the evening star,*
*they were true love written in stone,*
*they were never alone,*
*they were never that far apart . . .*
*. . . Hold them up, don't let them fall.*

—JAMES TAYLOR

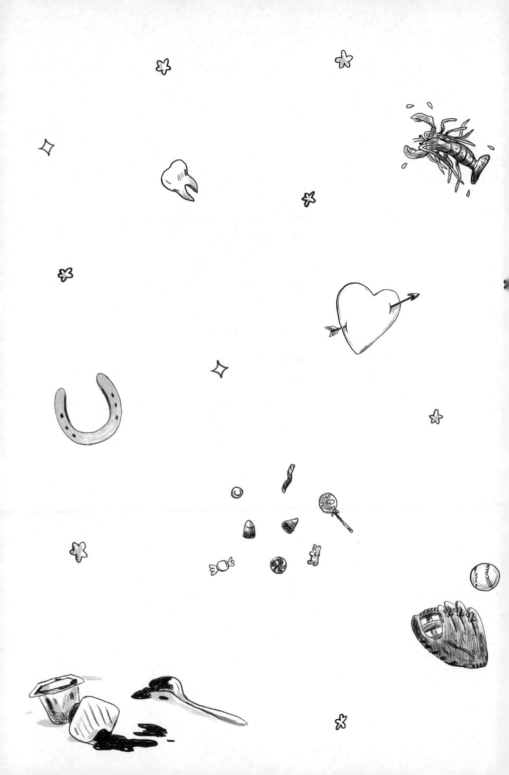

# 1
# Two Words
(school starts)

In late August, Tink got a new name. Her best friend, Jackie, renamed her. This was after Tink realized that none of her school clothes fit and her mother took her on a hellish shopping trip involving two sizes up, three bras-for-the-very-first-time, and four arguments about style that had both Mom and Tink in tears. On the way home, Tink convinced her mother to drop her at Jackie's with all six shopping bags, so they could have a fashion show.

Jackie had already been shopping—not because she had grown, but because she had insisted, and her mother said yes because Jackie was an only child. That was what Tink's mother said. She couldn't do as much when she had three girls between grades three and six to outfit, plus a first grade boy, all growing like weeds. Tink was just grateful that her mother had found two hours to take her shopping alone, without the whole circus. You could thank the bras for that.

The differences in Jackie and Tink's appearances in their first-day outfits, viewed in the mirror, worried both of them. Jackie was smaller, lighter, and, face it, flatter. Tink was too big. Tall, and "getting a figure," their mothers said. It was awkward.

Last year on the first day of fifth grade, they'd both worn flowered, ruffled skirts and pale blue T-shirts—twinsie best friends staking each other out, as if the kids they'd been in school with since kindergarten hadn't figured out that they were a pair. But this year the best they could do for twinsies was jean skirts and red polo shirts, even if Jackie's polo was from the boys' department and Tink's was borrowed from her mother. The only way they still matched was with their curly brown hair. Side by side they stood, Jackie on her toes and Tink slumping, and neither could tell which one was the problem. Neither, you might say. Or maybe both?

That night in the dark, Jackie voiced it. "I wish I needed a bra. I mean, I'll wear one, it's sixth grade, but I wish I had—"

"—the chest to pin it on?" finished Tink. It was the punch line of the jokey insult that went, "What do you want: a medal? Or the chest to pin it on?" Bushwhack had said that last year every five minutes.

"*So* not funny," said Jackie, not just meaning Bushwhack, although it was him, too—a boy Tink thought was actually quite funny. "I'm immature compared to you, Tinker."

"Maybe I'm too mature."

"You're lucky. Well, I make up for it in charm and charisma." So Jackie's mother said, Tink knew, and she was right.

"Everybody loves you," Tink agreed.

"Do you think Keith Kallinka will?" asked Jackie.

"Sure to," said Tink, as expected. "Do you think Will Wheeler will love me?"

"Sure to or he's a dodo," said Jackie.

Then Tink raised the question that was on her mind. "I'm too tall to be a Tinker Bell."

"Bess says your mom should have never saddled you with that name," said Jackie.

"Bess?"

"That's what I'm calling her now. James's kids get to, so why shouldn't I?"

Tink would never have gotten away with calling her parents Stevie and Tom.

That night was when Jackie worked out a whole new persona for Tink, also known as Christine Bernadette Gouda, to go with her new wardrobe. When school began, Jackie announced, Tink would be Chris, who was ever so much more grown-up and stylish after her summer than the girl the class had last seen in June.

Of course Tink hadn't done anything to *become* more stylish or grown-up all summer. What she had actually done all summer was hang with Jackie, whose mother had a new boyfriend and let Jackie sleep over more than usual because of it. Except for brief visits to grandmothers' houses in Maryland and New York (Tink) and Massachusetts (Jackie), they never got out of Connecticut, and didn't even get out of town except for occasional trips to the mall. They rode their bikes to the beach, walked to Clampett's for music magazines for Jackie and *Mad* magazines for Tink, and made up an elaborate bouncing game with a tennis ball against Tink's garage door, because if they just played the real handball rules Tink looked up in the library, Jackie got bored and wouldn't play.

And then Jackie had gone shopping and bumped into Maggie and Mitzie, two girls in their class, and uncharacteristically bought a pair of pants covered in tiny whales, which made Tink still more uncomfortable, since they were out of budget for a girl with a stay-at-home bookkeeper mother and a go-to-work housebuilder father. She had a vision of everybody showing up at school in clothes with tiny sea animals on them.

Into the dark of Jackie's room, Tink said, "But am I—"

Jackie said, "What?"

Tink wouldn't say until Jackie hit her with a pillow and then sat on the pillow and then tickled her, because Tink was embarrassed. But at last she opened her mouth and finished her question: "—pretty?"

Jackie considered the question for long minutes, even turned on the light to look at Tink's face, and finally said, "Cute. Maybe *becoming* pretty. Or maybe just going straight to grown-up gorgeous." To Jackie, grown-up *was* gorgeous.

"Thank you, Jacqueline," whispered Tink when it was dark again.

"Don't thank me, Chris," said Jackie. "Just make a little wish on my behalf for Keith Kallinka."

But Tink, who secretly thought Keith was sort of a fool, despite being the most crushed-on boy in the class, turned her thoughts instead to Will Wheeler, the second most crushed-on.

When school started, Tink told Ms. Cho that her nickname was Chris. But, two weeks into September, nobody was calling her that yet but Jackie and Ms. Cho. They still called her Tink, or Hundred Percent, a different nickname she'd been given, whether she liked it or not, by Bushwhack. Hundred Percent wasn't as good a name as Chris, but maybe it wasn't as bad as Tink.

"Bushwah, Chris!" Jackie would say, if she heard that. *Bushwah* was their sixth grade word, invented by Matt Alva, whose nickname (invented by himself) was Bushwhack. His friends were called the Farmers, but they were just a bunch of dorky boys with boring clothes, not the kind girls had crushes on. They had a lot of funny jokes, though, and Bushwhack made up words and insults. Yes, he was the same Bushwhack with the congratulations joke about the medal and the chest to pin it on. He also had these jokes in a situation where someone was wrong:

Close but no cigarette.

OR

Put another quarter in and try again . . . sucker.


AND, in a nonhumorous situation:


THAT'S as funny . . .

> . . . as a screen door in a submarine.
> . . . as a gum machine in a lockjaw ward.
> . . . as a rubber crutch.


There were a lot more endings, but they weren't what he was into this year. This year he was into insults.

In math Bushwhack sat right across the aisle from Tink. He didn't seem to have to think about math much. He sat there making up names to call people and muttering them under his breath to crack up the people who sat near him. Since sixth grade had started, Bushwhack and the Farmers had the class saying, "You eraser!" to each other, or "You combination lock!" Instead of getting mad at being called a name, the kids would just laugh.

Also this year, Bushwhack made up saying *bushwah*. It was such a spectacular word (and almost rude) that everyone in the sixth grade picked it up, even Jackie. It was so almost-rude that Ms. Cho and Mr. Bergman, the other sixth grade teacher, had already outlawed it, saying the kids couldn't use any words that weren't in the dictionary, so then they started just saying, "You know what Bushwhack would say." That got shortened (because the teachers weren't sure how they felt about the name Bushwhack) to two words: "You know . . ."

When they began getting teacher stink-eyes from saying that, they changed it to saying "Two words." That's what Tink said, because she was the kind of girl who didn't get in trouble. She'd never even gotten detention, and she wasn't about to start for one word, even as good a word as *bushwah*.

Jackie didn't bother saying bushwah to anyone but Tink. Maybe she didn't want Bushwhack to know she knew he existed. She smiled in her A+ way at the teachers and said flirty, charming things to Will Wheeler or Keith Kallinka. She was the one who started the whole "Roll Over" game. And the "Roll Over" game was what led to Will breaking his tooth.

Tink had never dreamed that today, in the second week of sixth grade, she'd be lying on the ground with the cutest boys in the sixth grade, rolling in the grass and singing.

What she dreamed of, when she dreamed of Will Wheeler, was what happens to Wendy in chapter one of *Peter Pan and Wendy*:

The window of Tink's room is ajar. Outside is her favorite kind of weather, warm and windy all at once. The wind whistles and smells of fall and grass and leaves and horse chestnuts. She is lying in bed, almost asleep, wearing a long white nightgown, with her long red hair in a long silky braid. (Just so you recall, Tink didn't have long red hair. Tink's hair was short and brown and curly.)

The window opens, and someone comes in. It is a second-floor window, so how does this happen? The boy who comes in can fly, that's how. He flies around Tink's room bumping into things, making the wind chimes chime, trying to wake her up. He needs his shadow sewn back on, and only she has the magic to sew it. It has come loose from his body, and he's lost without it. If she sews it, he'll take her flying to Neverland.

So she gets up out of bed and takes a needle from her pincushion. (She's the kind of girl who sews, which Tink is not.) She threads it with a strand of silver-gray thread, and she begins to sew. With her fingers she touches lightly along the back of the boy's head (she pictures Will's gold-brown hair), the back of his neck, his shoulders, down the backs of his legs to his feet. Somehow she doesn't hurt him sewing his shadow on. All those needle pricks, and not a drop of blood.

"Bushwah, Chris," Jackie would say to Tink, if she knew.

It was not the word Tink's mother would say. She'd have two words of her own for it, two words she said often lately. "Boy-crazy," she'd say. "This is when it all starts. Sixth grade."

★ ★ ★

Sixth grade was the first time Tink noticed that Will Wheeler had eyes of a color that was hard to name.

Sixth grade was also the first time a boy ever barked at her. You can't know how it feels if it has never happened to you.

It had happened last week, the first week of school, when she was riding her bike home up the hill, sweaty and wobbling. Keith Kallinka was riding by smooth and cool on the bus.

"Woof!" He barked out the window at her, and somebody else laughed, and barked along. She couldn't see the other person who barked. "Woof!" One known barker. One unknown barker.

Then the bus passed Jackie, who had already reached the top of the hill. They didn't bark at Jackie. They whistled.

"It's just as asinine. Boys are so immature compared to girls," Jackie complained when they got to her house. Her mother, Bess, just nodded. Bess didn't say anything, but she looked at Jackie the way Tink's mother looked at Tink when teachers talked about IQ, a way that made it clear Bess wasn't surprised Jackie had been whistled at.

Tink didn't say anything either. She knew Jackie was just as smart as she was, maybe smarter about some things the way Tink was smarter about others, but on the same level. But now she was realizing that other people thought

Jackie was pretty, while she, Tink, was something else. *Cute,* Jackie had said, because she loved Tink, but was that really true?

Tink wondered how it felt to hear whistling, now that she knew how it felt to hear barking. She kept thinking of all the things she could have done: yelled back "Bushwah!" or barked back or given the bus the finger. But she hadn't had the nerve. At the time it happened, she had been too busy pretending she hadn't heard to do anything at all. Anyway, she didn't want those boys to think she minded being barked at, any more than Jackie minded being whistled at. Even if she did mind, more than she wanted to admit.

What she *wanted* was a boy coming in her window at night, a hazel-eyed boy, someone who would say, "Only you. Only you have what I need." And she guessed something like that had happened today after recess when Will hit his mouth on the water fountain and was bleeding, a private moment when she alone could help him. She ran fast past everyone else into the girls' room—it was right there, next to the fountain—and grabbed paper towels and wet them under the faucet and brought them out and held them to his mouth. Anyone else could have done it, but he asked only her.

*Hazel* was a word she'd read in one of her romance novels. Her mother said it described those kinds of eyes that were half green, half brown. In Will's case it also meant speckled with gold. Hazel was what Tink thought—and kind of how she had felt at lunch today, a little mixed up, a little sparkly—when she looked at Will across the table where she sat with Jackie and the other cool kids. Tink wasn't cool, but they had let her sit there with them, because of Jackie.

She had imagined other things about Peter Pan besides sewing his shadow. She had dreams of him rescuing her as Wendy when she was on the pirate ship walking the plank, or rescuing her as Tiger Lily when she was about to be burned at the stake. The weird thing was, it wasn't the being rescued that intrigued her so much as the idea of rescue. Sometimes she imagined that *she* was the rescuer. But it was also nice to think that some boy might care enough to rescue her, and not just fly by and laugh or bark, but to put his life at risk.

This year in their class it was as if there were a circle of people playing Ring Around the Rosy and everybody who wasn't holding hands was outside the ring. Some of the outside people formed little groups of their own, but not enough to make a circle. Most of them were just in little pairs or triangles. Some were alone, just dots, loners, and leftovers.

Jackie was in the circle (Tink had been right about the whale pants being a clue), and she always brought Tink in, even if the person on Tink's other side—Maggie or Mitzie,

Keith or Will—was barely willing to hold on to Tink's pinky finger. That loose hand on the non-Jackie side let Tink turn, so she could see the outsiders. Sometimes things happened to make her want to let go of Jackie's hand and step out of the ring, such as the antics of the Farmers, who were in some wacky parallelogram, a clump of other boy dots—six or seven on any day—that Bushwhack had magnetized and named.

Tink—no, Chris—didn't want to be a dot of any kind. She wouldn't let go of Jackie's hand. And Jackie couldn't help it if the circle kids liked her. Why would Jackie, or anybody, step outside if she didn't have to? Tink wouldn't. She really wouldn't. And what would Jackie do if she did?

The "Roll Over" game had started today with *Brave New World*. That morning some of the elevated readers (they switched to Mr. Bergman for language arts) got to read this stupid book about this weird futuristic world. Tink didn't get much out of it except page 146. On page 146 this guy is standing over this girl watching her sleep. She's wearing a futuristic *Star Trek* sort of outfit with a zipper that goes all the way up.

"Or," Jackie said to the group, "all the way down." Everybody sat and read page 146, about this guy imagining things about that zipper. Then they went to recess and

Jackie wanted to act it out. She lay down in the grass and said to Keith, "Now you stand over me."

Tink didn't know what would have happened if he had done it the way Jackie said. Instead, while Jackie's eyes were closed, pretending she was the sleeping girl, Keith lay down next to her. And then Maggie Lindquist, who everyone knew also had a crush on Keith, lay down next to him, her golden hair on the grass. Next thing you knew, the circle kids were all on the ground, Tink included, giggling, side by side like sardines.

Keith started singing that song:

"There were ten in the bed and the little one said
'Roll over! Roll over!'
So they all rolled over and one fell out.
There were nine in the bed and the little one said . . ."

All together, outside in the hot grass, they rolled over. Keith, next to Jackie, pushed her as she rolled so that it was like she fell out. She jumped up and ran over to the other end of the row and lay down and started rolling again. Next it was Keith's turn to fall out.

It was stupid and crazy and wild and lovely rolling into the boys and the boys rolling up against them. At the end of recess they were covered with grass, hot and sweaty, and so thirsty they all ran for the water fountain. Tink didn't care why she was there; she was just glad she was, part of this wonderful *we* with Jackie and the rest.

She fell in line behind Will, watching Jackie sing "Roll Over" with Keith, when Bushwhack and one of the Farmers and some other kids who had been playing kickball came up. "Hundred Percent," Bushwhack said.

"My name is Chris," Tink said in her most dignified voice. She laughed in a way that was supposed to include Mitzie and Maggie, Jackie and Keith and Will, all ahead of her in the line. Her cool friends. Her new name.

"Christine Gouda," Bushwhack said cheerfully. "Gouda cheese. Hundred Percent fat!"

"I'm not fat," Tink said. But she wasn't thin and cute, either. Not like Jackie.

"I know," said Bushwhack, high-fiving her. "That's what makes it funny." He wasn't being mean.

Will and Keith nudged each other in the ribs. "Bushwhack," Keith said. "Why don't you go back to the farm?" For a second Tink thought they were standing up for her.

Bushwhack ignored them. "How'd you get all covered in grass?" he asked Tink.

"Maybe she was rolling in the grass at your farm," teased Will.

"Bushwah," said Bushwhack. His eyes were mad. When he leaned toward Will, Tink saw for the first time that Bushwhack was taller. But not cute like Will and Keith.

"Oh, Bushwhack, don't worry." Will shook his head. "Everybody knows *you* haven't been rolling with any girls."

Keith and Mitzie and Maggie laughed in an insulting way. Jackie gave Will a dirty look, but then she laughed, because everyone else was laughing. Then she stopped, with a guilty glance at Tink.

Tink wasn't laughing. She was watching Bushwhack. He seemed confused. Normally he would have said *Bushwah*, or even *You know* . . . but he said instead, "Two words."

Bushwhack picked the grass off the back of Tink's shirt and threw it at Will. He missed, because the grass hit the air and went dead, drifting down, so he threw it harder and more dramatically, making Tink snort with laughter, which embarrassed her. She subsided, and moved up closer to Will.

Bushwhack stared at Will. "Big Wheels, you've been rolling with girls?" Will acted as if he hadn't heard. Bushwhack's eyes narrowed. "What girls?" he asked.

Will didn't look at Bushwhack. "Jackie, Mitzie, Maggie . . ." He named all the pretty girls.

He didn't name Tink. He didn't even look at her. Bushwhack did. He frowned, and walked away. Tink could have shrugged, but instead she just stood completely still.

One by one, kids finished drinking and went back to flirting and insulting each other in the big, noisy hallway, waiting for the second bell. Then Will and Tink were last in line at the fountain, with everyone else just milling around. Keith and Maggie and Mitzie started giggling again and singing "Roll Over." Jackie stood against the wall near them, maybe waiting for Tink. Maybe waiting for Tink to do what she, Jackie, would do.

"Hey Will," Tink said, sidling closer to him as he bent and took a drink. "Did you like that game?" And again she sang "Roll Over," although she felt weird singing it just to him. Why hadn't he named her?

"Yeah," he said, wiping his mouth on the back of his hand. But he didn't move away from the fountain. He stood there waiting for her to stop talking so he could take another sip. Jackie and the other circle kids started to move off down the hall.

"Who do you like most in that game?" Tink dared to ask.

"Maggie," he said. "Everyone else in our class is a dog." But he said it looking right at Tink. *A dog.* Was he calling *her* that? They were the only two left in the hall. He turned around, turned his back on her. And then he bent over to take his second drink.

Tink looked at his shoulders, at the way his dark green T-shirt stretched over them as he bent to drink, at the tawny back of his hair, the wet edge of it soaked with perspiration against his neck. She moved closer. She moved a little too close. She reached out her hand.

He jumped. Or did she push?

A second later Will Wheeler turned, blood pouring down his chin, gushing from his mouth, streaming out from between his fingers. He took one hand away from his face and stared at it, appalled. His hand glistened red with blood. In the middle of all the blood was a little white thing like a pebble—part of his front tooth. Somehow he spoke two words, looking desperately at Tink. "Paper towels!" he said.

Will Wheeler had the most beautiful hazel eyes.

★ ★ ★

The intercom in the classroom let out a squonk. The sixth grade was back in their two classrooms, all except Will, and the rest of them were so nervous that they jumped when the intercom sounded. "Mitzie Schuman and Maggie Lindquist to the office, please."

Ms. Cho pointed at the door. "Uh-oh," said Keith Kallinka. "Trouble!"

Mitzie rolled her eyes as she and Maggie left the room. Tink knew that most of the sixth grade boys liked tiny little Mitzie with her brown pigtails and big blue eyes. She had three big brothers and just naturally knew how to bug boys into doing what she wanted, in a nice way. And Maggie had been Will Wheeler's best friend since kindergarten, just as Jackie had been Tink's. Tink hadn't been jealous of either of them before this year. Well, if Maggie and Mitzie were so great, where had they been after recess when Will needed paper towels?

Math was quiet because Will wasn't there in the chair behind Tink, drumming his fingers on the desk, tapping his pencil, and jiggling his knees. It was so quiet it was almost loud. It was sunny and warm, and Tink was still sweating. How long were they going to make them sit here wondering what was going on?

The intercom squonked again. "Keith Kallinka, Keith Kallinka to the office, please?" Maybe they needed help with Will's stuff? But Keith wasn't on Will's bus. No. They must want to ask Keith about Will's "accident." Squonk. "Jacqueline Messina to the office, please."

"Oh!" Jackie gasped and popped out of her seat, making big eyes at Keith, and they went out together. The office was definitely calling down all the obvious witnesses, the circle kids most likely to have seen what happened to Will.

Tink couldn't focus on math. The kids she'd been with at recess had been called, so why hadn't they called her name?

Not thinking whom she was speaking to, she said, "Will must really be hurt." Her eyes felt full of tears, and the pre-algebra blurred in the book on her desk.

"Two words." Bushwhack said it softly from across the aisle. Tink guessed he was feeling nervous like everybody else about what had happened to Will. Under his breath, he addressed Will: "You eject button. You toaster. You glasses case."

The reason these insults were funny was because they were stupid. The stupider and more everyday-odd the object was, the funnier it sounded. To Tink, anyway—and to the other kids who laughed at Bushwhack. Not to Jackie, and now Tink wondered for the first time whether the rest of the circle kids were unamused by Bushwhack as well.

It was what he did: dreamed up nicknames, invented clubs, drew cartoons the way Tink did (at night at her dad's drafting desk, with his pens), worked hard at science fair like Jackie, dealt out jokes, and made up funny insults, planning them ahead so they'd be there when he needed them. When it came to this kind of insanity, Bushwhack was the chief lunatic, in Tink's opinion.

Right now, she felt too serious to laugh, but Bushwhack kept going without any encouragement. He was on a roll. "You paper cutter. You bumper sticker. You cat dish."

"Excuse me, Motormouth?" interrupted Ms. Cho. "Could you focus your attention on pre-algebra?"

This merely sent Bushwhack into ventriloquist mode. "You remote control," he whispered. "You pillowcase. You doorbell."

Tink dropped her head and said, "You water fountain." She couldn't resist. He snickered, and she couldn't stop the corners of her mouth from turning up.

When she looked at her book again, there was a scrap of binder paper on it. *What's the worst insult you've ever heard?*

Tink thought about a time when her six-year-old brother Alvin had called her a name he'd heard at his friend Zach's—horny skank—causing Dad to invite him to a man-to-man powwow. She thought about various times when Jackie had called her a bobo or a momo or a schmuck (until her mother put the kibosh on that word). Tink's stomach curled a little, her brain sidestepped the word *dog*, and, remembering an old favorite phrase of her mom's, she stared down at the paper and recited it, even though she was lying about it being the worst.

*You disconnected piece of broken sewer-pipe,* she wrote. And on the other side, she wrote, *You?*

Out of the corner of her eye she saw Bushwhack's grin like a half-moon. The half-moon disappeared as he read the other side of the note. He wrote and passed it back.

It said, *I couldn't say it to a girl.* Hmm! What was the worst insult one boy could say to another? And who had said it to him? She didn't ask.

The intercom went off. "Matthew Alva," the office said. Bushwhack gulped, stood up, and left for the office. Tink waited. Everyone else had been called in twos. Weren't there any more suspects?

"Ms. Cho?" she said, raising her hand.

Ms. Cho turned from the board. "You can't go with Jackie everywhere she goes, Chris," she told her. Did everyone think she was just Jackie's tagalong?

"Just to the girls' room?" Ms. Cho sighed again, picked up the wooden pass, and handed it to her.

But the girls' room was not where she was going.

It was hot outside and their school was not air-conditioned. The two chairs outside the principal's office stood in full sunlight. Tink sat down in the other chair of disgrace, next to Bushwhack. He was hunched over and studying the palms of his hands, still dirty from kickball at recess. Tink gave him a once-over. He had thin brown hair, glasses, the beginning of zits on his chin, two pens inside his shirt pocket, a button on the outside that said "Captain Bushwhack" which he had made himself, baggy jeans, and old sneakers on very large, pigeon-toed feet. Bushwhack was laughable. But for once, he wasn't laughing.

"What did *you* do, Hundred Percent?" he asked.

She shrugged. "Waiting for my trial," she said.

He stared. "They called you?"

She shook her head. "Nope, I volunteered."

"That's bushwah," he said. "You didn't do anything wrong."

Laughable. "How do you know?"

He finally looked at her. "Because you wouldn't, would you?"

"How do you know?"

"To commit a crime, you have to have the three *Ms*. The Method, the Means, and the Motive."

"Oh yeah? And I don't?" She tried to look carefree. "Who do *you* think did it?"

"One of the Farmers?" he said. "Or maybe me."

"Maybe it was Jackie," Tink said, testing. "She was mad at him about the way he acts to some people—"

"Like she cares," said Bushwhack.

"Why wouldn't she, you—you—you mailbox?"

He grinned. "Good one."

She smiled, but just a little. She didn't want him getting the wrong idea about Jackie. "Jackie didn't push him," she said.

"Pushing would be the Method," Bushwhack said. "And if Jackie was mad at Will, she had the Motive, too."

"But Jackie didn't have the Means to push Will," said Tink. "She was standing on the other side of the hall, waiting with Maggie." She tried to say it as if she didn't care, the way she wouldn't if Maggie were her friend too, not just Jackie's. "Maybe he just tripped," said Tink.

Bushwhack shook his head. "He's not a klutz," he said, and then she was sorry, because Bushwhack was one. "The man is bushwah. He had it coming to him."

But he has such beautiful eyes, Tink thought to herself. "Why?" she asked.

"Why not?" said Bushwhack. "Do *you* think I pushed him?"

Of course she didn't, but she remembered now: He had been angry, too. "Do you have a Motive?"

Bushwhack crossed his arms over his chest. His shadow against the floor of the hot hallway was still and short, not long and thin the way Peter Pan's would be at night, in moonlight. "Meow," he said.

"What?"

"What do you mean, *what*?"

"You meowed," Tink said.

"Wheeler meowed at us on the bus," said Bushwhack.

*What's the worst insult you've ever heard?* She thought about who *us* might be. Bushwhack and his friend Alex Mott, who hadn't been anybody until he became a Farmer. They rode the bus together.

Something caught in her throat. "Will doesn't go on your bus," she said.

"When he goes over to Keith's house, he does."

"What did he mean by it?" By playing dumb, she was giving Bushwhack a chance to do the same.

His face went red with embarrassment and anger, but he didn't take the way out she was offering. "Come on, Hundred Percent. You know what it means when somebody meows at a guy. In front of all the kids on the bus, too."

Tink's mind hopped to the water fountain when Will had called the girls dogs. It bounced to the bus passing and someone yelling "woof." Now she knew beyond a shadow of a doubt: Will Wheeler was the unknown barker.

She said, "You know what Bushwhack would say."

He looked up.

"You know," she said. "Two words."

He shrugged, smiling.

They were silent for a long moment, so long Tink began wondering who'd speak next. She decided she might as well tell him the truth back. So she barked, "Woof!"

He stopped smiling.

"I beg your pardon," said Mr. Parisi. "What's all this animal noise out here?" Through the door came Mitzie, Maggie, Keith, and Jackie, like a sixth grade beauty contest. Everyone had been in the hall around the water fountain, but which of them had been right behind Will? Tink. She had the Means. Which of them had first mentioned pushing? Tink. She had the Method.

"Woof!" she said again. And there was the Motive. If she was going to be in trouble, she figured she might as well be all the way in trouble. She looked right at Keith as she barked. His eyes flared, and he shot a glance at Mr. Parisi. (What a fool.) Tink smiled. Jackie looked worried, but Mitzie looked at Tink the way she had for a while now, as though Tink were a rock in her path—barely patient, eager to get around her.

Bushwhack said, "Animal noise is what people of low IQ use to communicate." Tink could see he understood that she had the Motive, as well as the Method and the Means. But there was something else in his eyes, too. Something angry. Something sympathetic.

Mr. Parisi cocked his head and gazed around the circle of faces. "Mr. Alva, I presume you're here again for the way *you* communicate?"

"We all communicate," said Bushwhack.

"Pardon me?" said Mr. Parisi.

"Pardon *me*," said Bushwhack. "I guess I'm here about Will Wheeler."

"Me too," said Tink.

Mr. Parisi turned and looked at her. "Did I call you down?"

"I'm here about Will, too," she said firmly.

The way Keith was smirking, he seemed to like the idea of Bushwhack being in trouble for doing something to Will. Am*bush*ing him, maybe. Or *whacking* him. Clearly nobody had thought Tink should be a suspect, not even Jackie, who knew how Tink loved Will and knew about the barking. Had loved, that is. Tink suddenly knew that she didn't anymore.

Mr. Parisi told Bushwhack and Tink to sit in the chairs in front of his desk. He sat down behind his desk and folded his hands on top of it. "Miss Gouda, have you ever been in this office before?"

"No."

He studied his fingers, then looked at her hard with dark brown eyes behind glasses. His voice was gentle. "Why don't you tell me what happened to Will?"

"He broke his tooth on the water fountain," she said.

"What caused him to break his tooth?" Mr. Parisi asked.

"I think he tripped or something," said Bushwhack. "He banged his tooth on the spout. Maybe the water went up his nose and he jerked his head."

Mr. Parisi waited for him to finish babbling. Then he turned back to Tink. "What do *you* think caused Will to break his tooth?"

"Someone pushed him," she said.

"*Pushed* him?"

"It wasn't really a push. It was sort of a roll. A little rolling shove, from someone who didn't notice Will had his mouth open, about to take a drink."

"A roll? As in 'Roll Over'? You were playing, too?"

Tink nodded. Her stomach clenched with fear. Someone had told about their game! Even worse: As they were telling, they hadn't included her. Had any of them even noticed she was playing, with their eyes closed and the green grass all around them?

Mr. Parisi took a breath and seemed to consider the matter. Then he sent Bushwhack back to class. "Thank you for your thoughts," he said.

"You know—" said Bushwhack. He meant to say *bush-wah*, but wouldn't in front of Mr. Parisi. Bushwhack tried to say something to Tink with his eyes. Something funny. Something kind. He raised two fingers, meaning *Two words*.

She shook her head at him, and he left.

After the door closed, Mr. Parisi spoke to her quietly. "Christine, was it you who . . . rolled into Will when he was drinking?"

"Yes."

"Why?" He seemed genuinely curious, and not mean. Because of that she told him the truth, at least a small part of the true story of her crime against Will.

"Because I like him."

"Well, we all like Will."

"No." She folded her hands and made a small change, a change to something truer. "I mean, I *liked* him."

Mr. Parisi looked down at his own folded hands. He said, "Then why'd you push him?"

"I didn't mean to hurt him," Tink said. Was that true? She had pushed him, even without intending to.

"So it was an accident," Mr. Parisi said. He leaned back against his chair. "There are better ways to show a boy you like him."

"I know," Tink said. But did she?

If Will had asked her to sew his shadow on, she would have. If he had whistled at her from the bus, she would have smiled. But he had pushed her out of the circle—not physically, but with his words, with his list of everyone he liked that excluded Tink. So yes, she had pushed him back, in that moment of realizing that somebody she'd adored could ignore her, that somebody she'd adored could bark at her.

What she remembered, now, was the feel of his back under her hands when she quickly, sharply shoved him, and the way his head jerked when his tooth connected with the metal spout. She remembered his damp green shirt and his shoulder blades beneath it, under her hands.

Later, she thought maybe she should have acted differently with Mr. Parisi to stay out of trouble—cried, or lied—but somehow or other a little bit of truth had stood up for her better than a complicated, complete story. And maybe it was just as well that Mr. Parisi didn't know that she had been angry, or figured out why she might be.

Outside the glass doors of the entryway the first buses were arriving, lining up at the curb. Tink looked for her bus, which was number 21 when she was in kindergarten and had been ever since.

She couldn't think of any ways to show a boy she liked him through animal noises. Whistling at a boy seemed as bizarre as barking or meowing. Jackie might have purred, but that wasn't Tink's style. The other animal noises running through her head sounded like verses from "Old

MacDonald Had a Farm"—things she might yell at the boys on the bus if she were someone of low IQ. Imagine using animal noises—or words about animals—to insult people!

Tink realized that if Will flew in her window one night she might take the opportunity to push him off the sill. She felt tired of everyone, and scared of them at the same time. For the first time she was glad her school ended with sixth grade and they would all be somewhere else next year, at one middle school or the other.

But there was still all of sixth grade to get through.

She walked down the hallway and back toward her classroom. There was the fountain, right where it always had been. She felt thirsty, but she didn't take a drink. She walked away from the scene of the crime.

She was grateful that all she had to do was apologize to Will—and that Mr. Parisi wasn't going to call her parents. She *was* sorry, but she was angry, too, and worried, unsure how she would respond in the future if Will insulted her, and nervous about how the circle girls would act if they thought what she had done hadn't been an accident.

When she walked back into the classroom, Bushwhack was there in his seat next to hers. "How'd it go?" he said. The whole class was listening. Will's seat remained empty. He would not ride the bus today. He had gone home in his bloody, sweaty green shirt, and every person in the class from Keith Kallinka to the plainest Farmer knew Tink had bumped him, even if Bushwhack was the only one who knew she'd done it on purpose.

She had been in enough trouble for one day, so she knew she ought to placate Ms. Cho and stay away from words that weren't in the dictionary. "Two words" would have been so easy. But there was really only one word that could express what she was feeling. She said it so everyone could hear her. "Bushwah," she said.

When the phone rang, Tink got a bad feeling in her stomach. She knew it was Jackie, calling to get the full story. Although everyone had surely figured it out by now, Jackie clearly felt entitled to get it straight from the source.

JACKIE: Chris? Are you all right?

TINK (as if she didn't know what Jackie was talking about): Yes, sure!

JACKIE (whispering as if Tink's mother could hear): What did Stevie say? (She loved knowing Tink's mother went by her high school name, short for her last name—Stevenson.)

TINK: Don't call her that.

JACKIE: Bess says you can call her Bess. Does—YOUR MOM—know?

TINK:    No.

JACKIE (louder, happily): Really?? Mr. Parisi didn't call her?

TINK:    Yes, I have it right here.

JACKIE: What? He DID call her?

TINK:    No! It's right HERE!

JACKIE: Oh. Your mom's right there?

TINK:    Duh.

JACKIE: But Chris . . . (whispering again) Did you do it on purpose or was it an accident?

TINK:    What difference does it make?

JACKIE: Well, he's never going to like you if—

TINK:    He never is going to anyway.

JACKIE: Oh, come on.

TINK:    No, you come on! He never DID. He never WOULD.

Mom peeked out from the kitchen.

JACKIE: Do you know he broke his tooth? And it was a grown-up tooth? And he has to go to some specialist and get it fixed? Maggie called him, then she called me.

(And then Jackie called Tink, to make her feel worse?)

TINK (almost crying): Too bad!

JACKIE: Too bad? Then you DID do it on purpose?

TINK (crying):

JACKIE (gentler): Tink? Then you did?

TINK:    Shut up!

She shook her head at her mom to make her go away. What difference did it make whether it was an accident or not?

JACKIE: Wouldn't YOU want to know? He's been our friend since—

TINK:    He's been YOUR friend maybe.

JACKIE: But you ADORE him. You wouldn't do that!

TINK:    Who knows what I would do? Anyway, it's not like I planned it! Quit acting like you don't know why!

JACKIE (whispering to show off how in awe of the situation she was): Are you upset? About the barking? Is that what this is all about? He's just a dumb-ass boy, that's what my mom would say.

Well, goody for Bess. But Tink's mom came and hugged Tink, without even knowing why she was crying.

MOM:    Tell her you have to go wash the cat.

Tink laughed. She patted Mom to let her know she was okay. Mom let go of Tink, and Tink waved her back to the kitchen.

JACKIE: Are you going to apologize?

TINK (hotly): No! Well, they're making me. But I won't mean it.

JACKIE: But honey, he's hurt.

Tink knew Jackie called her honey to let her know she was wrong, exactly the way Bess did to Jackie twenty-five times a day.

JACKIE: Just make him a card. I'll take it over to him for you.

TINK (quietly): No. I have to go. I have to go wash my cat!

She hung up.

# 2
# Lobster Pot

(late September)

Jackie's mother had left her a note.

*J— Do the dishes. Soak in dishpan, then scrub. Put them away and do the sink. Everything PERFECT, girlfriend. I'll be home at four, and I want it beautiful. James at five w/ kids—and LOBSTERS. We're living it up! —Ma*

"Lobsters?" asked Tink. "Why?"

"It's sophisticated," said Jackie. "Somebody's trying to impress somebody."

"Well, I hope they're impressed then. See ya."

"Promise you won't leave," Jackie said, clutching Tink's arm.

Tink got a sinking feeling. "Why?"

Jackie dug in her claws. "Because. James is coming with his kids."

"And lobsters," Tink said brightly. "Dead or alive?"

"Oh, what do you *think*?"

"How do I know?"

"Haven't you ever had lobster?"

"No," Tink said. "Lobster is what my parents have when they get a babysitter and go out. They're expensive."

"They're sophisticated," said Jackie again.

"Well, I'm not," said Tink without regret. "Nobody ever brought any over to our house."

"Exactly," said Jackie glumly. She turned on the water and began running it into the white plastic dishpan. She squirted soap in to make the water bubble.

"So it's a special occasion, and your mom won't want me here," Tink said hopefully.

"She will," sighed Jackie. She shut off the water and began taking out dishes, soaping them, and stacking them on the counter next to the sink. "She thinks you're golden. 'Always such a sweet girl.' You remind her of herself when she was your age."

"I *do*?" Bess had fluffy hair and high heels, a big smile, a loud laugh, and a boyfriend with kids in middle school. She could dance. In other words, Jackie, all grown-up. "*Why?*"

"Um," said Jackie. It was unusual for her to blush, but she was blushing now, and it wasn't from the hot water. Tink could tell she wished she hadn't started on this. "Because she was the tallest one in the class."

"So?" Tink said. That was interesting, but believable enough. So Bess had been a tall version of Jackie when she was eleven like them. "So what?"

"And she said she knew how you felt, better than I do." Tink thought Jackie should have stopped after the tall comment, but she didn't seem to know how. "Like a fish out of water. In between, a little lost and not bloomed yet."

"I'm not lost!" Tink said. Then she said, "Yet?"

Something awkward had made its way into this kitchen. It was not the first time anyone had mentioned the ugly duckling concept to Tink. But Jackie never had. Jackie scrubbed hard at the coffeepot and hid her face. "She says it's easy for me, I don't know how easy I've got it, boys already calling up." The sinking feeling sank further: Boys called Jackie? Which boys?

"What does she think I'm in between about, anyway?" Tink asked. Did that mean she was *going* to bloom? Did that mean Jackie *had* bloomed? "What is this, a greenhouse?" Tink was just angry and hurt, she didn't expect an answer to that.

"I don't have any idea," said Jackie, angry too. She jammed the coffeepot upside down into the dish drain and stood squeezing the sponge before looking up at Tink. "Can I tell you something, Chris?"

She could be magnetic sometimes, calling her Chris, telling her she was cute. Tink had pretty quickly stopped believing in both things, but she couldn't say no to a new secret from Jackie any more than she could refuse a Milky Way.

"I'm not sure about James," Jackie said. "But I like his son Bobby."

"Oh, brother," Tink said. Here was some familiar ground. But: "If your mom marries James, won't Bobby be your brother?"

Jackie laughed and resumed soaping. "Stepbrother. Yeah, and he already has one stepsister, Amy, and she hates me. She hates my mom, too. And she'll probably hate you, too."

"Well, I'm not staying," Tink said. But she didn't say no way, no how. Amy and Jackie would be each other's step-stepsister?

"Yes you are," said Jackie. "Because now you're curious."

That was for sure. It beat whatever was going on at Tink's house: pizza and Friday night television, what a total bore, and the usual argument between Mom and Dad about sausage and pepperoni, and nobody getting enough pizza and having to try to fill up on salad, and the little kids stealing each other's crusts, and—oh, forget it.

"Besides that, what do you want *me* for?" she asked Jackie.

"Please," begged Jackie. "I'm so nervous, and you're so calm. You're reassuring. Stay with me."

It was the same thing Jackie said when she went to recess with the circle. They made her nervous, she said, and she needed Tink, she said, so Tink went along, because she didn't know what else to do. The circle kids were always hogging the swings at recess now, twirling and playing trolley cars, bumping together and swinging apart, flirting and giggling. One day when Jackie had a cold and stayed home from school, Tink got a tennis ball from her backpack and bounced it against the wall until a new girl named Eddie from the other sixth grade came and did it with her. Tink pretended she was too busy to join the circle, but the truth was she didn't know what would happen if she hung out on the swings with them without Jackie. But the next day that Jackie was better, it was back to the circle for Tink, because Jackie was her ticket in, and too bad for Eddie and anyone else.

Now Tink sighed and said, "What will you do to keep *me* from being nervous?"

Jackie said, "What are you nervous about?"

"Meeting your mom's boyfriend and his kids? Hanging around while you have some crush?"

Bess's car crunched the gravel in the driveway. Tink went into the bathroom to give Jackie a chance to tell her mother that Tink was here and ask if it was okay for her to stay. Tink studied her same old dumb face—brown curls, gray eyes, glasses—in the mirror, and wondered if change was coming. The only way her style had changed was asking the teachers to call her Chris. They did because she was new to them. But the students were slower to adapt.

She remembered how, when school started in September, some people looked better—that glow of cuteness on the faces of Keith and Will, Maggie, Mitzie, and on her own Jackie, too. Even though she'd been seeing Jackie all summer, she hadn't noticed her sudden cuteness until she noticed theirs. Could you see it if you had it yourself? Or did you have to wait until someone else saw it in you?

Tink could have stood in the bathroom all night feeling mad and sad and bad, but Jackie's mother needed the bathroom right away. "Who's in the potty?" she called, which meant it was fine that Tink was here.

Tink laughed, and caught her own smile in the mirror. Suddenly feeling fizzy at being included in this sophisticated lobster party, she drew herself up straighter and went out. Bess slid past, giving Tink a humorous little pinch on the chin as she went. She was all hair spray and perfume, rush and bustle.

"Stay!" hissed Jackie.

Tink agreed. But she frowned a little threat at Jackie: "For now," she said.

Jackie sighed.

"So you're the ambassador, Miss Tinker Bell?" Bess said, when she came out of the bathroom. "Wait, that's not what I'm supposed to call you, is it?" Tink thought Bess was like her own mother would have been without her father— dancing with her hips shaking to the radio and working really hard and doing everything in the house herself and knowing how to do everything—except without a husband to be grabbing those hips and getting swatted for it. And without all the other kids that came with having a husband, she guessed.

"You can call me Chris," Tink said to Bess. "Why am I an ambassador?"

"That's why I appreciate you, *Chris*," said Bess. "You won't just let me be glib."

Tink wasn't about to ask her what it meant to be glib.

"Someone who smooths the way between people is an ambassador," said Bess. "She helps make an event a success. She smiles through any storm. *You're* an ambassador because you wonder about what other people might be thinking and act accordingly. Unlike some people, who only worry about what *they're* thinking."

"Bess thinks she's funny," Jackie said, appearing from the pantry, lugging a huge pot, black with little white spots all over it. She set it on the counter and flicked the dish towel at her mother's rear.

"I just mean, it's nice when you're here," Bess told Tink.

"Bess thinks you should get along with people even if you don't like them," said Jackie. "She doesn't think of it as being fake." Well, even if Jackie saw right through Bess, she'd still learned the lesson.

"An ambassador takes the pressure off," said Bess. Tink would have liked to know what kind of pressure, but guessed she'd find out soon enough. Meanwhile she felt like an island in the sea, with two swimmers crawling ashore for refuge: Tink and her mother never talked about each other *to* each other the way Jackie and Bess were doing now. It gave her an in-between tense feeling that didn't seem like what an ambassador was supposed to feel.

"I'll share my lobster with you, Chris," Jackie offered. "You can even name him."

Tink gave her the stink-eye. She was *not* going to ask why you would name an animal you were going to eat. "Where are the lobsters coming from?"

"There's this place by the beach," said Jackie. "Did you really never have lobster before?"

Tink stared her down. She wasn't going to let Jackie make her feel dumb on top of everything else. "You are my ambassador of lobsters. You will have to consider what I'm thinking about them, and smooth the way between us." She didn't mention being worried that she wouldn't like lobster, and then Jackie wouldn't think she was sophisticated.

"With pleasure," said Jackie. "I'm going to go get dressed for Bobby. Coming?"

How did it feel, to dress for somebody else?

Now Bess was in the bathroom again, the door open to let out steam from the shower, the hair dryer running. Tink glanced inside as they passed: Bess was doing something fancy with a round brush to get her curls to go right. Was she getting dressed for James? Tink had never heard her mother say she was getting dressed for her father. Mom just plain got dressed and let her straight hair air-dry down. One of these days maybe Tink would get Bess to show her how to dry her hair somehow differently so it wouldn't stick out in a curly mess all over the world. Bess could be Tink's ambassador of hair, smoothing her head.

Jackie stood at her dresser, clamping her hair back in a fat barrette and tugging little tendrils of curls out around her forehead. She had lip gloss in a little pot, and a red striped sailor shirt. "Is that to make the lobsters feel right at home?" Tink asked. She didn't have anything to change into. She waved in the mirror. "Ahoy, Larry Lobster?"

With Jackie's hair up like that, she and Tink did not look remotely similar. This was the problem with Jackie lately, the thing that made Tink most uncomfortable: Jackie knew things Tink didn't know. Maybe she should stop hanging out with Jackie, so she didn't have to see how ignorant she, Tink, was. Or maybe she should stay, to learn what Jackie knew.

Jackie looked at Tink, said "Hang on," and went out. She came back with a blue and white polka-dot shirt that looked like something Bess would wear to work. "Try this on," she said, and reached down and whipped the tail of Tink's shirt up to show her she should take it off. Tink turned her back and pulled the bright green polo shirt she was wearing over her head. She buttoned Bess's shirt and looked in the mirror. Her bra showed a little through the shirt. But Jackie turned her aside and unbuttoned the shirt three buttons from the bottom up, and tied the shirttails together at Tink's belly button, and bloused the shirt out at the top. The bra didn't show then, but Tink's stomach did.

"Ugh," said Tink. She pulled the knot a little looser and tugged it down to the top of her shorts.

"Nice," said Bess from the doorway. "You're getting a cute figure." Then she went away again. But Tink felt funny. *Cute* described her figure? Not her face? What about the shirt? What did it mean to get any kind of figure?

Jackie stuck her pinky finger in the lip gloss and spread some on Tink's mouth. "Go MWAH, Chris," she said.

Tink went MWAH, and the lip gloss spread around a little more. She had it licked off before they heard car doors slam. Bess went dashing down. They could hear lots of big merry hellos, and then some squealing from Jackie's mother, and then yelling. "Jackie! Tink! The lobsters are here!"

Jackie put her hand on her stomach. "I've got butter-flies. Come on." She rolled her eyes and ran down the stairs. Tink trudged down after her.

There were lobsters on the kitchen floor, five of them. Two of them were trying to fight, even though they had rub-ber bands on their claws. James and Bess were standing in the middle of the floor kissing. Outside the open back door two kids were trying to look like they didn't notice. Jackie cleared her throat in a big way, and her mother stepped back from big chubby James, mussed the curls back from his forehead as she pushed his head away, and narrowly missed stepping on a lobster. "Whew!" she said, either about the kiss or the lobster.

Then suddenly Bess and Jackie were shrieking and jumping around the floor to avoid the lobsters. It was a very darling fuss, observed with a grin by James and open-mouthed stares by his two kids and Tink. That Bobby was cute, all right, as curly-headed blond as his father, but tall and slim. "This is my son, James Jr.," James said.

"This is our lovely Tink," said Bess. "Jacqueline's dearest friend."

"You can call her Chris," said Jackie.

"Hi," said Tink. "Nice to meet you."

"You can call me Bobby," said James Jr. That made no sense. The daughter was short and round-cheeked and chubby and had a straight dirty-blonde ponytail and freckles. Very strange. Was she even a member of the same family? Then Tink remembered she wasn't, not by blood, anyway.

"And my stepdaughter Amy," James said, waving her in. "Two eighth graders at once!" he told Bess with a dizzy head-shake.

"I'm called Bobby, too," said Amy. She stepped forward and leaned her head on Bobby's shoulder, to get a rise out of him. Funny! He shrugged her off. "I'm his ex-wife's daughter," she added, explaining to Tink. "That's why we're the same age."

James and Bobby didn't like her saying that, Tink could see that without x-ray vision. "God, Amy," Bobby said. She made a phony sad face, rolling her eyes, in a fair imitation of Bobby. Tink smiled, and heard Jackie make a little sighing noise behind her. Tink thought how that sighing noise meant she and Jackie would laugh about Amy later, afterward, when they were going to sleep in the dark. Was that what ambassadors did—smooth first, laugh later?

Jackie picked up a lobster. "Hey, Ma," Jackie said in her deepest voice.

Bess scooped a lobster from the floor too. "Hey, Jack," her mother replied. "Where'd all the water go?" They made the lobsters do a little dance at each other. The two of them were the life of the party; that was the plan, Tink realized.

"I dunno, man," said Jackie to Bess in her lobster voice. Then she went over to Tink and said in a completely different voice, "I am the ambassadah of the lobstah! Gweetings, human!"

"So you're a lobster," Tink said to the lobster in a sneery voice. "*Not* what I was led to expect." And she turned and walked out of the kitchen onto the back porch, because she understood what Jackie meant about the butterflies. It was all so freaky weird: Jackie's mother getting smooched by this old man, James. And his cute son seeming perfectly miserable with his own family. (Tink had never thought about being happy or miserable with her own family; they were just *there*.) And the stepdaughter, who probably should have been miserable, because, wait a minute, what did it mean to her to be here with James and his girlfriend and the girlfriend's daughter (and the girlfriend's daughter's best friend)? But somehow the stepdaughter was making an enormous effort to not be miserable, even if it looked like James and Bess, Bobby and Jackie might become a family that didn't really include her.

Were people really like this? Everybody in Tink's family was just how they seemed to be: loving each other if they really did, happy if they really were. Nobody cheating. Nobody acting. Nobody needing ambassadors to be understood, especially not lobsters. Certainly no wild animals tied up and being teased in a habitat that must have been as odd to them as the moon. Tink imagined how the lobsters must feel, and thought pizza was better, even if nobody got enough.

In the backyard the sun was shining down on some corn Jackie and her mother were growing there, because they didn't have little kids that would ride bicycles into it, and Tink went outside and looked at an actual ear of corn that was still growing even though it was October.

"Want to play catch?" Amy asked her.

"With what?" Catch would be better than whatever was going on in that kitchen. Catch would be more of being an ambassador than acting like a member of an audience.

"Me and Bobby bring our gloves everywhere," Amy said, and went to their car and got them out. "You can use mine."

Amy squeezed her hand into Bobby's glove and pulled a baseball out of the pocket of it. She may have been two years older than Tink, but she was easily four inches shorter. Tink saw that wearing Bobby's glove made Amy think she had him in her hand, as if he were hers.

"Let's play High Pops!" said Amy.

"What's High Pops?" said Tink.

"Don't you play softball?"

"No."

Amy threw the ball up so high they both had to look straight up at the sky to follow the arc. When she realized Tink wasn't trying to catch it, she dove for it, catching it even though the big glove was flopping on her hand.

Probably Tink should have taken Bobby's glove, since she was closer to his size. Not that Amy was offering. Not that it would have made Tink any better at throwing or catching. She was okay with a tennis ball bouncing off a brick wall or garage door, but a baseball plummeting from the sky was swift, rock-hard, and slippery. Nevertheless, with each toss, Tink's ball went higher, and Amy had to wait longer for it to come back down.

Tink didn't know what made her say it. Maybe it was the cackling from inside the kitchen that made her feel left out. Maybe it was getting better at High Pops. Maybe it was feeling worse about being an ambassador. It was after

Bobby came out with a lobster in his hand that had had the rubber band removed from its claw, then turned back into the kitchen when he saw Amy and Tink were just playing ball. "Jackie's got a mad crush on him," she said.

"But she's only in sixth grade!" said Amy.

"She's 'mature,'" Tink said, making it clear that mature was what grown-ups said, not her own opinion of Jackie. Yet she couldn't shake the feeling that Jackie, in the kitchen, was having a different kind of fun than Amy and Tink in the yard. The ball fell into the corn, and she climbed in extremely carefully and retrieved it without harming the stalks. Amy stood looking toward the kitchen for a moment after Tink emerged from the garden, with a sort of unspoken *oh*. Tink thought: If Bess and James got married, and Bobby and Jackie crushed on each other, Amy would always be left out.

"Will the lobsters fight?" Tink asked. She tossed Amy the ball.

"Wouldn't you?" said Amy, and threw it back harder. Tink caught it, and laughed in surprise at herself for managing to do so. This felt real. She and Amy didn't need an ambassador to smooth the way between them.

"What I don't get is, how do they kill them?" she asked.

"Didn't you see that big pot in there?" asked Amy. "It's full of water, and it's going to boil. Then they stick the lobsters in, head first."

Tink shuddered. "Why that way? Is that normal?" Tink felt like a different person today, a too-tall person with a new name, an insane person, and maybe even an unkind one. Maybe the meanness came from her vision of the lobsters, head down, diving into the steam and boiling water.

"Who knows what counts for normal around here?" said Amy lightly. Then she threw the ball—right over the back of the garage.

"Oops," said Tink aloud. They both gave the same short little laugh.

Suddenly everyone came tumbling out of the kitchen as if the lobsters were chasing them, screaming and giggling.

"What are you saying oops about?" Bess asked Tink.

"Amy can't find the ball. It went behind the garage."

"Well, Jackie, Bobby, go help her find it!"

Behind the garage were lots of bushes. Bobby held them out of the way so Jackie could go through before him. "What did you athletes do with my ball?" he grumped. This was all just so *boring*, you could see that's what he thought, and he made the word *athletes* sound like a swear word.

Tink didn't know what Jackie thought, beyond the fact that Bobby was cute, which was true: curly light hair, big dark eyes, long eyelashes, plus he was the kind of slender person Jackie got crushes on. Tink watched Jackie make up her mind to entertain Bobby and Amy, to get them both to like her, by teasing them as if they'd known each other for years.

It was impressive. Jackie said, "Geez, Bobby, just use your claws." She stuck her arms out straight and held her hands like lobster claws, leaned over from the waist and hung her straight arms down and groped around for the ball. "You too, other Bobby," she said to Amy. "You, too, lobsterface," she said, to bring Tink into it, too. Tink realized what Jackie was doing: She hadn't done a good job of being an ambassador of lobsters for Tink, but she was doing her funny best to smooth the way between her mother and herself (her family) to James and these two unrelated kids with their strange relationship (their family). Tink (basically Jackie's family, but not technically) was helping a little with Amy (technically Bobby's family, but only technically), that was all.

Here we go again, Tink thought: Here I am in a group of people I wouldn't be with if it wasn't for Jackie. She tried to imagine a group somewhere that *she* could bring *Jackie* to. But she wasn't sure that Jackie would want to come to her group, anyway. Who would be in it? People like Bushwhack and that new girl Eddie and Amy? Jackie wouldn't want them. So who liked the right people? Who liked the wrong people?

The question was, since when had either of them needed anyone else? Not this summer. Not in fifth grade. Not anytime before. So why now?

Tink found the ball and threw it, too hard, to Amy, and it went over her head back into the bushes. Amy slumped toward the bushes after it, but she wasn't quick enough.

"Oops!" yelled Jackie cheerfully. "Uh-oh. Problem. Trouble!" She and Bobby jumped into the hedge together to find the ball.

Amy's eyes met Tink's. She said gently, "Throw from the shoulder," and showed Tink what she meant. That was nice of her, but Tink had lost patience with Jackie. Try as she might, apart from playing ball with Amy, she didn't feel like she was smoothing anything, certainly not smiling through a storm. Maybe if Jackie had done a better job as ambassador of lobsters, instead of using the poor things to make a darling fuss, Tink would have felt more like staying.

"I don't want to play anymore," she said. Amy took a breath, then turned to help the others find the overthrown ball. Tink knew they wouldn't want her, and wondered why Amy had come tonight. Where was Amy's mother, and why weren't she and James still together? What did Amy's mother think of Bobby's mother? What did they both think of Bess?

Everybody's backs were turned away from Tink as they all clawed the bushes. When she turned she saw Bess and James in another lip-lock.

She darted past the knot that was them and slipped into the kitchen. In an instant, she picked up the back end of a lobster and slid it into the white dishpan that Jackie had left empty and rinsed in the sink. And she took that lobster in the dishpan right out the front door and marched away down the street, the sidewalk hard under her sneakered feet, stomping away as fast as she could, through the speckled yellow light from fall leaves, carrying a pan with a lobster inside.

"Chris?" James called out the door behind her.

Tink froze. Somehow she blocked James's view of the lobster with her body. The low light and a helpful bush hid his view of the dishpan as she set it down and looked back. She didn't know where everyone else was. James came out on the front step and shut the screen door softly behind him. He walked toward her, so she went back to him, to keep the lobster hidden.

"You okay, kiddo? Going someplace?"

"Just home," she said. "My mom needs me."

"Oh! Thought you were joining us for dinner. Which, if I'd known, I'd have brought you your own lobster."

He didn't know she'd *taken* her own lobster. His eyes were kind, though, so she said, "That's nice of you. But I don't think I eat shellfish."

"I see. Well, catch you later, hon."

"Bye," she said. She walked away slowly, waiting to hear him close the door before scooping up the pan with the lobster in it.

The beach wasn't far, not a mile away. By the time they would have figured out there was a lobster missing, she'd made it to the beach, pulled off the rubber bands in frantic horror, and dumped the lobster off the jetty.

Tink hurried to toss the dishpan in a big green can that said VOTE YOUR TRASH HERE! Only then did she feel the slightest bit guilty: Bess was going to be quite ticked off when she found out it was gone, and she'd definitely think Jackie had done something with it.

Tink walked to the library. "What are you doing at the library?" Mom said on the phone. "I thought you were at Jackie's for lobster."

"Well, now I'm at the library," Tink said. "I need a ride."

"O-*kay*," Mom said slowly. "Anything else you want to tell me, Tinker Bell?"

"Don't call me that," said Tink. But she didn't mean it.

She went into the bathroom and checked in the mirror to see if she was still the same. Bess's polka-dot shirt had come untucked long ago, from playing catch or chasing balls through the corn or rescuing wild animals. The stomach of the shirt was damp from carrying the wet dishpan against it. Tink made lobster claws in the mirror. She made a lobster face at herself and made herself laugh, which was a funny thing to observe in the mirror. It surprised her. She was bad: She had stolen a lobster. She liked herself for doing it.

She went outside and stood there leaning on the cold iron banister of the front steps, waiting for her mother. The sun was going down, and it was getting cool, and she realized she was hungry. Also she was beginning to wonder about herself—her good girl, Tink self that now had committed two crimes just in this very new school year, when it was still warm enough to wade into the water at the beach.

Mom pulled up in the red station wagon with the big dent on the back door from the time Kitty had gone wild with the basketball. Mom's straight hair was in a messy braid down her back. She had obviously jumped right in the car the minute Tink had called. Her face was full of questions, but Tink hurried to distract her.

"I'm starving!" she said. "Did you guys eat yet?" She hoped not.

"What happened to the lobster dinner?" Mom asked. Tink shrugged, and slumped into the front seat. For once, no little kids were in the back seat, which meant Dad must already be home. Even so, Tink knew enough to be touched that her mother hadn't let any of the kids come with her. Tink pushed the curls back from her hot forehead and held the backs of her hands to her eyes for a moment. Tears had sprung there, shocking her. Her mom said, "Are you wet?"

"A little."

"Well?" Mom knew there was a story.

Tink spat it out. "I stole a lobster and dumped it back in the Sound." She looked down at the wet spot on her front.

"Are you serious?" Her mother stared ahead at the road.

"Ma? Did you ever have any friends cuter than you?"

Mom glanced in the mirror. "What do *you* think?" she asked, and tucked a strand of hair back.

This was *not* what Tink meant! "No, you're beautiful!" she said. "I mean, people who know how to . . . make the most of themselves?"

"Make the most of themselves? Where did you get those words? Let me guess." Her mother took a breath. "Honey, Jackie doesn't have all the answers. She's making her own way, different from you." She looked at Tink and said, "You're a beautiful person. You know, you saved a life today!" She was Tink's mother. Of course she would say Tink was beautiful. When Tink didn't answer, Mom turned and looked at her, and there was a sparkle in her eyes. "Bess is going to have a conniption."

Tink could have cried, but instead she smiled. She was thinking about the moment when she'd held the dishpan down to the surface of the water and turned it sideways to let the lobster slosh out of it. Its claws had sprung wide open, as if it was looking for something to grab on to. The Sound was cool and blue and clear. She hung over the water to watch the lobster sinking down into the gloom. Back where it belonged again, back home like Tink. She felt like—like crying, but also laughing, like smiling through the storm, like an ambassador of lobsters. She wondered: Does an ambassador ever forget that the foreign land he's learned so much about isn't the place he's from?

★ ★ ★

The phone rang.

TINK:    Hello?
JACKIE: Honey, did you take a lobster?
TINK:    Why, is one missing?

To herself she said, "I will never tell you, never never ha ha ha ha ha ha ha it is too funny, I am too funny!"

JACKIE: Well do you have any foggy idea what happened to the dishpan?
TINK:    Excuse me, Sherlock Holmes? Next thing, you'll be telling me beloved BOBBY is missing.
JACKIE: Ah, me.

She had been saying this since they saw *Romeo and Juliet*. Juliet says, "Ah, me," after Romeo says, "See how she lays her cheek upon her hand. O, that I were a glove on that hand." It made them just about pass out, because they wanted Romeo to want *them* that way. Or Bobby, if it were Jackie. As for Tink, well, there wasn't anybody she wanted to want her that way. Not anymore.

TINK:    O, that I were a claw upon that lobster.

Jackie told a big long story about how she and Bobby went and sat on the front steps while everybody else was in the backyard until Stupid Amy came and wrecked the great moment of romance.

TINK:     Well, what was she supposed to do? Stay in the backyard with the make-out king and queen?

JACKIE: She wasn't supposed to be there anyhow, so she could just entertain herself!

TINK:     Or, is that what I was there for? To entertain Amy? Bushwah!

JACKIE:

TINK:     Hmmm?

She waited, tapping her foot.

JACKIE: That ambassador thing? Well, it was definitely better when you were there playing High Pops or whatever that game was.

TINK:     We were just playing catch.

JACKIE: Not according to HER. All night long: "Come on, Bobby! Don't you and Jackie want to play High Pops?" She's so abnormal!

TINK:     No, she was cool. I like her for calling it High Pops. She was trying to make it sound funner to you guys.

JACKIE: You were SUPPOSED to be the ambassador, not the disappearer.

TINK:    I had to go. I forgot I had to—

JACKIE: What? Make up a good one.

Did she think Tink was a liar?

TINK:    My mom needed me. I'm not making it up!

JACKIE: For what? To be your mom's extra pair of hands?

TINK:    I am not her extra pair of hands. Anyway, I'm supposed to go over and get Jessie from the Hugheses'. You could meet me. Walk down.

Again she tapped her foot. It was risky, daring Jackie this way. Take it or leave it, she was saying to her friend.

JACKIE: She'll never let me.

TINK:    Why? Because a lobster was missing?

JACKIE: She just hates me is all.

TINK:

JACKIE: She DOES! You sit there thinking I'm wrong, but I'm not. I am just In. Her. Way. She wanted to have her BOYFRIEND over, not his stupid kids, but he brings them because I'M here, so I won't be the third wheel, but then he brings Amy.

TINK:    So Amy got to be the third wheel. I know how that feels.

JACKIE: If you'd just stayed until dinner, Bobby and I wouldn't even have been missed. You'd be playing High Pops, and they'd think Bobby and I were too, all of us behind the garage.

TINK: What were you and Bobby doing when they found you?

JACKIE: Trying to get away from Amy. Maybe he would have kissed me. Tell me the truth, Chris. Where'd you GO?

TINK: To the beach. Just me and Larry Lobster. It was like Romeo and Juliet.

Jackie started laughing and couldn't stop. Tink had never been this mad at anybody, even her sisters, and it was all because of how Jackie dragged her in and set her up and all she was doing was using her, and Tink let her because otherwise her life was so boring!

TINK: But Larry and I didn't die at the end. We both went home to be with our people.

JACKIE: Me and Bess, there are only two of us. If we don't get along, things get ugly fast. Sometimes we just need—

Suddenly Tink had never felt so sorry for Jackie. Rats. She didn't want to be sorry for her, but how could she not be? Downstairs was her own dumb family, not only Mom but

Dad and all the kids. Stupid pizza fight or not, with her own family, no smoothing was needed, no matter how rough things got.

TINK:     An ambassador. I know. But they already had you. And James was nice. So . . . What happened to the other lobsters?

JACKIE: What do you think? The pot, and melted butter, and lemons squeezed in.

TINK:     Oh, poor Larry!

She started laughing and couldn't stop until her mother made her GET OFF THE PHONE AND GO GET ALVIN OUT OF THE TUB AND PUT HIM IN HIS PAJAMAS OR NO PHONE PRIVILEGES FOR A WEEK!

# 3

# Chocolate Pudding

(mid-October)

One day Tink got to school long before the buses. She'd ridden her bike, and she had her father's socket wrench in her backpack to take the front wheel off to lock it safely to the bike rack. The wrench felt cold and heavy and silvery in her hand. She hadn't known how long it would take her to ride her bike to school, it had been so long since she rode her bike, so she was too early. She wished someone was around to see her tighten every part of her bike all over again just to hear the clicking and ratcheting sounds the wrench made.

It was Monday. Mr. Joseph the custodian must have been there, because the door was unlocked, but Tink didn't see him. It was ghostly quiet with nobody but him yet. She went in. Inside, the bricks gleamed orange and shiny under the hallway lights. It was so early it was practically still dark and bluish outside. All the color was still inside.

After Mr. Joseph and Tink, Mr. Parisi got there next. She guessed every day it must be like this, but she didn't know because she had never been here this early before. The bikers started coming. And the teachers drove up in their cars. She saw Ms. Cho staggering down the hall with a box of pine branches she must have sawed off some trees over the weekend, for some project Tink hadn't heard about yet. Tink walked the entire school, which went in a square, just looking at everything and feeling strong and able and early and ready, before she finally came back around to the two sixth grade rooms, open doors across from each other on opposite sides of the hall, and she found herself taking a deep breath.

When it was just her, she sometimes felt beautiful. She liked herself. Alone, she was a sugar cube, settled, with firm edges and strong corners. But when other people were around she thought that some of them were better— smarter, funnier, cuter, thinner, hotter, cooler—and she felt herself come apart a little, like sugar on the kitchen table, spilled from a spoon.

Something worse happened when the whole class was around. She felt like some people were *not* better than her. She didn't want to think *she* was the smarter, funnier, cooler one (she sure wasn't cuter, thinner, or hotter). But she had to admit there were people she wouldn't go sit with or talk to. She couldn't get interested in them. Worst of all, she worried what people would think if they saw her with them. Tink hated the way it felt to be so aware of how she seemed to other people.

Only Bushwhack was in their classroom so far. He had this clear plastic cardholder with a pin on the back for his Captain Bushwhack badge, which had replaced the Captain Bushwhack button, which mustn't have seemed big and noticeable enough. The cardholder was on his desk. He was drawing intently on a little rectangle of card with one of the red pencils from Ms. Cho's desk. The red pencil was going to need to be sharpened again, Bushwhack was pressing so hard. He glanced up when Tink came in. She rolled her eyes and said, "Monday. School. Bushwah," as if school were a drag, even though she was really feeling glad to be there.

He said, "I am a Hundred Percent in agreement."

The buses began puffing in along the driveway. Soon the whole empty place filled up with noise and the sun got higher so there was color outside and inside. Orange buses. White paper. Sneakers. People.

Everyone was supposed to go to their classrooms before first bell to put their stuff in their cubbies and get their books out for their first subject. Lunches were put away, squishy paper bags and clanking metal lunchboxes, and if you realized you had the wrong lunch and needed to switch with your sister there was still time to go down the hall to grade five, as long as you moved it or put the pedal to the metal or went full steam ahead, whatever Ms. Cho advised. Today she told Tink, "Make like a banana, and peel out."

Kitty had arrived on the bus and was in her fifth grade classroom. She gave Tink her lunch, and took her own. "Moron," she said.

When Tink got back to her class, lots of seats around hers were still empty. All the buses weren't there yet, plus sometimes the walkers came in late, plus sometimes sixth graders were the crossing guards so they were late, plus sometimes people showed up even after attendance had been taken.

Ms. Cho got rolling early anyway, because she had a lot to do, a lot to do. Now she handed Tink a pile of lunch menus. "Put 'em on the desks," she said.

Tink got busy, padding around the classroom bestowing lunch menus, which were as good as a dictionary of jokes as far as Bushwhack was concerned. She never saw anybody get such a kick out of the lunch menu as Bushwhack did that morning. He read it and burst out laughing. Then, watched by Tink and a growing number of others in the class, he dramatized it for them.

"Chicken cutlets!" He threw himself across his desk facedown, thumping the desktop, then slumped so low in his chair that his feet stuck out all the way under Mitzie's chair, saying "Tater tots!" in a voice both exhausted and excited. Mitzie, her nose curled up, kicked at his foot. In response he said, "Milk!" the way someone in the Sahara desert says "Water!" and melted out of his chair right onto the floor. The knees of his scruffy pants absorbed the dust the classroom floor always gave off even right after Mr. Joseph cleaned it—white and dry and chalky. Then he rolled in the aisle, laughing hysterically and gasping out the words "Chocolate pudding!" as if it were the last straw in a long list of complaints instead of what it was: everyone's favorite dessert, so brown it was purple, so creamy it stayed in your mouth for long wonderful moments, so treasured that many fine trades could be made with it. You could get such prizes as pretzel sticks in a box or homemade chocolate chip cookies or—best of the best—Fritos, not in somebody's mother's clear plastic baggie, but in the little orange snack-size bag they sold at the deli for $1.25.

"Mr. Alva," said Ms. Cho. "Please do whatever is required to compose yourself."

"Sanctuary!" said Bushwhack from the floor.

"Just go," said Ms. Cho. Since the second bell hadn't rung yet, he just went, without taking the wooden bathroom pass. He didn't come back all through attendance.

When the second bell rang everyone was supposed to be in their seats, and that was when Ms. Cho passed out even more things: pre-algebra, *To Kill a Mockingbird*, science fair proposal, week schedules of homework, this week's art project: draw a pine tree. (The branches, Tink thought.) She made announcements, too: oral reports from people with names K–A today, permission slip for the trip to the Museum of Space, fifteen dollars.

Tink remembered about oral reports K–A. (Ms. Cho, who had lived her life at the beginning of the alphabet having to go first, had reversed the alphabet for her class.) Tink had worked on it over the weekend, because hers was this week. Her name wouldn't come up until Tuesday or Wednesday, fine with her, so this morning she could sit back and cool her heels and witness the spectacle of Keith Kallinka giving his report, and she intended to enjoy it.

The second bell rang.

When Tink next glanced across the aisle, Bushwhack was back at his desk. He had returned there silently and must have stayed there since, his head down, drawing his usual cartoons of superhero farmers. Classroom doors were shut one by one all down the hall, and school got quiet the way Tink always kind of liked on Monday morning. It was okay to settle into the smell of pencils and the feeling of doing something with your head after a weekend of too much TV and wearing yourself out raking leaves and fixing bikes with your father's socket wrench or fighting with your sisters and brother. She wasn't proud of the raking or fighting or TV, but the bikes: For the first time her father had taught her to undo the nut that held the bike seat rod, and to adjust the seat up or down. She and Kitty and Jessie and Alvin all sat higher on their bikes now. They had grown, and Tink had been put in charge of all future adjustments.

Tink pulled out a sheet of notebook paper and began a drawing of a superhero girl on a bicycle. She was giving the girl the kind of hair she would have loved—long, sleek, shining braids streaming in the wind—when Bushwhack murmured from across the aisle, "Nice ears."

"It's *hair*," she muttered back without looking up, and went back to drawing. It felt companionable, now, both of them cartooning, waiting for the day to get going. Cartooning, they had been informed by their snooty art teacher, was all well and good, but sixth graders were ready for some real genuine fine art.

"Okay," yodeled Ms. Cho. "This morning we'll be starting with the *K*s. Yes, Keith, there's still time for the boys' room, just take the pass, that's right, and are you feeling okay?"

"Stomach cramps," said Keith, grabbing himself around the middle and heading out the door at a rapid pace.

"Two words," said Alex Mott, and everybody waited to see if Ms. Cho would say anything about it in the seconds that followed.

The door swung shut on the diminishing sound of Keith Kallinka's footsteps, but still stayed partly open because he'd been in too much of a hurry to close it. Will Wheeler mumbled some comment about Keith unbuttoning his fly halfway down the hall, and Jennifer Marx had just gotten up to close the door when it happened.

THE LOUDEST SOUND IN THE WORLD.

Like a plane crashed on the playground.

Like an earthquake brought all the pine trees down onto the school roof.

Like the furnace and boiler in the basement dropped all their metal gears and pipes and parts exactly at the same time onto a giant sheet of metal and then it was run over by tanks.

Like the sound of all these things was broadcasted over the intercom system.

SOMETHING FELL in a collapsing, avalanching vibration of thudding crashing, very close by and ridiculously shaking the school.

Everyone screamed and Keith Kallinka came running back to the classroom as if monsters were chasing him, actually holding onto his pants and trying to button them as he ran, but nobody laughed because everyone was frozen.

Then the loud blarting of the fire alarm began.

"Wow, what's going on in this place?" said Keith.

"Hush!" With scary calm Ms. Cho closed the hallway door behind Keith and opened the door to outside and followed them out. They all knew the drill: They stood and filed out, no pushing, no panic, down the classroom steps and across the lawn to the sidewalk.

"Sit on the curb," Ms. Cho said, her voice shaking. "Study the pine trees. We'll draw them when we go back."

"This is not a drill," said Meghan Lin, chewing a fingernail.

"There's no smoke," said Alex Mott.

"Quiet," said Ms. Cho.

Other classes came out, too, and the teachers huddled together to compare notes. But they were just as clueless as the students. The kids in Tink's class smooshed together so everybody could surround Keith. He was just sitting there breathing quietly. He said, "What time is it?" Jonas MacDonald told him nine twenty-four A.M. He said, "We're going to draw pine trees?" Everyone just looked at him.

"He's lost it," said Will Wheeler.

"What happened, Keithy?" asked Maggie.

"I won't have to do my oral report," said Keith. He started giggling, his smooth cheeks pink and his blond hair pushed back from his perspiring forehead. "The bathroom fell down," he said.

"What are you talking about?" said Jackie.

"He's delirious," said Jonas.

"The ceiling fell in?" Tink asked.

"Not exactly," said Keith. "I don't know. No. It caved in."

"The walls?" asked Bushwhack.

"Not exactly," said Keith. "I don't know!" He covered his face with his hands.

Ms. Cho came back, with Mr. Bergman on her heels. They studied Keith Kallinka in particular, taking him aside and talking to him privately, too far off for anybody to eavesdrop. The kids all made themselves busy looking at the pine trees. Mr. Bergman came over with some art paper and a can of pencils and gave them to Jennifer to pass out. He said, "Take a shot at those pine trees while we wait for Mr. Joseph and Mr. Parisi to check the school." He handed Donna a stack of books for them to draw on. Keith came back and took a piece of paper and a pencil and sat on the curb with the others.

The other classes were reading or writing or having early recess, everyone outside and waiting for what would happen next. You might think: How could the sixth graders think about pine trees? It was just what they did. They couldn't think about the other thing. And once one of them was drawing pine trees they all did. It was a way of being together.

After a while Ms. Cho walked over to Keith and put a shaky hand under his chin, pushed his hair back, and looked into his eyes. Then she looked hard at the rest of them until they turned back to the pine trees again.

All of them had spent their lives drawing Christmas trees this way: You made a point near the top of the paper, then swooped down to one side, then cut back toward the middle with a horizontal line, then made another swoop down and to the side, going out farther from the center this time, back and forth until you got to the bottom of the paper or almost to the bottom. Then you did the same thing on the other side, matching up the swoops and horizontals until the last horizontals met at the bottom in one straight line. Then you did the trunk and added your balls—oops, the *Christmas* balls, the decorations!—by drawing them onto the points of the branches.

A real pine tree was nothing like that. Whatever made Tink think she knew what a pine tree went like, the upper branches reaching up, and the bottom branches hanging down? At what point on the tree did they stop reaching up and start hanging down? She looked back and forth from her tree to her paper, and meanwhile Keith Kallinka began trying to draw, trying to act normal and busy, while Mr. Bergman and Ms. Cho observed him while pretending not to.

Mr. Parisi came out with Mr. Joseph, and the lower classes began filing back inside, bewildered but resigned: Nobody tells little kids anything. Mr. Parisi came to their class last. Keith looked up and smiled, kind of daffy, and Mr. Parisi took a step backward. "You're—uh—you're okay then, Mr. Kallinka?"

Keith lifted up his arms and flexed his biceps. They were about the size of half a tennis ball. He said, "Yeah."

"A hundred percent?" asked Mr. Parisi.

Everybody looked at Tink, and Bushwhack giggled, and Ms. Cho gave him a glare.

Mitzie said, "Why aren't you asking Matt Alva if he's all right? Wasn't he in the boys' room, too?" Tink noticed that Mitzie didn't call him Bushwhack. Did she think he was annoying the way Jackie did?

"Is that true?" said Mr. Parisi.

A deep line creased the place between Ms. Cho's eyebrows. "No," she said. "You went before the bell, didn't you, Matt?"

He said yeah. Tink couldn't help nodding, too. And Keith Kallinka said, "I was the only one in there."

Mr. Parisi asked Bushwhack, "Did anything seem strange when you were in there?"

Bushwhack looked like he wanted to laugh. Will Wheeler said, under his breath, "Just himself. That's strange enough."

"Save it," Mr. Parisi told him. "Mr. Joseph was in there and mopped this morning, but he didn't turn on any water or flush a toilet. He didn't push any doors open. Did you hear anything rattling when you were in there?" He was asking Bushwhack.

At first Tink didn't know why Mr. Parisi and Ms. Cho didn't just ask Keith and Bushwhack to go to the office. Then she realized that they were watching the rest of the class to see their reactions. Everyone in the class was potentially guilty. "But what happened?" she asked. "What fell?"

"The whole bathroom!" said Keith Kallinka.

"Like an avalanche?" asked Bushwhack.

"Chris was the first one in this morning." Ms. Cho said.

"You think *she* sabotaged the boys' bathroom?" asked Mitzie.

"Why would I do that?" Tink asked in horror. No Motive, that was her.

Jackie said, "How would she *do* it, anyway?"

"That's the question," said Mr. Parisi.

"What's the question?" asked Jonas. "Why or how?"

"The how is easy enough," said Ms. Cho. "The bathroom is all held up by nuts and bolts. The bolts hold everything on the wall—the toilets, the sinks, the urinals, the dividers, the doors . . . even the paper-towel holders. Somebody took all the nuts off the bolts."

Mr. Parisi cleared his throat as if he thought maybe she shouldn't give away any state secrets (but Tink already knew there were urinals in boys' rooms, and she didn't even have a brother in the upper school). Ms. Cho said, "These are smart, mature sixth graders, Mr. Parisi, and I would like their input."

Mr. Parisi's shoulders sagged ever so slightly. Tink thought he didn't want input, he wanted a culprit. And if none of the sixth graders was the culprit, well then he'd just mosey along. "Let me know their thoughts, then. I may want to talk to a few of them individually to get their views." He went back into the school.

Tink gulped like Daffy Duck. But what did she have to feel guilty about? She studied her pine tree drawing. It was all wrong. Bushwhack spread his paper over a big book, and she couldn't miss seeing that the branches of his tree looked like branches, like the bones of a skeleton, like a tree, not just lines. Hers looked like a collapsing haystack.

"It must have been vandals who got in here over the weekend," said Ms. Cho. "The World Series, you know, and lots of people around here went a little crazy. Some windows got broken at a bar downtown. Do you think someone could have decided to sabotage the school?"

"Sabotage?" Bushwhack seemed to taste the word as he repeated it.

"I'm so glad you asked, Matt. That's a wonderful, incredible word. It comes from the French word *sabot*, which means a wooden shoe."

"It's *zapata* in Spanish," said Jackie in her A+ way.

"Same word," said Ms. Cho. "Some people thought French workers threw their shoes into machines when they went on strike. But it really just means—" She pulled out her cell phone. "Treacherous action. Deliberate subversion. Obstruction of normal operations."

"It obstructed mine!" Keith Kallinka said. Will Wheeler and certain others cracked up, falling onto the sidewalk on their backs, getting covered in the fuzzy, sun-baked dirt.

Ms. Cho said, "Better get on with those drawings. We'll have to make up this time on Friday." She looked at her phone and went inside. Everyone turned back to their drawings, but the nervous chatter went on.

"Poor Keith!" said Maggie.

"Soon as he got in he had to take a—" said Jonas.

"He took a little bathroom break to get over the World Series." That was Will.

"A bathroom *break,* get it?" said Alex Mott.

"A few things got broken around *our* house this weekend," Mitzie said.

"I thought my dad was going to have a heart attack," said Keith.

"My brother went running out the door and straight into the woods, screaming like a maniac," said Jennifer.

"My mom cried," said Keith.

"My mom slammed the kitchen door so hard two coffee mugs fell right off the shelf," said Jennifer.

"My mom lost twenty bucks to my dad," said Will. "So she made him take us out for pizza."

"My dad lost five hundred bucks," said Bushwhack. He had turned away and was working on his pine tree again.

"Five hundred bucks? I bet he was mad," Tink said.

"You should have seen *my* dad," said Jennifer. "His face was bright red."

"Mine's was purple!" Keith giggled.

"Mine was like a bull, pawing the ground," said Jackie, who didn't even *have* a dad.

"And all us kids started screaming," said Will.

"I just got under the bed," said Bushwhack to Alex below the hooting, but Tink heard. Had Bushwhack needed to hide from his father?

Ms. Cho came out again and people started asking her about the bathroom. "Who could have come in over the weekend?" asked Maggie.

"Were there any windows broken?" asked Meghan.

"No," said Ms. Cho, and she just shrugged at Maggie. "No doors were jimmied either, that's what Mr. Joseph says."

"Where were all the nuts?" Tink asked.

"In a row along the back of the sink," said Keith. "I had just noticed them when . . ."

"Two words!" said Tink aloud to herself. She stared right past her sketch paper at her toes and matched them up with the grate over the sewer drain below her feet, which was just where she happened to be along the curb, and looked down into the drain, at the puddle and mud at the bottom, at the reflected piece of sky shining up out of the dark.

"My sister's bed," Bushwhack went on telling Alex.

Jackie asked, "How did the vandals do the sabotage?"

"With a wrench, Mr. Joseph says," Ms. Cho said.

Bushwhack just kept on drawing, making his pine tree even better. "She's at college, so he wouldn't think to look there. He went completely loony."

"Did they just whack the toilets and stuff off the wall?" said Donna. She was kind of dumb, Tink thought.

"No, they undid the nuts," said Jonas.

All the stupid boys cracked up. Whack! Nuts! Bathrooms!

Alex said, "How long did you stay under the bed?"

"The game was Saturday. So it was practically all weekend!"

"Yeah, right," said Will Wheeler. He had heard, too.

"Ask my sister," Bushwhack said angrily.

"About nuts?" asked Will.

"The one at college?" Tink asked.

Bushwhack shook his head. "The other one. My little sister." He had a sister in Tink's sister Jessie's class, third grade, just eight years old. "She brought me food the rest of the weekend. Otherwise I would have starved to death hiding. She went down to 7-Eleven with the only ten dollars I had left, plus a dollar of her own."

Tink stood up and brushed the back of her skirt. "What'd she buy?"

"Chocolate pudding."

"All weekend long?" asked Alex.

"Where's your dad now?" Tink said.

"At work."

Ms. Cho was standing on the threshold of the classroom, balancing on her little striped Keds. Tink went over to her. "Ms. Cho," she said softly. "What if Keith had been right next to the stalls when they fell, instead of going out the boys' room door?"

Ms. Cho pressed her hands together.

"You mean smooshed?" Tink asked. Jackie appeared at her elbow. Tink looked at her and shrugged. Jackie shrugged back.

"They could have hit him or landed on him," Ms. Cho said. Keith was really small. Tink imagined a sink or stall collapsing on *her*—the cold, heavy porcelain sink crashing down, the metal dividers keeling over sideways.

"Is he lucky to have made it out alive?" she asked.

"Unscathed," Ms. Cho said lightly. "All fingers and toes and limbs intact. No broken bones or lacerations." Her voice shook a little. Tink could tell she was just pretending to be calm, cool, and collected.

"He could have been crushed," said Jackie.

"Ms. Cho," Tink whispered. "Can I talk to you a minute?" She glanced past Jackie at the kids on the curb, trying to find a way to say what she needed to say without . . . "There won't be time for more oral reports until tomorrow, right?"

"Is that what this is about? You're not on the schedule for today anyway."

"No, Keith is," she said.

"Even I couldn't do that to him today," said Ms. Cho. "He's an absolute bundle of nerves."

"So is Bushwhack," Tink said. So was Ms. Cho.

"Well, *Matt* won't give his report until Friday."

"Ms. Cho," Tink said again. "I probably shouldn't tell you this, but I don't know what to do."

"Trust yourself, Chris," Ms. Cho said. Her black eyes went sharp and very serious. "You usually do the right thing."

She still thought this after Will Wheeler and the water fountain?

Tink leaned in. "Matt's dad lost a lot of money on the World Series and Matt spent the weekend hiding from him, under a bed. He would have died if his sister hadn't brought him food." Jackie's stillness at Tink's side was proof of her surprise: at Bushwhack's situation, at Tink for telling the teacher about it. Tink felt Jackie there as solidly as if Jackie had taken her hand.

"So that's it," Ms. Cho said. "That's what's eating him."

"He was here first thing," Tink said. "He must have snuck out of his house early and come to school to get away from his dad."

Ms. Cho looked away. "And I'd been thinking . . . Well, never mind. You were right to tell me, Chris."

"Okay," Tink said. And she knew three things for sure: One, Ms. Cho had suspected Bushwhack of unbolting the bathroom right down to the nuts. Two, now Ms. Cho didn't think he'd done it. Three, she, Tink, thought he might have. With her socket wrench.

Her stomach hurt. Had Bushwhack's growling stomach led him to check her backpack for lunch when she had gone down the hall and left it open? Hadn't he seen her take the lunch out to go swap it with Kitty? She wished he *had* found her lunch, instead of the socket wrench.

Ms. Cho narrowed her eyes at Jackie. "Your discretion is of course a given?" she said.

"What do you think I am?" asked Jackie.

"Hmmm," said Ms. Cho. "I'm putting my faith in you, Jacqueline." She hadn't made any such threatening statement to Tink, and Jackie looked hurt. But Tink was the one who had pushed Will. And Tink was the one who had brought the socket wrench to school!

Ms. Cho went on, looking intently at both of them, "No one could know who would go to the bathroom next. I know it's the upper school bathroom, but it could have been a kindergartener. And even Keith could have been seriously hurt."

Her heart pounding, Tink went past Ms. Cho into the classroom to her cubby and got her backpack. "Going somewhere?" said Ms. Cho.

"Just back to draw," Tink said as casually as possible. "My colored pencils are in here." She felt Ms. Cho's trust, and it worried her. She wasn't so angelic! Ms. Cho didn't know what she had in her backpack besides colored pencils.

She went back out and sat in her place above the sewer, and said, "Bushwhack, I crave a boon." It was what he made the Farmers say when they wanted any stupid thing, like help with math or a drawing of a speeding race car. He was a fair leader, though: He said it to them, too, when he wanted anything. Usually the correct answer was "Pray ask," but Bushwhack just looked up at her, surprised.

"I need to get this stupid tree right," she said. He saluted and moved over to make room on the curb. She leaned closer to him.

"Whoo-whoo," said Keith Kallinka.

"Shut up," said Jackie.

"I saw your pine tree before," Tink said, without looking at Bushwhack. Now Jackie was tickling Keith Kallinka, while Tink was embarrassed just to be sitting *next* to a boy. But Jackie was distracting Keith . . . Smart girl! Tink dumped the colored pencils and the wrench into her lap, into the fold of skirt that hung between her legs, and hid them there.

"You're a decent drawer, Hundred Percent. You're, like, an artist."

"Then what are you?" she asked. "I think you're better."

"I'm an engineer," he said. "That's what I am—someone who figures out how things go together."

And come apart?

She said, "Okay well, I can't figure out how those pine trees go together. Look, this part goes up, that part goes down. They're nothing like Christmas trees. I can't get the shape at all."

He sat on the curb with his foot wedged into the grate over the sewer to steady his knee under his drawing. "You have to *look* at it to see how it goes together," he said, as if it was that easy. "It's just a big stick, see, and it's got branches going off in all directions." Tink gave him her green pencil out of her skirt. He used it to gesture above her drawing, not drawing on it the way certain art teachers would. "Not just side to side like a Christmas tree, but frontwards and backwards, too."

She couldn't see how to draw that, so she said, "Just do it on the paper. I don't care. I'll start over later." He began to draw, his head down, floppy hair hanging over the paper. For the first time all day maybe he forgot he'd slept under his sister's bed. Tink was glad.

"But that's not all there is to it, it's not just branches going frontwards and backwards," she said. "Some go up, and some go down. How do you get it not to look like some big pom-pom or hairball or something?"

"Well duh, Hundred, the tree is too tall to come out looking like a ball."

She laughed. He drew, while Tink took the socket wrench out of her lap and hid it against the curb, under her knees. "How do you know which ones go up and which go down?"

"Look at the tree," he said. Tink saw him glance down. She thought how Bushwhack had understood when she pushed Will into the water fountain, how he hadn't gotten critical over her angry, hurt act. How could she fault him for doing what he had done? Nobody had gotten hurt. Even Keith Kallinka was just basking in the glow of attention. The person who had gotten hurt was Bushwhack. He was the one hiding under the bed starving all weekend. She let him see the wrench by poking it out from behind her knee.

He flinched when he saw it, and looked up at her face to see what she meant by showing it to him. "Some branches sag, some don't," she said. What she meant was, *I know, but it's okay.*

"Weight," said Bushwhack. Or did he say, "Wait"?

Tink flipped her paper over and began not just drawing the pine branches coming off the tree at the right angle but trying to show that they were so long they weighed themselves down—the longer ones hanging down the heaviest, the shortest, newer ones poking up toward the sky. "The bigger they are, the harder they fall," she said.

"What are you doing with that wrench?" he whispered.

She said, "Waiting for the bell to ring."

It rang. She dropped her dad's silvery wrench with a clang through the rust-colored sewer grate and into the silty mud at the bottom of the drain. It sank slightly, halfway into the puddle, wrinkling the reflection of the sky. Tink scooped her colored pencils out of her skirt and shoved them into her backpack. If anyone looked into the sewer, they could see the wrench. But who would? And how would they know where it came from? They wouldn't. Just in case, Bushwhack and Tink hung around picking up their papers. Jackie hung back, too, waiting for Tink without knowing why, and the three of them—plus Keith, who waited by the door for Jackie—were the last ones into the school.

Tink dropped her pack on the floor of her cubby and grabbed her lunch bag, and Jackie got the little pineapple-shaped purse that held her lunch money. Keith and Bushwhack were buying lunch, Tink guessed, since they didn't pick up anything and were already halfway down the hall. Jackie and Tink hustled to catch up. On the way to the cafeteria/auditorium, which Bushwhack had renamed the cafetorium, they passed the boys' room. Mr. Joseph was folding up a MEN WORKING sign.

"Open for business?" said Keith.

"Keith, you still have to go?" asked Alex.

"I went before—" Keith began.

"Nobody wants to hear any more about your functions, Kallinka!" Jackie said.

"What a sewer grate I am," said Bushwhack, in line ahead of Tink. "What a spiral notebook. What a screw top." Then he added, "I forgot my lunch *and* my lunch money."

Tink said, "Well, I bet you already had enough of *that* dessert."

"It kept me alive all weekend under the bed," said Bushwhack.

"Thank God for that," said Keith Kallinka, rolling his eyes.

"Have half a chicken cutlet," offered Jackie.

"And half my peanut butter sandwich," Tink said.

"You can have my milk," said Will Wheeler, ahead of them. "It's disgusting anyway."

Jennifer shook her head at Will, and handed over her straw.

Donna offered a banana.

Bushwhack said loudly, "All I really want is—"

Tink slipped back to the lunch counter, cut the line, fished a dollar out of her skirt pocket, and handed it to the lunch lady. The lady placed a little cup on Tink's tray, but she picked it up and passed it. "Give it to Bushwhack." Hand to hand it went up the line.

Tink never appreciated Jackie as much as the moment when she said, "He can have my pudding, too."

"Two chocolate puddings?" said Bushwhack. "I get two?"

And then everyone did it, five more people, one after another, all the ones who had hot lunch and a few who had dollars: Jennifer, Donna, Alex, Jonas, even Keith Kallinka. Which answered the question, Tink thought, of whether the class was actually thankful that Bushwhack had survived the weekend. By now they had all figured out how he had spent it. Somebody had to give him a tray for all his food.

"Kallinka," complained Will Wheeler. "What does Bush-face need with your pudding? If you're not hungry, I'll—"

"Too late, Wheeler," said Keith. Impressive.

Bushwhack balanced the heavy, pudding-laden tray across the cafetorium to the table where the Farmers sat. Mr. Parisi saw him and said, "Big appetite today, Mr. Alva?"

"Who doesn't love chocolate pudding?" said Bushwhack.

Tink called Jackie because she wanted to know if she was suspicious.

TINK:     Who do you think did it?
JACKIE: Keith Kallinka, his own silly self?

So she thought he was silly too? No longer in love? Tink guessed Jackie was in love with Bobby now.

TINK:     To get out of his oral report?
JACKIE: Quite seriously, no. He doesn't have the balls.
TINK:     Jackie!

Hysterical laughter. Mom, passing Tink with a giant basket of laundry, shook her head. She could tell Tink and Jackie were laughing at someone.

JACKIE: Who do YOU think it was?
TINK (airily): Oh, some thug over the weekend. Nobody WE
              know. Maybe some angry ex-student returning to
              haunt Mr. Parisi.

From the bedroom doorway, Mom gave Tink the stink-eye.

JACKIE: Whoever it was, it was worth it. What a noise!
TINK:    What a racket!
JACKIE: What a din!
TINK:    What a ruckus!
JACKIE: What a kerfuffle!

Jackie really *was* as funny as Bushwhack.

TINK:    You're kind of a goof. But seriously—wasn't
         it loud?

Her mother asked, "What was?"

TINK:    MOM.

Mom asked, "Can I talk to you please? About a message the
parents got from Ms. Cho?"

TINK:    Er—okay. Jack, I've got to go.
JACKIE: What message? Is it about the bathroom or some-
         thing else?

Tink got nervous. She asked Mom, "Is it about the
bathroom?"

Mom said, "Yes, do you know anything about that?"

JACKIE: Not the chocolate pudding situation?

Tink didn't want to talk about that with her mother there.

JACKIE: You know. The great lunch donation?
TINK:　What made you give him yours?
JACKIE: You did, twerp. And I'm sure you had a good rea-
　　　　son, right?
TINK:　Yes.
JACKIE: You don't have to tell me what it is. I can guess.

Tink thought, Jackie had been standing there listening to her tell Ms. Cho about Bushwhack. So what was the big surprise?

JACKIE: Is there something you want to tell me?
TINK:　Mom, I'll be off the phone in a second.

Oh no. Did Jackie think she liked Bushwhack? Mom came into the hall with the empty basket and looked at Tink quizzically.

JACKIE: Tinky, sometimes you're just right. You were
　　　　right to tell Ms. Cho. And you were right about
　　　　the chocolate pudding. That's why you're my best
　　　　friend.
TINK:　Am I? Is that why?

Tink meant: Am I still your best friend? And she thought, She called me Tinky. It made her feel warm in her heart. But Jackie said nothing. Did she know what Tink was thinking?

Mom chose this moment to insist that Tink get off the phone once and for all and talk to her about the bathroom. "What's been going on at school with the boys? First I hear that Will Wheeler got pushed face first into the water fountain. Next thing, the boys' room is collapsing like a house of extremely heavy cards."

Tink shrugged to hide the fact that she was quaking inside, not able to even consider what her mother would say if she knew that both of those things were her fault. She asked, "Mom, what happens if you borrow something from somebody and then you lose it?"

"Like what?"

"Like a, um, a library book? I took this big book to school for my report and it fell off my bike into a puddle."

"Fell right out of your backpack?" asked Mom.

"Out of the bike rack. It was too big for the backpack."

"Where is this book now?"

"I had to throw it away," said Tink. "It was wrecked. You know how it rained last night? All the sewers were full." Why had she mentioned the sewers?

Mom gave her a narrow look. "Well then, I guess you'd have to borrow against your allowance to make things right. How much is it going to set me back?"

"Like, fifteen dollars?"

"Hmph!" snorted Mom. "Be sure you go right down after school tomorrow and pay it."

But Tink didn't go to the library the next day. She went to the hardware store and bought her father a new socket wrench, just like the old one.

# 4

# Pregnant Girlfriend
## (Halloween)

Bess had decided that now that Jackie had turned twelve (quietly, enviably, celebrating with a dinner alone with her mom during which she got her own glass of wine), she could be home at night alone in the evening sometimes, but that wasn't Tink's mom's idea of good parenting. "*You're* not twelve yet," she said, "and I wouldn't care if you were. And we're *certainly* not testing this on Halloween. Let Jackie sleep over here if her mother goes out."

*Her mother.* Not Bess. It wasn't Tink's first hint that Mom had cooled on Bess. Mom had gotten a few digs in since the lobster dinner. Or maybe Tink had only now become aware that the relationship was cool, and maybe always had been. Oh well. Did Mom have to love who—or what—Tink loved?

Lobsters aside, Tink still loved nothing more than having Jackie in the little roll-out bed in her room. It was something she and Jackie both understood: loving having your own room, but also loving having someone else there—someone you chose, not some sibling. "But Ma," Tink said, trying to be understanding, "doesn't that make you feel like you're babysitting while her mom goes on a date?"

"Is it still that same man?" was all her mother said. She meant, that same *twice-married* man. The odds were bad, that's what Tink had overheard Mom tell Dad.

"Yeah. James," said Tink. They were in the laundry room, looking through the plastic bins of Halloween stuff for white face paint Jessie wanted for her costume. Tink was pawing through stuff that was mostly too small, and all too stupid, to be a Halloween costume for herself.

Mom didn't say anything bad about Bess. She just pulled another bin off the shelf and dropped it on the floor. She didn't say "poor kid" about Jackie (Tink had overheard that, too). She did say, also probably trying to be understanding, "I would have loved to have had a buddy like you in sixth grade."

"Jack's my buddy, too," Tink said.

Her mother said, "Lately she's a different kind of buddy to you than you are to her."

"Maybe she's the kind of buddy I need," Tink argued. "She's smart, and she's not a fool, except when she's trying to be funny." Tink was trying to sound wise—wise in the sense of intelligent, not a wisecracker. "She shows me stuff I wouldn't figure out for myself otherwise."

"That's for darn sure," said Mom, stunningly fast and sarcastic.

"What does that mean?" asked Tink, getting anxious.

Mom jiggled her knees, glancing away. "You're different since school started," she said. "I wonder whether you're trying too hard to keep up with Jackie. And you always seem to get mad when you're on the phone with her."

Tink blinked. "You think I'm different because of Jackie?"

"Then what is it because of?"

Tink felt a swirl of confusion all through her chest, fingers of it pushing at her ribs. She took a short breath and said, "Everybody thinks they know everything about me. Well, they don't!" She knew that wasn't answering Mom's question. "Anyway, it's not Jackie's fault."

"You know," said Mom, "sometimes when girls have been friends for a long time—"

"It's *not!*" roared Tink.

Mom didn't even look startled. A line appeared between her eyebrows and then went away. She kept going through the bin. After a moment Dad appeared in the doorway from his little office next door. "Everything all right?" he asked, looking from one of them to the other.

Tink made an expression with her mouth, a little sucking-in of one cheek that meant *sorry*. Mom raised her eyebrows, which meant *okay*. Dad went back to his work.

Mom tried to have the last word. "Think about it," she said.

"*Mom,*" said Tink.

Jackie always came to Tink's house to go out for Halloween, and Tink thought Jackie liked the getting-ready part just as much as the going-out part. This year Jackie decided to bring music so "We can all get funky dancing while we're getting ready." She announced this to Tink on the bus on Halloween as she was getting off at her stop, and didn't even give Tink a second to say yes or no, as if it wasn't Tink's own house Jackie was bringing the funk to.

Fifteen minutes after Tink got home from school, Jackie showed up at the door with her little green plaid overnight bag, which had her pajamas in it and her tooth-brush, and her notebook she always wrote in before bed, and her stuffed monkey and her birthday iPod in her hand. (Needless to say, Tink didn't have one of her own, but maybe for her birthday in November?)

"Somebody's ready to trick-or-treat!" Jackie told Tink. She was already in a party mood, and for a tired instant, Tink felt like she just wanted to do her homework.

Mom came to the front door and hugged Jackie just as hard as she usually did (Tink was paying close atten-tion) and even gave her a little more attention than usual, pulling back to look at Jackie's face and say, "How are you? How's your mom?"

"Fantastic!" said Jackie, about both, Tink supposed.

Mom wouldn't be so quickly settled with. "Your mother is always fantastic," she said quietly. "But all this means big changes for you. A man with kids of his own."

"I love them!" said Jackie brightly. In the case of Amy, that was a lie. In the case of Bobby, she meant it differently than Tink's mother probably thought. "Big happy family," she went on.

Mom cocked her head to one side and hugged Jackie to her again, and this time Tink saw a hollow look in Jackie. All of a sudden Tink was alarmed. From the expression on Mom's face over Jackie's shoulder, Tink could tell Mom knew Jackie had doubts about that happy family. Tink felt a thump of love go out to both of them. Poor Jackie, she thought. And she was proud of her mom for being nice.

The kids came thundering down the stairs. Jessie yelled, "Yay, Jackie's here!"

Alvin picked up her bag as if he was the bellboy in a hotel, and Kitty cried, "Hey, you brought your music?" Jackie made a little fancy bow.

To Tink, Jackie said, "Mitzie and Maggie and Meghan are getting ready at Maggie's house. They asked me, but I said no. They were talking about meeting later. Okay?"

Tink tensed up. Mitzie and Maggie and Meghan hadn't asked *her*. Just as well, because she wouldn't have wanted to go. Halloween was something that happened here, at home. It always had, so far.

Jackie said to Kitty and Jessie, "You girls ready to get funky?"

"What?" said Alvin.

"*Dance*," said Jackie, and did a swooping hip move that was obviously a copy of Bess—as was the word *funky*.

If they got ready at Jackie's house they could have eaten those chocolate-covered almonds Bess always had, and danced without an audience of siblings. But Jackie was opening her suitcase on the family room floor and letting Jessie and Alvin play with the monkey, while Kitty thumbed through the iPod, which was not full of awful little-kid junk the way Dad's was (loaded up for entertaining Jessie and Alvin—and even Kitty—in the car, and devoid of the rock and soul and funk Tink had learned to like, courtesy of Jackie, who had learned it from Bess).

But it turned out to be okay that they were there, because all they did was try to hog Jackie's attention, trying to show off how well they could dance, while Tink bumped around quietly behind the chair. She needed to figure out how to dance. Mitzie had begun talking about how she was going to have a boy-girl party for New Year's and have dancing. Jackie was sure to go, and that meant Tink would have to, too.

It wasn't that Tink didn't love music. She really did. She lay in bed at night and listened to the old CD player with some headphones from a plane trip her father had taken, until she fell asleep, but the idea that you were supposed to get up and move somehow confused her. Now she tried to imitate what Jackie did, and sometimes Kitty, and even once in a while Alvin, although he mostly did the butt dance. Jessie was at least as bad as Tink, but she could sing along better.

"That's where your soul is," Jackie told her. "In your singing."

"Where's your soul, Jackie?" asked Jessie, pleased.

Jackie swung her hips around and stuck her chest out and asked, "Where do you think it is?"

"You sound like Jonas," Tink said disgustedly. Jonas MacDonald banged his pencils on the desk all day as if they were drumsticks, and went home and read *Rolling Stone* magazine. He used to bring it to school, but Mr. Bergman took it away from him and probably read it on his lunch break in the teachers' room. At first Tink thought maybe Mr. Bergman thought *Rolling Stone* was about his favorite band, but then he told her he was just a big fan of any music. He also did not pass up the opportunity to advise her on what Rolling Stones song to look up next. First he had told them all to listen to "You Can't Always Get What You Want." Then, when Tink—with Jackie tagging along— had asked for another recommendation after liking the first, he suggested "I Am Waiting," "Jumpin' Jack Flash," and "As Tears Go By." Next he said "Honky Tonk Women" and "Tumbling Dice." And Jonas himself had chimed in for "Start Me Up" and "Let's Spend the Night Together," but Mr. B nixed that last one, which made them listen to it anyway. It was good, and raised some interesting questions between Tink and Jackie about its meaning.

"What's wrong with Jonas?" Jackie asked now.

"That's what I've been wondering," Tink said.

"But why?" Jackie said seriously. "He's cool."

"You think so?" asked Tink. "Well, everybody else thinks he's a freak."

"Define 'freak,'" said Jackie.

"He thinks he's cool," Tink said, a little nervously, because she'd thought she knew who was liked and who was just there. "He thinks he knows so much about so much." Jonas was an expert on wars as well as music, and knew about such things as bombs and guns and fighter jets. Also he wore button-down shirts that he thought were stylish and the other boys in the class were just plain uncomfortable about. Or maybe not? Tink had thought Jonas didn't fit in, and now she was worried that she had it wrong. "He's weird," she said dismissively, testing.

Jackie shrugged and did not shoot her down.

"Is that who you like now?" Tink asked her.

Jackie wiggled her eyebrows at Tink. "I'd rather groove with Bobby," she said. She didn't really mean it when she used words like *groove* or *funky* or *far out* or *boss* or *keen*. She collected them from wherever she heard them—Bess laughed at old-fashioned words that people used to use to be cool—and used them to be funny, instead.

"Ooh, Bobby?" said Kitty, not knowing who he was, but knowing his was a new name in the world of Tink and Jackie. "Have you danced with him?"

"My soul's in my butt!" said Alvin, shaking it.

"Stop saying that word," said Mom, coming in. "Isn't it time for everybody to start getting ready for trick or treat?"

Alvin was going out as Swamp Thing. He wore green clothes streaked with black paint, and green streamers that Mom had crinkled and tattered so they looked like seaweed. His face was covered with green and black goo, too.

Jessie was going to be a dead princess. White monster makeup and a princess costume.

And Kitty was going to be a mummy, wrapped up in three rolls—"that's three thousand sheets," she reported—of toilet paper. She wanted to go out with Jackie and Tink, but Mom was making her take the little kids. Good. Kitty, Jessie, and Alvin would be like *Night of the Living Dead,* a bunch of zombies walking down the street.

Jackie and Tink were going to be pregnant ladies. Jackie's idea. A fat stomach and big bazoomas. It was an easy laugh for Jackie, who didn't have any of her own, but not for Tink. She had actual bazoomas now, and her stomach was round already. She didn't like the idea of extra padding, and when she went upstairs to borrow her mother's big bra, stuffed with socks, she thought she didn't look pregnant, just fat.

When Dad found her standing in his and Mom's closet crying at her reflection, she begged him to let her go trick-or-treating in his army uniform jacket.

It wasn't easy. At first Dad just plain said she couldn't borrow his uniform jacket for her Halloween costume. "Why not?" Tink wailed. "I've got to change my costume, and I have to change it now! Jackie's waiting for me and we're supposed to go in like, five minutes!"

"Should have thought it through better, my friend," said Dad.

"How did I know I'd hate being pregnant so much?" He just stared at her. "Dad. Please. I can't be a bum without your jacket."

He was never like this. He helped her do things, helped her make things, liked her ideas, laughed with her, not at her. But now he was staring at her in a skeptical way. He was hesitating. "Why do you have to be a *bum* with it? What bums have you ever seen, anyway?"

"The guys who hang around by the train station," Tink said. "They're veterans. They wear their own army stuff and they smell like drinking."

"Stevie, is this true? What are you letting her go to the train station by herself for?"

"Don't be ridiculous, of course I don't," said her mother. Tink let it drop, didn't explain how she and Jackie went to the station to get the weekly free newspaper, the one with the sexy ads in the back.

Mom was on her knees sewing Jessie into her costume, which was one of her own long fluffy slips done up to look like a princess dress. She was both fitting it to Jessie and putting it on her for the evening, all at once. Jessie, standing on Alvin's toothbrushing stool, kept taking her crown off and on because the elastic was pinching her chin, and bashed her mother on the head every time she moved.

Dad said, "Anyway, how do you know what drinking smells like?"

Tink said, "They have flasks in their pockets, that's why the drinking smell. Jackie says it's gin."

"How does she know? Now listen," scolded Dad. "If those guys are bums, that's their business. God knows what they've been through, and it's no wonder they're half crazy, if that's what the problem is. But my uniform jacket is not going to be worn by some kid pretending to be a bum. I served my country in that jacket, and it's worthy of respect."

"But the bums served their country in their jackets, too," Tink said. She didn't understand.

Dad read her confusion. He stared into her eyes for a moment, then said, "Just be a soldier. I'll grab my old infantry cap, and you can wear my uniform."

Jessie said, "Women in the army have their hair in a bun. I saw it on a commercial."

"My hair's too short for a bun!" said Tink. "I have to be a man." She wasn't thinking clearly—of course there must be female soldiers with short hair—but it had sounded so much easier to be a guy, even if it was a guy bum.

"Stevie—" Dad was reaching the end of his rope.

"Can't I be a guy soldier, if I want to?" demanded Tink. "Like G.I. Joe or something?"

Mom's voice was even. "Wait 'til I'm done here, Tinker Bell, and I'll do you a mustache with my eyebrow pencil."

"Go get it, Tink. I'll do it," said Dad.

"You're going to draw me a mustache?"

"Who better?" he asked.

When Tink came down to the kitchen, Jackie was standing there pregnant, hands cradling her basketball-shaped stomach (in fact it *was* a basketball), arching her back to show her phony bazoomas (the decorative pillows from Bess's bed), and doing the Mexican hat dance for Kitty and Alvin, jumping from heel to heel, to make it all bounce.

Dad and Tink examined her from all angles and determined that, despite being 4'11" and baby-faced, Jackie could really be having a baby. "Can I borrow that eyebrow pencil?" she asked. She quickly lined her eyes, emphasized her eyebrows, and practically punctured her cheek as she twirled the pencil around and around to make a beauty mark. Even if Bess didn't allow her to wear makeup out of the house, Jackie was an experienced maker-upper.

"So grown-up you are, Jackanapes," said Dad.

"Let me do you a mustache, Tommy," said Jackie.

"Tommy!" said Alvin. None of the kids ever called Dad that, only Jackie.

Dad shrugged. He sat down at the kitchen table so his face was nearer Jackie's. Tink felt a twinge of jealousy when Jackie held her father's chin in one hand and drew a mustache under his nose with the other. He would never let *her*. She would never even try.

When Jackie was finished, Mom put one hand on her hip and studied Dad's face. "I can't tell if you're a good guy or a villain," she said.

Dad pretended to twirl the end of his mustache, and tried to act mysterious.

Jackie, being shorter, stood in front of Tink when they went to doors to trick-or-treat. The people at the doors all rolled their eyes when they saw her belly and bazoomas. A little girl, pretending to be pregnant! Funny! Then they saw Tink—tall, with her short curls and mustache and army jacket hiding her girliness—and the eyebrows wrinkled.

"I want to go home," Tink said after five houses.

"Why?" said Jackie.

"Jackass, they think I'm really a boy. They think I'm the one who got you pregnant!"

Jackie laughed so hard that if she'd really been pregnant she'd have had the baby right there in the street. "You're right!" she howled. "You look like a man who could make me great with child!"

This made Tink's heart sink lower than her fat, pregnant reflection had. "Terrific," she said. "Whatever makes *you* happy." She fumed as they tramped along.

They didn't last ten more houses. After six or seven, Tink couldn't take the stink-eye looks. "I don't want to do this anymore," she said. "I want to go find my sisters at least. Then we can still trick-or-treat, but if I'm with little kids I can act like the babysitter."

Jackie said, "But we're supposed to meet Mitzie and Maggie and Meghan!"

In answer, Tink licked the back of her hand and rubbed off her mustache, pulled off the infantry cap and stuffed it in her pocket. "I'm not being a man with a pregnant girl," she said. "I'm not being a man at all."

"Well, why didn't you just stay being a pregnant girl too?" Jackie demanded. "You're the one who changed. Or a lady soldier?"

"Because I didn't like it! It was too real! I'm too grown-up! I'm too tall and big and everything!" She didn't mention her bazoomas. "I'm not going out for Halloween anymore. There's no law that says I have to. I'm too old for this."

"How can you be? I'm older than you."

"But you don't look it."

Jackie stuck her chest and belly out, standing under one of the streetlights in full view of some other kids coming down the sidewalk. "Don't I look real? You said I did."

"You look like a pregnant sixth grader! I look like a grown-up!"

"That's not my fault!" Jackie said.

"It's not my fault, either!" And Tink sobbed, finally, which made her even angrier.

Jackie stood still. "All right," she said. She pulled the basketball out from under her shirt and bounced it. "Hey, how do they look without being pregnant?"

"You just look like you have boobs," Tink said. "So what?"

"I wish," Jackie said. "Well, I can dream, can't I?"

"Geez, you will one day," Tink said.

"*One day.* For now, it's Flatty Patty," said Jackie. "Well, find me some youngsters so this evening isn't a total bust. Get it?"

"Look, if you still want to go out with Mitzie and Maggie and Meghan, there's time. My dad'll drive you up there." Tink stared into Jackie's eyes, daring her. "You probably want to," Tink added. "Don't you?"

"They're being *bunnies*," Jackie said with disdain. Mitzie and Maggie were always, always something cute. Meghan, who was tiny and cute naturally, was usually something mean and ugly. This year she was being a bunny, too?

"A pregnant lady trick-or-treating with three bunnies!" mocked Tink.

"I'm out with *you*," said Jackie.

"In other words, your mom made you go out with me, not them?" Tink asked her.

"Bushwah! Is that what you think?"

So it was true. "Now it's your choice," Tink said. "You can go out with them and come back here after trick or treat. Bess won't ever know."

Jackie put her hand on Tink's arm. "It wouldn't seem like Halloween if we didn't go out together. Besides, my mom's not even home. She doesn't give a— But your parents are home and they're both so into it."

"You mean you like how they helped with your costume?"

Jackie knew what she was asking. "I love your family, Tinker Bell, but not without you. You're my girl. Don't be a dodo."

Tink wondered, What about next year? It seemed to her that Halloween was ending, for her anyway.

She tried to imagine what kind of evening Bess might be having with James. They were going to some probably cool and sophisticated Halloween party as foxes. It sounded sexy and funny to Tink. Last year her parents had gone to a party as dice. All night long Dad kept saying to Mom, "Baby, let's roll."

When she had heard that, Jackie had said, "Your dad is so swayve." It was her way of making fun of the word *suave,* so that Dad seemed silly and corny, not smooth and cool. (Tink thought Jonas MacDonald was swayve, but it seemed like maybe Jackie thought he was suave.)

"Yo! Hallowieners!" Jackie went pelting down the sidewalk to catch up with somebody. It was Alvin, Jessie, and Kitty, at the next corner. Big whoop. Tink trudged along with her pillowcase holding treats from just twelve measly houses banging against her leg.

"Monsters!" Jackie said to them.

"Jackster!" said Kitty.

"We're here to protect you from the big kids," said Jackie.

"You *are* the big kids," said Jessie.

"What happened to being an army man?" asked Alvin, rubbing his upper lip to indicate Tink's missing mustache.

"It was stupid," Tink said. How could she explain? She was so relieved not be an army man anymore that she could have cried. Try it sometime: Dress as a big old realistic grown-up when your cute little friend is being something even more cute and little and totally unrealistic. "I think I'm getting too old for Halloween," she said.

"Just too tall, that's all," said Jackie regretfully.

"Does that mean if you're short you can go out for Halloween forever?" asked Kitty.

"As long as I want to," Jackie bragged.

"Your mom's tall, though," Tink said.

"Yeah, but I don't take after her," said Jackie. This was the closest she ever came to mentioning she had any of her father in her bones.

Tink had her father's army jacket warm around her.

At home at last, Tink looked in the mirror and wiped off the gray streak that was left of her mustache. Looked closer: Yes, that was a zit starting, right at the lower edge of her nostril. She wetted a washcloth with the hottest water and held it, steaming, to her face, pressing away the zitness and sniffing up her tears. Then she dried her face on a cool, soft towel and went downstairs to steal some Milk Duds from the little kids.

★ ★ ★

JACKIE: Hello? Complaint Department. May I help you?

TINK: I *do* need help. You know how I dance? I mean, you know how I can't dance? There's going to be that party at Mitzie's, and everyone else already knows how to dance but me, and I'm afraid that I'll have to just sit there when everybody else is dancing.

JACKIE: Just listen to the music, my soul sistah.

TINK: I AM listening.

JACKIE: Don't you FEEL anything?

TINK:     I do, it just doesn't make my body move.

JACKIE:  Just tap your foot when you hear the beat. Do it now. Your mom's always got that crazy radio station on in the kitchen. What's playing?

TINK:     It's just the stupid news. Wait . . . now . . . it's some old thing.

JACKIE:  Oldie but goodie. Tap your foot, sistah. Are you standing up?

TINK (getting up): Now I am.

JACKIE (being a cheerleader): Good! Now move it around while you're tapping it.

TINK:     Move WHAT around?

JACKIE:  Tinky! You're so adorable. Your foot, dopey.


At least she hadn't called her Chrissy.


TINK:     I am NOT adorable. Yeah, I'm doing it, so?

JACKIE:  Now move the other foot around.

TINK:     This is where I get messed up.

JACKIE:  Why, do you only WALK with one foot? Just keep the first foot tapping, and let the other one go along.

TINK:     Are YOU dancing?

JACKIE:  To your radio? No, just the music inside my head.

TINK:     Better not tell Mitzie about that. She'll have something to say to you.

JACKIE: She's nice, really.

TINK:   No, she isn't. She's, like, the normal police, and the rest of the world is abnormal.

JACKIE: Oh stop.

TINK:   No, seriously. She asked me, "Do you think people your size normally eat five fun-size Milky Ways for lunch?"

JACKIE: She's never said anything about being normal to me.

TINK:   Well, there's a reason for that.

JACKIE: Oh yeah?

TINK:   Yeah! What would you know about being normal? No, Jack, that's not what I mean. I mean, of course she's not going to say anything mean to you.

JACKIE: Listen, if she wants ME to come, she'll have to ask you too. I'll kill her if she doesn't. Now, are you moving and grooving? How about your hands? What are you doing with them? Are you snapping your fingers? Making fists? Jazz hands?

TINK:   Should I snap my fingers?

JACKIE (sighing): If you must.

TINK:   At the same time as tapping my feet and holding the phone?

JACKIE: It was your idea.

TINK:   I'm such a bad dancer I'm going to have to stay home whether she asks me or not.

JACKIE: Wait for a different song to start. Then practice in the mirror.

TINK: I don't want to have to WATCH myself.

JACKIE: That's the whole point, sugar plum.

MOM: What do you need to dance on the phone for?

TINK: You think this looks like dancing? I don't.

MOM: Just interested in dancing for no reason, huh?

TINK: Why. Shouldn't. I. Be???

She ran downstairs, out the door, into the yard, yelling her words.

# Horses, Ponies

(Christmas/New Year's)

Some days Tink felt like magic was happening inside her, like she really was growing up into something better, brighter. Her twelfth birthday felt like that: a late November Saturday with just days to go until Thanksgiving break. Her grandmother took her to lunch and gave her clothes money and a charm for her bracelet (a *C* for Christine—or Chris—as if Granny had somehow divined that Tink wanted to leave her childhood name—and self—behind). Jackie had come to dinner and a sleepover, and Bess, instead of dropping her off in the driveway, had come in to wish *Chris* a happy birthday.

It had been a while since Bess and Mom and Dad had met face to face. Tink exchanged nervous vibes with Jackie, suddenly aware these factions would never have connected in regular life without their daughters to haul them together. Everyone was too much lively and laughing, too much trying and smiling, too much pretending they were friends—for her sake, and Jackie's. Tink wondered if they'd always acted this phony (she'd never noticed before), and if they minded.

"Yes, I *do* have a new boyfriend!" Bess exclaimed to Mom.

"There must be a long line of contenders!" Dad said, a comment that made Mom blink the way she did when Alvin pointed at fat people in the grocery store.

"You're the sweetest man!" said Bess. "If only I'll be as lucky as you, Stevie!" That made Dad blush and Mom blink more.

Afterward, when Bess had left to meet James for dinner and Jackie was in the bathroom, Tink had mumbled, "Mom, do you and Dad think Bess is slutty or something?"

"Tink!" said her mother. "What kind of a word is that to use?" Well, Granny had used it at lunch, when she talked to Tink about the clothes she hoped Tink wouldn't buy with her money. After lunch, Granny had taken Tink to Bloomingdale's and together they had chosen an outfit Mom would never have sprung for financially. It was, Granny said, classic and charming and age-appropriate, which meant, Tink assumed, not slutty.

"But what does slutty mean?" Tink had asked Granny, whispering in the fitting room, where Granny sat on a little stool and played lady's maid, taking clothes off their hangers for Tink to try. (The selections were fifty percent hers and fifty percent Tink's—Granny's rule.)

Granny's eyebrows had knitted together before she answered, "Too available."

That definition came back to Tink after Bess said good-bye with a chiming sort of giggle, gave them a wave, and headed off to see "her sweetheart."

Dad said, "There she goes, on her toes, all dressed up in her Sunday clothes." Mom rolled her eyes at his corniness (or at Bess's too-availability?) and Jackie narrowed her eyes ever-so-slightly: Were they making fun of her mom?

Then Kitty said, "Are you *never* going to open your presents?" and Tink felt saved. There she found more to make her feel magically mature—including an iPod mini of her own. And that night, lying in bed, with Jackie dozing off practically in the middle of a sentence about Bobby's cheekbones, of all things, Tink felt twelve in a very good way, and went to sleep feeling older.

But some days she didn't know what was wrong with her. It was like, how long have you got to listen to the list? The last day of school before break was that way. Tink looked in the mirror and just felt disgusting. It was Christmas-time though, no matter how she felt, so she reached for something seasonal. She pulled out the outfit Granny had bought her at Bloomingdale's.

The skirt was red and flippy, and had a little matching bolero that hid her chest. Which was good. There was a white blouse that went with it, but Tink couldn't find it anywhere. And her mother didn't know Tink was looking for it. She tore her room apart searching, while Mom raved and screamed that the bus was coming down the road. She kept yelling until Tink grabbed the first thing she saw—a brown T-shirt with thin white stripes—and flew out the door trailing the bolero over one arm.

She finished putting it on as she slid into her seat on the bus, already exhausted at eight thirty-five A.M., and Jackie said, "How are you doing your hair for the class picture?"

"Class picture?"

"Class picture. The special one for the sixth grade, because we're graduating. Is that how you're doing your hair?"

Tink didn't know if she'd even *brushed* her hair, not that it made any difference whether she brushed it or not. It was just a frizzy mess lately, no matter what she did, the same way she was sweaty all the time no matter what she did, the same way her shirts were too tight, the way she just kept getting taller even if she already *was* the tallest girl. Taller and klutzier.

Jackie had her hair up. It looked formal, pulled tight into a bun on the top of her head, with little corkscrew curls hanging down in front of her ears. Tink's hair might do that if it was longer—but it wasn't. And if her mother had thought of a hairdo for her, as Bess obviously had for Jackie—but she hadn't. And if Tink had even remembered they were taking the special sixth grade class picture—but she hadn't.

"You look cute, Chris," said Jackie, backtracking. "I like that skirt and vest." She didn't mention the striped T-shirt. "I have a barrette you can borrow, if you want to."

She was so obvious. "Don't call me Chris," Tink said.

She had a sudden vision of what the day was going to be like. Will Wheeler might say the same thing he'd said last time she'd worn this red skirt, about how maybe they could get her to climb the monkey bars. She put her hands over her ears, just remembering. Now that his teeth were fixed, she often felt like knocking them out again.

The other girls now on their way to school were going to show their best side the way Jackie was. They were going to give Tink a long, hard look. Some of them might even try to make her feel better about what she was wearing, the way Jackie had, making suggestions or offers of help. Because Tink so clearly needed help.

She got a sore throat just thinking about it. Maybe she was getting sick, maybe she should have tried to stay home from school. Too late now.

"You don't look as hot as you think you do either," she told Jackie furiously, and kept staring at her long enough to see her brown eyes fill with tears.

"Don't be snide!" Jackie said, just like her mother.

"Get lost, Jackass," Tink said. But Jackie didn't act mad. She just looked at Tink hopelessly, like she saw right inside her, like she didn't know what to do with her, as if Tink were her responsibility. She had been looking at Tink like that a lot lately.

At school, Jackie's desk had a little red envelope on it. Tink's didn't. She scanned the room for others and saw them on the predictable desks: Will Wheeler, Keith Kallinka, Meghan Lin, Maggie Lindquist, and—this was a surprise—Jonas MacDonald. Not Mitzie, and so when Tink saw the others talking to Mitzie through the day, she figured she knew what they were talking about.

In line to have the class picture taken, she said to Jackie, "I guess the invitations went out."

For once in Jackie's highly verbal life she didn't have anything to say.

Tink said, "For a boy-girl party, it seems like chopped sides. Too many girls." They both knew Meghan Lin was the one girl too many. Why Meghan, instead of Tink?

Jackie kept her voice light. There were people around. "She *had* to invite Jonas," she said, without explaining. Jonas was outside the circle enough to have given Tink hope when she'd seen the envelope on his desk. "And she told me I could invite someone." Tink got hopeful again, and it must have shown on her face. Jackie knew her mistake immediately and said, "A boy. Bobby."

Tink stood there like a tree stump, like a mailbox, like any of Bushwhack's inanimate objects. She whispered, "Jackie, did you even try to get me invited?"

"She said she was going to," said Jackie. "I don't know why she didn't. Maybe she still will."

They both knew better than that. What was Tink supposed to say: How hard did you try? When did she say she was going to ask me? Why don't you ask her if she's forgotten someone? "Two words!" she said miserably.

Jackie leaned closer and said, "Chris. How could I pass up the opportunity to get him on his own, away from everybody?"

"You'll be with all of *them*," was all Tink could say. And she added, "Don't call me that anymore!"

But Jackie went on whispering in her ear about Bobby, having it both ways: having Tink as her best friend, and getting to go to Mitzie's party, too. Well, it was what Tink had known in her heart since September. She was outside the circle. Now she wasn't even clinging to the edge.

Tink said, "You can't have it both ways, Jackie." Her heart thumped, but she stood firm.

Jackie stepped back and looked into her face. "Meaning what?"

"Meaning, I'm your best friend, and I'm not invited. And you don't want to invite me, you want to invite Bobby. But Mitzie doesn't want me to come anyway. So what are you going to do, Jack?"

Jackie stared at her.

"You're going to go without me, aren't you?"

Jackie's mouth turned down, and her eyes filled with tears again. She nodded sadly. But she nodded!

The photographer lined up the sixth grade on the risers in the cafetorium that were already set up for the holiday concert that night. Tink had to stand in the back in the center, between Bushwhack and Will Wheeler. Mostly hidden, thank goodness. Jackie was in the first row in a chair, her ankles crossed one over the other.

The photographer had a parrot puppet on his shoulder and kept telling them to watch the birdie.

"This guy's a birdbrain," said Joey Butler to Bushwhack, his idea of humor.

"Apparrotly," said Bushwhack, and he cracked himself up so much he had to jump off the back of the risers. They all had to move over, teetering, to let him up again. Tink's bolero cut under her arms, where she was sweating.

The picture did not get taken fast enough, but at last it was over. Tink went into the bathroom to see how it would look to take the bolero off, but her t-shirt was too tight. She put the bolero back on and shuffled off to homeroom.

She went and stood in front of Ms. Cho's desk, where she hoped nobody could hear her. "My throat hurts, and I think I have chills," she said. "I don't want to go out to recess."

"Couple of cuties *you* got to stand between, and that whole back row," murmured Ms. Cho quietly. "You know, you're going to be quite lovely when you get older." Tink straightened up, stepped away. Just because Ms. Cho was going to let Tink stay in didn't mean she had to think she knew her so well.

"I always have to stand for class pictures, my whole life," was all Tink said as she walked away.

"My whole life, I never got to stand," said Ms. Cho.

"Me neither," said Eddie Dewey. She had a boy's name, Eddie, short for Edwina. She had been in the front row, the chairs on the floor, sitting daintily with her ankles crossed between Meghan and Jackie, not standing with boys like an ape the way Tink had. Tink didn't really know Eddie. She had come from another school in September, and they were in different groups for most subjects, because Eddie had learning difficulties.

Tink didn't bother trying to speak to Jackie when she came back, walking slowly into the classroom, chattering to Mitzie and twirling one of her curly-hair pieces around her finger as if she wanted everyone to look at it. She slid her eyes around the room and looked away when she got to Tink. Tink wished the bell would hurry up and ring so the class could go out and leave her in peace.

"You like horses, right?" she asked Eddie Dewey. The notebook on Eddie's desk had horses drawn on the front.

They looked like she had drawn them, hard-to-get-right legs and all.

"Yeah. Do you?"

"They're okay," Tink said. And Jackie was whispering with Mitzie, so Tink whispered to Eddie, "Once a horse peed on me."

"What?" Eddie laughed, and Jackie couldn't help it: She glanced over.

Tink held one side of her red bolero vest up to hide her face and said, "I took these riding lessons once? And I dropped my crop. I had to get off the horse and pick up the crop, and when I was down there under the horse—"

"Oh, no!" Eddie laughed, a bigger laugh than you'd expect from such a small girl. It surprised Tink so much she laughed back.

Ms. Cho raised one eyebrow. Then the bell rang, and recess started. Everyone left but Tink, and Jackie didn't even look back to see what she was doing. Just as well. Eddie glanced back, but when Tink didn't move she did this sort of mouth-shrug and went out. Tink ignored Ms. Cho and sat reading her book for twenty minutes until everybody came back. Then Ms. Cho began getting out the cupcakes the mothers had made for the holiday party and announced, "Remember, folks, tell your parents the pictures will be given out at the end of school in June." June was a long way off, but that didn't help: Tink would still have to see the picture sometime. Even if she became magically gorgeous, cool, and slender by the end of the year, in time to enter middle school, the picture from today would be there to haunt her.

Mitzie got two cupcakes and brought one to Jackie. When Tink saw that, she took the one she had picked up automatically for Jackie to Eddie Dewey instead. "Those riding lessons?" she said to Eddie in a low voice. "They were from the Y. We had to take that old blue Y bus all the way up to the hills where the stables were, and every time, by the time we got there, I was so sick I practically barfed."

That loud laugh again! Since when was Tink this funny? Since now, she guessed. Eddie said, "I have my own horses."

That seemed unlikely. It wasn't the kind of school where people had their own horses.

"You should come riding over vacation," said Eddie.

"Riding? Me?"

Jackie had icing on her nose and her curl wrapped around her finger, and she was smiling at Will Wheeler, because he was pointing out the icing on her nose.

"Well, you took those lessons, right?" said Eddie.

It was easier to just say yes. Actually Tink hadn't been kidding about how close she always was to barfing at the end of those bus trips to the stable. The time she'd gotten peed on was on one of the rare days when she'd kept lunch down long enough to climb on the horse.

"Get it off," Jackie was saying to Will Wheeler. He touched her nose with his fingertip.

Tink asked Eddie, "What day?"

Eddie said, "I'll call you."

When Tink got home from school that day, her mother took one look at her and said, "Weren't those pictures today?"

"So?" Tink said.

"Oh, honey," Mom said. "I'm so sorry. I forgot. And you went to school all—"

"I love this outfit," Tink interrupted. She had, before today. "But do I have to wear it to the holiday concert?" Accidentally on purpose, there was chocolate icing on the skirt.

Her mother nodded her head as if she were thinking to herself. "No, I can get creative," she said, adding, "if you want." She gave Tink the nervous, questioning look she had been giving her a lot lately.

"Okay," Tink said, near tears. For once in her life, instead of the usual fight, she just let Mom put something on her: a black velvet dress of her own that was too long for Tink—"like a midi dress," said Mom, not wanting to hem it, because it would leave a mark and Tink would be taller soon anyway (like it or not). Mom had to take it in, not sewing but pinning it with safety pins under Tink's arms, and for once something wasn't too tight *and* seemed to hide her chest. The dress looked okay, the black making her white face look somehow nicer, and her frizzy hair looked nicer, too, once Mom pinned it back so it only frizzed out *behind* her. And she lent Tink some little dangly screw-on earrings that would hurt brutally, but not until later.

"What do you think?" Mom asked. Her eyes in the mirror were uncertain and hopeful.

"Fine," Tink said, and Mom exhaled, and Tink laughed a little.

At school, in the brightly lit hallway outside the girls' room, where the plate-glass windows reflected everyone's images full-length, Tink saw Jackie, with her hair done up even higher than that morning, the curly pieces even stiffer.

"Are you wearing hair spray?" Eddie Dewey asked her flatly, making it clear what she would think of Jackie if she said yes.

Jackie said nothing to Eddie—whose thick brown ponytail hung flat and sleek down her back, with a black satin bow in it—and pulled on Tink's elbow. "You look nice, Chris," she said in her ear.

Tink tried to pull away. "Quit calling me Chris," she said.

"Your real name's Christine, right?" asked Eddie.

"I mean it," said Jackie. "You *do*. Elegant."

"Oh yeah?" Elegant just meant tall.

"I was trying to help," said Jackie.

"Well, don't."

"Anyway, I'm not the only jerk," said Jackie.

Eddie said, "She's coming riding, at my house. I have horses, you know." Which made Tink wonder again if they were really hers.

"I've seen them," said Jackie. Which reminded Tink how sometimes now Jackie rode the bus that Eddie and also Keith Kallinka and Maggie did, going home with Maggie. Tink wondered what they did at Maggie's house.

"I've never asked *you* over," Eddie said to Jackie.

"Your loss," said Jackie.

Eddie made a face. "Two words," she said.

Tink felt impressed. Jackie was annoyed with Eddie, enough to be a snot to her? Eddie didn't care what Jackie thought, enough to make a face at her? Well.

Jackie angled herself and Tink away from Eddie. "Are you really going riding?" she asked.

"Why shouldn't I if I want to?" said Tink.

Nobody answered.

Over vacation Tink's family went to Granny's and then skating at Misty Manor, and Tink spent the night at Jackie's. Jackie was still going to Mitzie's party on New Year's Eve, as far as Tink knew, but they didn't bring up the subject, and neither of them apologized. Bess gave Tink a big hug and a "Long time, no see enough of you," and the girls were nice to each other, and afterward, Tink thought to herself that the night was about one-quarter fake and three-quarters real, and that was a decent percentage.

Bess let them make nachos with dripping, oily orange cheese and sat chatting with them about Christmas presents. Jackie had gotten noise-canceling headphones, which Tink thought would have been a better present for someone living in *her* house. What noise was there at Jackie's? She told them about her favorite present, a porcelain pig that was a speaker for the iPod mini. Bess had received pearl earrings from James, and was acting like it was the next best thing to an engagement ring, but Tink thought pearls sounded boring. After they ate, Bess let them watch a reality show Tink's mother said was too mature for Kitty and Jessie and Alvin, while she went to her room to talk to James on the phone. Jackie and Tink stayed in front of the TV, and by its light Jackie asked Tink what she thought Sleeping With People meant.

Tink said carefully, because she wasn't entirely sure, "There's more involved than sleeping," which made them both laugh hard.

Jackie said, "You always crack me up," so Tink didn't have to really answer.

At the commercial, Tink asked, "Did you ask me to sleep over to make up for me not being invited to Mitzie's?"

"No, because I wanted you to sleep over, stupidhead," said Jackie. And at the next commercial, she said, "What more than sleeping is happening? Sex?"

"I guess," said Tink uncomfortably. They both knew what sex was, of course. But how and when and why people "had" sex perplexed them. "Do you have to go there?" she added.

"I just wondered what you know," said Jackie. "People have been asking me as if *I* knew."

Tink could guess what people. "Ask your mom," she said.

Jackie shuddered. "I asked her once already. I'm not starting that conversation again."

Jackie seemed to want Tink to tell her. This confused Tink because she thought Jackie must know better, what with Bess having a boyfriend and all. Her own parents having sex was unimaginable. "Why not?" Tink asked.

"She won't tell me about having sex yet," said Jackie. "She doesn't want me to get any funny ideas." Tink could see that happening, with all those boys liking Jackie. It made her stomach feel weird. Jackie added, "I know what it is, but I don't understand why people do it."

"My mom isn't worried about me," Tink said. She thought of something she'd heard her mom say to her dad about Bess "sleeping around."

"Well," said Jackie. There were so many things she could have said after that *well*. Finally she went back to an old favorite. "You're more mature than I am. That's what Bess says."

She called her mother Bess all the time now, never Mom. As predicted, Tink's mother hadn't liked it when she heard Jackie doing it on Tink's birthday. "Don't try calling me anything but Mom, unless you want me to call you Stinker Bell," she had said. (Dad had said, "Don't call her Stinker Bell, or I'll call you Irene," which had made Tink and her mother look at each other cross-eyed, their way of acknowledging his craziness.)

"What do you think I'm so mature about?" Tink asked. "You mean because I wear a bra?" She was trying to put the pieces of the puzzle together.

"So do I," said Jackie.

"Yeah, but you don't need to," Tink said.

"So? Do you think it's slutty or something if I wear one?"

"Slutty?" That word again. Too available? Because she wore a bra?

This reminded her of something Granny had said on Christmas: "According to your mother, you and your friend are becoming quite boy-crazy."

"So?" Tink had asked Granny, crossing her arms over her chest.

Mom had exchanged glances with Granny. "It changes things!" she said. "Your energy goes where your focus is. If you're crazy about, say, bugs, maybe you're going to become a scientist. If you're crazy about, um, color, maybe you'll be a painter. But if you're crazy about boys, you could wind up losing yourself to other people."

"But there are so many cute boys," Tink had said.

Granny and Mom had laughed. "This is true," Granny said. "But it's about more than cute. It's about being your best self. And you can't do that if you're just following Mr. Cute around."

Her mom hadn't ever—wouldn't ever—use the word *slutty* (maybe because her own mother *did* use it). Tink didn't believe Bess slept with anybody except maybe James. And she didn't know what any of that had to do with Jackie. So what did any of it have to do with being slutty?

Jackie was still talking. "Yeah, because it's lingerie and I'm flat. But still Bess says at my age it's appropriate even if I don't have anything to put in it."

"I'd rather be like you than me," Tink said sincerely. She felt so far from Jackie right now, and didn't see what having to wear a bra had to do with boys at all. Unless it was about choosing the bra color or whatever, as if a boy was going to see it. Ack! She pushed her mind away from the thought.

"No you wouldn't," Jackie snapped.

"Everybody likes you," Tink said.

"Who? Bushwhack? Eddie?" Jackie demanded. "Did they say so?"

"No." Tink didn't even bother to be indirect. She was shocked at the people Jackie had named. She couldn't believe Jackie was jealous of people who were outside the circle. "I meant Will and Keith and Maggie and Mitzie."

"That's because they don't know the real me. But you do, Chris. I'm such a phony."

"Bushwah," Tink said. But Jackie just looked at her. Tink didn't know what to say. Her mind felt blank at best, achy at worst. The pieces were not fitting together into any shape she could recognize. She said, "Stop calling me Chris, once and for all."

"But in the summer you said you wanted people to see you differently. Not like—"

Tink knew: not like some green fairy, even if she had been Tink's favorite character when she was little, even if she still did love the real book of Peter Pan (not the Disney version) and the whole idea of Neverland and sewn-on shadows and flying and pirates and rescue. Being called Tinker Bell was even more ludicrous now that she was so tall and bazoomy and everything, everything. But being called Chris didn't feel believable either. She had thought about it. Chris sounded like someone who could scuba dive and knit mittens and had boys just naturally liking her, calling her up all the time. Chris was who Tink would have liked to be, but wasn't. Maybe in about twenty years.

Jackie's shoulders rose and fell. She waited for Tink to say something or do something, and when nothing came to Tink, Jackie lay down. Then she turned over and went to sleep in fifteen seconds the way she always did, in the middle of a sentence, then BAM, out like a light. Tink lay awake, missing her music, and looked at the things stuck up around Jackie's mirror, which reflected the light from the streetlights. She could see Jackie's sunset poster, her peace sign sticker, magazine pictures of that actor she liked—the one with all the hair on his chest—a picture of Jackie with Bess when she (Jackie) was in third grade, and the gift tag from the pale blue sweater she'd gotten for her birthday from Bobby and Amy. (She had folded it so you couldn't see Amy's name.)

What part of herself was Jackie phony about with the circle girls? What couldn't she, or didn't she, tell them? Tink didn't know anymore. She did know they had started getting together on the weekends, going to the movies or the mall, limiting the number in the group to what their mothers could hold in their cars. Tink had seen the four of them—Maggie, Mitzie, Meghan, Jackie—once when she and her mother were at the mall, and dragged Mom into the store's fitting room to hide so she didn't have to be ignored or, worse, hear their excuses. Would it be different now if she had been able to somehow become whoever Chris was supposed to be in Jackie's mind?

In the morning there was bustling around, because Tink's mother had to come get Tink early or she (Mom) wouldn't get done what she needed to get done that day. It turned out that Kitty was going to a friend's house all day, and Mom needed Tink to be her extra pair of hands, looking after Jessie and Alvin. Tink wondered if things would have gotten more peaceful or settled between her and Jackie if she'd been able to stay even for breakfast, but go she must. And for the rest of vacation week, neither of them picked up the phone.

The morning of New Year's Eve, Eddie called. "I have to babysit Walter Warner the Third tonight," she said. "Do you want to come and sleep over? Walter Warner the Second and his wife are going to be out real late. They have sheets that cost five hundred dollars."

"What about riding?" Tink was sort of stunned: a whole sleepover, when she had never even been to Eddie's house after school?

"Come earlier. We can ride this afternoon, then go to Walter's. He just lives next door." She didn't say which Walter, the Second or the Third. It must be both.

"Let me ask," Tink said. It was a grand offer, but she felt bossed. She held her hand over the phone and said to her mother, "Say no!"

"Why?" Mom whispered. "Don't you like this girl? Somebody besides Jackie might be fun."

Tink huffed. "I've got my period. They've got five-hundred-dollar sheets," she said, thinking that telling her mother she and Eddie were babysitting would be the nail in the coffin of the evening at Walter Warner Whichever's house, and that the thing about her period would seal the deal. Mom would never let her take a chance at some stranger's house.

Too bad she was exactly wrong about the effect her period had on her mother. It backfired completely.

"Don't be silly! We have ways to deal with this," Mom said. "Say okay."

Eddie lived in a small house on a country road across from a big red barn with a field full of cows behind it, then Christmas trees growing behind that. Eddie let Tink in the front door and immediately took her to the kitchen to see the horses. The windows of her kitchen (empty, dark, with no brothers or sisters or parents home) looked out on green grass and horses (fat, brown, shiny). There were five of them, each more beautiful than the last, something Tink appreciated even though she had never been one of those girls who drew horses all the time or read books about them. She had only read one: *Black Beauty*, which was narrated by the horse itself, and was pretty good.

As soon as Eddie stepped inside the fence, the horses trotted over and surrounded her. Even though she was so small, she didn't seem worried. It turned out she had carrots in her coat pocket, and the horses knew it. She handed Tink a little handful—she had broken them all up into little chunks—and told her the horses' names as Tink fed them, her palm raised to their smoochy velvet hot lips.

The horses were all named after old fogey singers. The black one was Dean Martin. "Dino," said Eddie. Three brown ones with white spots were Frank Sinatra, Perry Como, and Sammy Davis Jr. And the little one—white, with brown spots—was Johnny Mathis. They all had boy names, but Tink could see that some of them weren't boys. "Did your parents name them?"

"We only just got here in August," said Eddie.

"Didn't you bring the horses?" Tink asked.

"No," said Eddie, as if Tink were stupid.

"Aren't they yours?"

"Of course they are!"

"Oh," Tink said, as if she got it. But she didn't.

"Can you really ride?" said Eddie.

"Of course I can," Tink said, as if Eddie were stupid.

Eddie looked at Tink with one eye closed. Then she led her into a little shed full of horse things and gave her a helmet to wear and a saddle to carry. Tink actually was very good at saddling up a horse. That part was done standing on solid ground, where she had liked to be after the long bus ride to riding lessons. "It's easy with such a baby horse," she said.

"Johnny's a pony," said Eddie. She stuck her foot in the stirrup and swung her leg over Johnny's back, gave a little nudge with her heel, and got the pony to go out the door. Tink followed, feeling left behind.

"Do you want me to ride?" she called.

"Johnny's the only one I'm allowed to ride," said Eddie. "When nobody's around, anyway."

"Where is everybody?" Tink asked, but Eddie wasn't listening. She was urging the pony to go faster, heading for a little wooden jump at one side of the yard. Tink walked into the yard a short distance, feeling awkward, picking her way around horse poop.

"Can you do this?" Eddie yelled, and Johnny jumped over the jump. Eddie didn't even bounce. She just leaned forward and sailed over the jump from her perch on the pony's shoulders. Together they turned smoothly and leaped the jump from the other direction. Both their pony-tails flew up almost vertically, froze completely for a second, then flopped down at the same angle and rate. Finally the pony came bounding over and stopped before Tink. Eddie swung down. "Your turn!" It felt like an order. It was an order.

Tink pretended she knew what she was doing. Left foot in the stirrup, then throw the right leg up and over. But the horses at her lessons must have been taller: Johnny's stir-rups were shorter, Tink went up faster, and her right leg flew over his back so fast and far she would have fallen off the other side if Eddie hadn't grabbed her leg. "He's short!" Tink said breathlessly.

She grabbed for the reins and jiggled them, but Johnny didn't move. Eddie called, "Nudge him!"

Tink nudged, and Johnny practically shrugged. "Johnny," said Eddie in a warning voice. Tink nudged again, and he began to trot. She bounced, but it was okay, because she focused on the top of Johnny's head between his pointed, velvet-plush white ears, and held on with her knees, since she didn't dare let go of the reins to hold on to his mane. "Good!" said Eddie.

"YAY!" Tink yelled, pretending to be enthusiastic. She took a chance and looked around the ring, getting used to the pace.

"Try the low jump!" invited Eddie.

"No," Tink said. Only she didn't feel that she could refuse.

Eddie didn't choose to hear her, anyway. "It's over here!" she said. She had climbed up onto the fence and was sitting there watching Tink. She didn't have to say "Bet you can't." It was all in her eyes.

Johnny trotted toward Eddie, and Tink had no choice but to go along. "Come on, Johnny!" Eddie urged him, and he moved faster, his rhythm changing. Tink's knees came up along his sides with the bouncing, and it got harder to hold on to him, and just when she realized that the stirrups were too short he jumped.

Somehow she stayed on, saw the fence sinking down around her and the sky coming up bright beyond it, saw the bars of the jump beneath Johnny's shoulders and felt the hard thump of his front feet on the ground, then his back feet on the ground, then her rear on his back, and then they were down.

"Attagirl!" yelled Eddie, as if she were a teacher or a parent, as if Tink were some other girl, not herself. Tink thought: This can't be me. "Try the big one!" Tink told herself she wasn't scared of Eddie; she could just call her mom and she would come get her. Eddie moved to the part of the fence opposite the big jump and called to Johnny, and Johnny went running to Eddie, as if he thought he could get away from Tink, and jumped.

Everything that could be wrong about it was wrong. He didn't go straight, for one thing, but at an angle, because Eddie had judged her position on the fence wrong. And Johnny's front feet seemed to come down a long time sooner than his back feet, so that he made a slippery slope from his tail to his nose. Tink slid down the slope and landed on his neck, and finally did let go of the reins to hold onto his mane. Then his back end came bashing down, and he seemed to reel under her. Tink slid to one side and nearly went over, the pony with her. One foot came out of the stirrups and she was ready with it, ready to leap away and aim for the ground. Then somehow Johnny landed and Tink managed to stay on his back. She could have gone on riding, but she decided to try to get off, even though Johnny was still walking. This was not a good idea, and she almost fell to the ground, while Johnny kept on going, dragging her. As all this was happening, someone began yelling, "Edwina! Edwina!"

Tink stood in the dirt in the middle of the ring. Johnny trotted away from her. One bar of the jump had been knocked down in the kerfuffle, and Eddie was trying to leverage it back into place too quickly. It fell and clanged.

There was a shout of outrage. The gate of the ring swung open and a woman came through. She was short and chubby and wide, with brown hair pulled back into a small round knot, and her face was as red as her red flannel shirt, and her jeans were tight. She was mad. "What's a great big girl like that doing on a little pony?" she roared. "Edwina, don't you have the sense to see when a rider is wrong for a mount? What kind of a risk do you think you're taking?" As she roared, she marched across the ring. All at once she nabbed little Johnny by the reins, quit yelling, and stood murmuring to him and gentling him.

But then Tink realized that the risk the lady thought Eddie was taking was with the *pony*, not with her, Tink. "I'm sorry," Tink said. "I didn't know I was too big or I wouldn't—"

"I'm not angry at you!" the lady said, but she *was* angry. "Ed*wina* should have known. Ed*wina* should know better!"

And now bossy, nervy Edwina was terrified. "I'm sorry, Mom. I'll take Johnny back in and put him up, and I'll do everything perfect. But don't make her go home, Mom."

Going home would have been just fine with Tink, but there was something about this exchange that stopped her cold. Eddie's mother stood there, the reins in her hand, the pony blowing horse breath on her head. Through her teeth, she said, "No. You told Mrs. Warner that you'd find an intelligent friend to babysit with you. It's New Year's Eve. I'm not going to tell her she has to stay in. And this girl seems to have more sense than you do. That can't hurt."

"I might have to leave," Tink said. "I told my mom I'd call and check if for sure it's okay for me to stay."

"Call her and tell her it is!" Eddie pleaded. "You're the intelligent friend!"

Tink felt neither intelligent nor like a friend, but Eddie apologized as she unsaddled Johnny and wiped down his fur and rubbed him with a brush. "I'm really sorry," she said. Tink wasn't sure she could believe anything Eddie said. Was she actually sorry, or just sorry her mother caught them?

"You'll be sorry if you set me up again," she said boldly, and shook her finger in Eddie's face.

Eddie grabbed her wrist and gripped it so hard it hurt. "You know what *I'll* do?" she said. "I'll punch you out."

For some reason Tink was interested. There was something going on over at this house that was dramatic. She said, "I can punch harder than you," although she doubted it. She had seen Eddie lifting giant buckets of horse water and pushing big horses around.

Suddenly Eddie wasn't angry. Maybe she even liked it that Tink fought back. There was something about her

Tink liked: Eddie didn't know she was cute and little, and she wouldn't like it if you said she was. She wanted to be big and tough. Maybe she thought she was.

"All right, I'll stay," Tink said, feeling powerful. "I guess you're stuck babysitting, huh?"

Before Eddie could answer, there was a shout, and a scrawny blond boy dashed in and threw himself at Tink, grabbing her shirtsleeve and hanging from her. "Happy New Year!" he hollered. "What's your name?"

"Joe Montana," Tink said, for no reason. He was her father's favorite football player, long gone and in the Football Hall of Fame, wherever that was. "You must be Walter."

"Joe Montana, the San Francisco Forty-Niner?" he asked. "In my stable?"

Tink glanced at Eddie. "*Your* stable?"

"You didn't think it was *mine*, did you?" said Eddie. "Richie Rich here owns the whole place."

So that was it. "What's your real whole name?" Tink asked, to hear him say it.

"Walter Warner the Third," he said. "And I'm six and a quarter years old."

"Then I'll call you that," Tink said.

Eddie looked jealous. "This is Tink," she told Walter.

"Is that your *real* name?"

"No. It's Christine."

"Christine what?"

"Christine Bernadette Gouda."

"Call her Tink," Eddie said.

Walter Warner the Third looked at Tink. "Can I call you Christine Berna—Christine—what?"

She could tell he wanted to call her something different from what Eddie told him.

"Call me Tinker Bell," she said.

"I don't want to," he said.

"Then just call me Joe Montana," she said.

"Okay," he answered, grinning up at Tink. She had a little brother. She knew what to do. She grabbed his hands and pulled them up to give him the idea he should jump. He jumped, and landed on the ground.

"No," Tink said. "Here, walk your feet up to my knees." She took his hands again, and carefully he put one foot on each of her knees, leaning back to balance there, his legs stiff, his eyes wide. "Now walk up my arms all the way to my shoulders." His eyes widened even more, and Tink laughed. Eddie stood there with her arms crossed, looking impatient, intrigued. Walter walked up Tink's arms to the shoulders, until he was almost upside down. "Now flip!" Tink said. Still holding her hands, he took his feet off her shoulders and flipped down to the ground, onto his feet.

"Yes!" His face glowed. "Do it again, Joe!" She did it again.

Eddie turned and went back to taking care of Johnny, probably annoyed that Tink was getting all the attention. She was too short to flip Walter like that. "Call her Hundred Percent," she called.

"No, don't," Tink said, laughing.

"What would I call her that for?" said Walter. "She's the world's best quarterback! And she's sleeping over at my house too, right?"

First they had to have dinner with Eddie's mother, who cooked amazing cheeseburgers, but made them clean up afterward. "So you're not a rider?" she asked Tink. "What do you like?"

"My bike," Tink said. "And reading." She didn't know why she said that, but she remembered as soon as she did about Eddie's learning difficulties. So she added, "And drawing, like Eddie."

Eddie looked hopeful, but her mother zeroed right in. "Reading!" said Eddie's mother. "What a concept!" She was criticizing Eddie. "What do you read?"

"*Mad* magazine," Tink said. In fact she read all kinds of books. Besides, her father said *Mad* represented the finest in American letters. But let Eddie's mother think she just read trash. Eddie laughed into her glass of milk.

Her mother's brow wrinkled, not quite a stink-eye, but only because she was trying to be polite. "Where do you ride your bike?"

"All over," Tink said. "For miles and miles. I come by here all the time. I ride by here and across the Post Road and all the way to Burying Hill Beach, and back home again."

"Does your mother know you do that?"

Eddie was rolling her eyes and shaking her head.

Tink kept a smile on her face and said coolly, "My mother has confidence in me. Just ask her."

"Maybe I will," said Eddie's mother. Tink just shrugged. She knew her mother. She liked Tink to be an adventurer. Not Eddie's mother. She had rules. First Eddie had to soak the dishes while she packed to go next door to Richie Rich's. Second, Eddie had to go back and scrub all the dishes and then dry them and put them away. It wasn't a Bess/Jackie situation where Bess was always teaching Jackie how to raise the standard; Eddie's mother just bossed her. And Tink wasn't allowed to help because she was the guest and entitled to privileges.

"What's the point of having someone over if you're just going to have to get in trouble about them and then wait on them hand and foot?" Eddie grumbled, pacing outside the door while Tink went to the bathroom, after her mother finally left. Tink reminded herself again she could call her mom anytime. She had made it this far. She would hold out until she saw Walter Richie Rich's house.

Eddie had been acting like Walter's house was some kind of palace, but it was just a really big house. It was white on the outside, with pillars in front of a circular drive-way made of lots of little white rocks that would hurt your feet if you walked on them barefoot. Eddie hustled them toward a side door.

There was an actual cook in the kitchen, who looked peeved when Eddie came in. Eddie didn't say hello, so Tink didn't either, just headed up a dark little carpeted staircase with the same kind of paneling on the walls as Tink's family room at home. Thinking this made her feel homesick, for the first time tonight. She wondered what everybody was doing at home, whether the little kids were going to bed, and who Kitty had decided to have spend the night, and whether her mother was already grating the cheese for the fondue she always made on New Year's Eve. She would come if I asked her, thought Tink. I can always leave. It's just a phone call away.

Her mind briefly flitted toward Jackie at Mitzie's party, and she grabbed it and tried to pull it back to her own reality. It was no use. She missed Jackie. She tried to picture the party. It was hard to imagine the circle kids together somewhere other than school. What were they doing? Maybe dancing in Mitzie's basement TV room, which Tink knew from the long-ago birthday parties when Mitzie had been obligated to invite all the girls. When had *that* kindness ended? When boys came into the picture? She imagined them—Will and Keith and Jonas, Jackie and Maggie and Mitzie. Even Meghan. And Bobby? It was even harder imagining him being with all of them while she, Tink, was not. All that came to her mind was the picture Jackie had dreamed of—of her and Bobby slow-dancing in Mitzie's basement with the lights turned low.

Tink's heart felt pressed tight, wedged under her ribs, from feeling so left out. There was another hurt, too, that came from the idea of Jackie dancing with Bobby, their arms around each other. Somehow that made her feel most left out of all.

The stairway came out in an upstairs hallway, where Eddie started calling "Whoooooo!" like a ghost.

Luckily Walter Warner the Third wasn't the sort to be spooked.

"Eddie! Joe!" He threw his arms around Tink's waist, then Eddie's. "How do you like your popcorn?" He sounded like Tink's father offering his boss a burger from the grill. Good manners. Not like Eddie's.

"With butter and salt, please," Tink said.

"No Gouda cheese?" said Eddie slyly.

"Actually it's *really* good with Gouda cheese," Tink said.

"Hold on," said Walter. They stood in the hallway at the top of the stairs and didn't say anything as Walter ran down. "Hailey?" Tink heard him say. "Miss Hailey, please? Could you make us some popcorn? Butter, salt, and a little sprinkling of Gouda cheese?"

Tink heard the cross-looking cook laugh in a nice way. "Okay, honey," she said.

"Great!" He was so sweet. "Ring your bell and I'll come down and get it." Then he came pounding back up the stairs. He said, "So, would you like to see your room, and then we can play Twister or watch TV and eat some popcorn? Sorry I'm not allowed to play ee-lectronic games after six at night. Or we could play Sorry."

"I'll Sorry *you*," said Eddie.

"Sorry is an excellent game," Tink said. She liked the way Walter said things, as if words tasted good in his mouth.

"Yes it is," said Walter. "Eddie fears me." He flexed his miniature muscles inside his little shirt. "Do you want to see your beds?"

Eddie nodded. Couldn't she speak? Five-hundred-dollar sheets. Tink wanted to see what those looked like. "Follow me!" said Walter. He led them to a room with striped bedspreads neatly turned down to reveal plain old pale blue sheets, which were the first thing Tink noticed, since they were the whole point. But they politely looked around, checking the view out a front window at the stony driveway, in shadows, through pretty lace curtains. There was a TV all to themselves, and a bathroom just for this room.

"Why do those sheets cost five hundred dollars?" Tink had to ask.

"Because they are Egyptian cotton, my mom says," said Eddie. "They are four hundred and fifty count. Their maid Marlena told her."

"What does four hundred and fifty count mean?" Tink asked.

"It means expensive and luxurious." Eddie sighed happily.

"Come see *my* room," said Walter.

Walter's room was the first sign Tink had seen that it was any use being as rich as Eddie said the Warners were. He had a beautiful bunk bed of dark shiny wood, with soft-looking navy blue flannel-covered comforters on it. The top bed looked pretty lived in, but the bottom was where Walter kept his games and books, just strewn happily all over the place. His games looked good and new, because he didn't have little brothers and sisters trashing things, and his books were many and beautiful.

Tink made herself walk around and look at some baseballs he had there with important baseball players' signatures on them, and a picture of a beautiful blond woman—"That's Mom," said Walter—and, best of all, a giant poster of the Alps, with a little wooden mountain climber hanging from a string. "Look how he goes up," said Walter, and carefully demonstrated how to jerk a bead at the bottom of the string exactly the right way, to make the climber ascend his line.

"Excellent," Tink said.

Then he took them on a tour of the house, to please Tink (and to Eddie's annoyance, because she clearly just wanted to move into the guest room). This took practically an hour. It had an indoor pool, that's all Tink really needed to know. Everything else blended into patterns of pale gold and white stripes and navy blue things with stars and paintings of animals and sailboats. Lots of boring furniture and brass lamps. But finally in the kitchen, Hailey the cook had the popcorn ready, just perfect, with some shredded cheese on top (who knew or cared if it was really Gouda), waiting for them.

"Can we eat upstairs?" asked Walter.

"Not in that guest room!" said Eddie, before Hailey got a chance to speak.

So they took the popcorn and some Cokes into Walter's room and he laid out Sorry, but they only played for the length of time it took to eat the popcorn and drink the Cokes. Eddie didn't take well to being Sorried, even though Sorry was just luck really. It was Tink's idea to play Twister instead. Walter put a little music on, just pushing some button, so that playing Twister would be the way it was on TV, like a party. This made Tink think about Mitzie's party again. If it was her party—horrifying thought!—she'd have preferred Twister to dancing. Were any of them really dancing with each other? She bet Keith Kallinka was entertainingly bad at Twister *and* dancing.

Walter was small, and Eddie was too—strong and practically a gymnast—so it wasn't long before Eddie grabbed for a red dot with her left hand and knocked into Tink's ankles, toppling her. Out. Tink pushed some books aside and curled up on the bottom bunk. One minute it seemed like she was watching them play Twister, and the next Eddie was jostling her awake. "Don't go to sleep! You're supposed to help me babysit!"

"She is," said Walter. Tink pretended to snore, and he thought it was fun to cover her up with the soft blue coverlet. "Good baby," he said, and Tink giggled.

Eddie turned on his TV. "We're going to watch Times Square from eleven to twelve, right?"

Would Walter still be up then? Would Tink? She didn't think so.

"What's that?" asked Walter.

"It's *Times Square,* New York, where the ball comes down at midnight," said Eddie. "Don't you know anything?"

Tink could have thrown something at her, but instead she let out a loud phony snore. Walter laughed. He put on a show with some family of singers and came over to move books out of Tink's way so he could hoist her feet onto the bed. One by one he took off her shoes. Darned if she didn't start feeling really, truly sleepy. Darned if the coverlet wasn't soft and warm and dark blue. Darned if it didn't please her to fall asleep there, where a reassuring and familiar crunch told her there was a plastic sheet on the bed, like on Alvin's, rather than the five-hundred-dollar sheets. Maybe it was a five-hundred-dollar plastic sheet, she thought as she dozed.

"We're going to play something else," said Eddie. "So wake up. It's not even nine thirty."

"I don't know how," Tink said, her eyes closed. She had had just about enough of being bossed.

"You don't even know what we're going to play!" said Eddie.

"I bet you're going to pick," Tink said. She was done, "right through the middle," Bushwhack would say. Or Jackie. Or anyone else she knew with a sense of humor. Anyone else but Eddie.

"Why shouldn't I?"

"It's not even your house," Tink whispered so Walter wouldn't hear. He was watching the singers.

"It's more my house than yours!" hissed Eddie.

"Walter?" Tink asked. "What if I fall asleep right here?"

"Really? Here? That'd be great!" said Walter.

"No!" said Eddie. "Babysitters sleep in the guest room."

"Well, *you* can, Eddie," said Walter. "*She's* not the babysitter, she's my friend." So Tink conked out right then and there, feeling protected by a six-year-old. Six and a quarter.

"I hope you have a very happy New Year, Walter," she said just before she fell asleep. She felt safe knowing that the next morning she'd get up and look out Walter's back window at the fields and woods, and that Hailey would fix something nice for breakfast, and that Dad would come and get her at ten and take her home, and she wouldn't ever have to spend the night with Eddie again.

The phone rang on the afternoon of New Year's Day. It was Jackie, screaming into Tink's ear. Tink was so relieved to hear her voice (even screaming) that she talked to her despite everything.

JACKIE: HAPPY NEW YEAR, SUGAR PLUM!
TINK:   Hello? Is this Aunt Judy? Aunt Judy, is that you?
JACKIE: No, this is not Aunt Judy.
TINK:   Is it Ms. Cho?
JACKIE: No sir, it is not. It is I.
TINK:   Jacqueline Q. MacGillicuddy?
JACKIE: Have you missed me?

*Missed her* didn't begin to describe it. But there was no way she was going to let on to Jackie.

TINK:   Did YOU miss ME?
JACKIE: YES. At Mitzie's party—
TINK:   Stop.
JACKIE: —Will told me—
TINK:   Stop. Stop.
JACKIE: Stop what? We were at Mitzie's, and Will—

TINK:    I'm going to hang up.

JACKIE: Why?

TINK:    If I was meant to know what happened at Mitzie's party I would have gone to Mitzie's party. And if I was meant to go to Mitzie's party, I would have been invited.

JACKIE: Maybe I was meant to tell you!

TINK:    I don't care. I'm not part of your little group, and that's that. La, la, la.

JACKIE: MY little group? What makes you think I'M part of it?

TINK:    You were there, weren't you?

JACKIE: It wasn't like I wanted to be.


Stab to the heart! It was starting to worry Tink how many lies she and Jackie were telling each other, just to try to stay friends. (She and Eddie had told each other lies in order to try to be friends—and look how well that worked out.) Jackie had been thrilled to have been invited to Mitzie's party. Tink was devastated not to have been. But neither one could say so. That didn't stop Tink from wanting to pick at the scab the wound had left.


TINK:    Then what'd you go for?

JACKIE: I was curious. What'd you go to Eddie's house for?

TINK:    Why shouldn't I?

She felt a pang of satisfaction. Was Jackie possibly hurt that Tink had found another friend (not that Eddie had become a friend)?

JACKIE: Did you even WANT to?
TINK:　　Yes. At some point I did want to.
JACKIE: Are you sorry you went?

Now how had she figured that out so fast?

TINK:　　In about five hundred ways.
JACKIE: I'm sorry I went, too. My mom said I should have done something with you, and she was right.
TINK:　　What was she right about?

Tink's mother had said she was glad Tink was finally doing something with someone else besides Jackie.

JACKIE: Mom said they were only nice on the outside, so they were like their mothers. They were only nice to me because they wanted to find out more about me, and once they were done watching, they'd push me back out.
TINK (because she didn't know what else to say to that, got overly literal): So they watched you dance with Bobby? Big whoop.

JACKIE: Bobby wasn't there.

TINK:

JACKIE: Well, you can't expect an eighth grader to come to some kid's party he doesn't even know.

Tink felt too relieved that it had just been sixth grade boys at the party to be annoyed on Jackie's behalf that Bobby was a no-show.

TINK:   Can't say I'm surprised, can you?

She knew that was a little vicious.

JACKIE: His loss. So I took pity on Jonas's bony heart.

Tink took pity on Jackie's and let the subject of Bobby drop.

TINK:   You danced with Jonas MacBonas? Did EVERY-ONE dance?

She couldn't help herself: In spite of everything, she wanted to know who Will Wheeler had danced with. Who could blame him if he danced with Mitzie or Meghan?

JACKIE: Keith tried to dance with Maggie for a little but she got embarrassed and stopped.

TINK:    So you were the only ones?

JACKIE:  Yeah. They're insecure, that's what Bess says. Are you mad at me for going?

TINK:

JACKIE:

TINK (relenting again, avoiding): Is Bony MacBonas a good dancer?

JACKIE:  Sure. Mitzie's dad played actual records. He had a Rolling Stones one. I danced with Jonas until . . .

TINK:    Until what?

JACKIE (choking up): Until Mitzie's mom came in and turned off the music.

TINK:    What? Doesn't she like the Stones?

JACKIE:  She didn't like the way Jonas and I were dancing. She turned up the lights and made us stop. Then she made everybody play Twister. She said I was out of hand, and she didn't know what my mom did with me.

TINK:    Idiot. Did she tell your mom that? We played Twister too.

JACKIE:  NO. But Mitzie said she knew that tone of voice, and when her mom talked like that I could forget about being allowed to come to any of her parties again.

TINK:    What an idiot. Didn't anyone say anything to her? I would have told her where to get off!

JACKIE:  I wish you HAD been there.

TINK:    I probably wouldn't have. I'm just talking tough.

JACKIE:  At least you think that way. You know what Maggie said?

TINK:    But Maggie's better!

It was true. She was the best one. No wonder Will Wheeler liked her. Everybody did.

JACKIE (sniffling): At first she was nice. She said "You're a good dancer" to me, and asked if I'd had lessons.

TINK:    What did you say, you were self-taught, a natural soul sistah?

JACKIE:  I said yes. It seemed like a better answer. So she asked who I took lessons from, and I thought she'd think I was lying if I said music videos, so I said my mom.

Bess could dance, too, that's what Tink had observed.

JACKIE:  Well, she made this face and was like "SIGH, why does it always have to be you who turns things to the slutty side, Jackie?"

TINK:    To the what side?

JACKIE:  To the slutty side! That's what she said: to the slutty side.

It was the kind of thing Mitzie would say, not Maggie. Tink felt terrible, because she thought Maggie was sort of right. She wondered how exasperating Jackie must have been to get Maggie to say that. She had seen Jackie shake it. That was part of the reason she couldn't dance the way Jackie could. Then she thought how upset Jackie must have been about Bobby, to be that exasperating. But she also felt terrible because she sort of hoped that if Maggie and the others didn't like Jackie then Jackie would stick around with her, Tink, some more.

TINK (finally giving in to desperation): Want to come over?

She was embarrassed to agree with Maggie. But she couldn't help wanting Jackie back to herself.

JACKIE: Do you want me to? After all that?
TINK:     I don't know what you're talking about. See you at
          the corner.

# February 14th,

## (Valentine's Day)

Oh thank God. The day was finally over.

It was finally not Valentine's Day anymore. Valentine's Day had ended when the bell rang.

Some people had had a great day of love and pinkness and romance. It was only a year since their fifth grade teacher, Mrs. Anjone, had brought one of those big mailboxes to put the valentines in, so she could check before passing them out to make sure everybody brought a valentine for everyone else. Apparently that was phony and babyish, according to certain girls who were now in the sixth grade, certain circle girls who said it was insulting to offer people valentine love if you didn't really mean it, and even Ms. Cho had announced that they were too mature for mandatory Valentine's Day. She asked them to be kind, and to keep it private. There would be no public valentine boxes.

Now there were cubbies. And if there wasn't a red or white or pink envelope in your cubby, it might be on your desk. Or your chair. Or in your backpack. Or in someone's hand. There could be valentines anywhere. Or, as it turned out, nowhere at all. Not for Tink.

In January, Jackie and Tink had had another fashion show, featuring the new clothes they had gotten for Christmas, and had come up with a few outfits for Tink that still fit (not the red skirt and bolero). Jackie had encouraged Tink to ask her mother for some new things, but it was expensive to keep a growing weed outfitted, Mom said. Still, on Martin Luther King Jr. weekend she had taken Tink shopping at some secondhand stores. And in the Presidents' Day sales, she had bought her a new sweater and jeans at the mall. She had also opened up her own dresser drawers and closet to find some "basics" for Tink— things in neutral colors like black and white that didn't look mommish, but fit. Today, for Valentine's Day, Tink had come to school in black leggings and a black jumper worn over a red button-down shirt so that the gaps between the buttons didn't show. This morning she had felt, if not cute, then not a mess. She felt put-together and comfortable. And on the bus, when Jackie had stuck her red velvet hair band into Tink's hair, Tink had accepted the kindness.

Lately Jackie had been pushing so hard for Tink to be called Chris that she had wondered which name might be on a red or pink or white envelope, if she got any. What was the goal of all this encouragement from Jackie? Tink asked herself. She thought she knew. Jackie wished she hadn't been alone at Mitzie's party. She wanted a friend in the circle, so she was trying to make Tink cooler.

But it hadn't made a difference after all, to the circle boys and their valentines. On top of Tink's disappointment about that, she was anxious that her lack of interest from the boys would push her so far out of the circle that even Jackie couldn't pull her back. The only reason that Jackie was still on the edge of things herself, Tink thought, was that the New Year's party had been such a dud for all those in attendance. According to the boys, its only redeeming quality had been Jackie—the life of the party, said Keith Kallinka, as he and Will thoughtlessly brought it up in front of kids who hadn't been there. "Dud firecrackers," muttered Bushwhack. Alex Mott sputtered, "Stocking stuffers." It was Jennifer Marx who whispered, "New Year's *balls*,"— and that was the one that made Tink laugh most of all. Mitzie and Maggie sniffed and opted to remain silent, and as usual, Meghan went along.

So Jackie was back in. For how long? Tink wondered. Until the next time somebody decided she was slutty? Tink herself did not know what to think about that. She felt guilty that she had understood what Mitzie and Maggie meant about Jackie dancing with Jonas. But she also noticed they hadn't called Jonas any names—not even swayve.

The sleety, freezing January weather had made the playground such a treacherous, icy mess that the school was kept inside for recess pretty much the whole month. Mr. Bergman had initiated a complicated game of trivia baseball, involving leagues and teams. The team Jackie was on, including know-it-all Jonas MacDonald, was in the lead (despite the handicap of having Maggie on their team, too) when a late January thaw melted the ice off the blacktop. Since then, the circle kids had gone back to the swings, Jackie and Tink included. Jackie made everyone call Tink Chris, and they did. The tension kept mounting until Valentine's Day.

Now at last it was three o'clock and school was over, and it could just be plain old February 14th for the rest of the day. No more red and pink and lace, but plenty of white: Tink was sitting in her classroom feeling like the unpicked last rose of summer, just about wrung out with crashed hopes and green jealousy, gratefully jotting down a math assignment because the idea of sitting somewhere quiet doing pre-algebra equations suddenly felt like a cozy, nice, calming activity, something to look forward to. There seemed to be some dust on the classroom window below the cock-eyed venetian blinds, against the darkness of the pine trees, except—hey—the dust was moving because—hey!

"HEY! IT'S SNOWING!" Somebody yelled it right out. "HEY!" It was Tink. She was the one who yelled it, blowing off her tension, and Jackie yelled, "Whoo-hoo!" right after her, not to be left out.

It was so exciting everybody got out of their seats. Maybe, like Tink, they were so relieved to be thinking about something white instead of pink or red, to be thinking about what was going to happen later instead of what had happened before, to be feeling happy right there instead of wanting to just go home fast, it couldn't happen fast enough, so she could cry and put aside her fantasies.

You know which fantasies. The ones where Will Wheeler sent a valentine, even if she hated his guts, or brought a chocolate rose in a plastic wrapper, or slipped a red Charms lollipop into her desk. Or Jonas MacDonald. Or even Keith Kallinka. Somebody? Anybody?

And you can imagine the reality, too. Jackie and Mitzie and Maggie and Meghan wearing little smug smiles all day, huddling off into the girls' room at lunch to whisper and hug each other and love themselves, as if they'd never had a single disagreement. United by their success with boys if not by friendship. Bushwhack and the Farmers keeping their heads down all day, mumbling among themselves how Will and Keith were nothing but doorknobs and postage stamps, lightbulbs and gumballs. ABC gumballs, Already Been Chewed. Free with your purchase of one gallon of gas.

Then the girls like Tink—and face it, there were more of them than there were of the successful others. Nothing wrong with any of them. (Well, nothing wrong with most of them.) The ones who came to school not daring to hope—not out loud anyway, not even out loud in their own heads—for a valentine. It wouldn't even have to be Keith Kallinka. It could have been anybody. (Well, almost anybody.) Maybe there could be a second tier of people. Somebody besides the beautiful ones could have a crush, could get a valentine. Or the beautiful ones could be sweet, could send valentines to other girls who were only inside the circle once in a while. But no. Those girls sat at their desks pretending to care about the snow, fighting frowns, sinking into the empty-mailbox feeling they had been try- ing to stay afloat above, all day.

The bell rang, and Tink bolted for the door. This was not like her. Her usual way lately was to pretend, to watch, to wait and see if Jackie was going home on her bus or Maggie's. Not today. Tink just took off, didn't even get on the bus. She left with the walkers, and if Jackie—or Ms. Cho, or anybody—called Chris or Hundred Percent or Tink or anything else after her, she didn't hear them.

It wasn't as if she ran out the door crying or anything like that. Bushwah. She hardened her crushed-up heart. *Do not pass Go. Do not pass Will Wheeler face to face. Do not pass Jackie with her secret smile.* How many valentines had she gotten? Who were they from? Tink didn't want to know. As long as possible, she would put off going home, where Mom was no doubt wondering how the day went. Maybe that would be the worst of all. There were times when her mother's understanding and sympathy just made her want to roll into a ball under the bed and never come out.

She gave herself a destination—the library downtown—and she went there. Tink wanted to be walking in the snow and feeling it fall on her eyelashes and her chin and her knees. She wanted to be downtown with the wet sidewalks and snow reflecting, falling at a funny angle, in the windows of the stores and OPEN signs. She wanted a red Charms lollipop, she had wanted one all day, ever since she had seen them sticking out of Maggie and Mitzie and Jackie's desks first thing that morning. She wanted the magazine rack at the library, and a quiet corner where she could read *Seventeen* and *Mad* and do pre-algebra and absorb her red lollipop out of the view of any library personnel.

But she had not counted on Bushwhack.

There he was, reading *Popular Mechanics* in the tattered armchair she'd been aiming herself at. How had he gotten there? *When* had he gotten there? She was so surprised her mouth popped open, the lollipop making a sucking sound.

Bushwhack looked up. He noted the red lollipop. "Valentine's Day is retarded," he said.

She closed her mouth and nodded. You would have thought he could come up with a better insult than that. It may have been the plainest, dullest, rudest thing he'd ever said, a word that was even more forbidden at school than bushwah, despite being in the dictionary. Tink agreed with him completely.

"Who's the lollipop from?" he asked.

She didn't want to tell him she'd bought it herself. "My secret lover," she said. "Mr. Clampett." He owned the store where she'd bought the lollipop.

"It's his wife I'm after," said Bushwhack, grinning. Good. Now they were back in familiar territory. Mrs. Clampett weighed about three hundred pounds and seemed sort of bearded, and if you stood there and tried to read a comic she *screamed* at you.

Bushwhack went back to *Popular Mechanics*. Tink felt like asking him what was in it, but instead she walked away, feeling the floor quiver under her. There weren't any more armchairs. She went and sat in a hard yellow chair next to a long wooden table, where two old men were examining a map of California. She started drawing. She used to just draw, but after Christmas, what with indoor recess and trivia baseball, she'd spent more time on her cartooning, inventing new characters and making up stories to go with her pictures.

She was doing a series of cartoons about elephants that patrolled the jungle, seeming normal, but who were actually made of leather, and hollow, so that by day they carried children and at night the children came out and ruled the jungle.

Cartooning was a relief, a refuge. But the two old men seemed to want to talk to her. "Do you know the date, young lady?" one asked.

She should have just said the date. But she said, "It's Valentine's Day."

"Valentine's Day!" said the other one.

"I didn't get any," said the first one.

"Neither did I," Tink said.

The second one snorted and chuckled.

"What's so funny?" she asked.

Just then Bushwhack appeared, offering his open pre-algebra book in both hands as if it were a plate of pancakes. "What did you get for—"

"Nothing," said the laughing old man. "She didn't get any valentine. And I'd like to know why not, young man!"

Bushwhack usually had at least one or two words, but his mouth just hung open with none coming out.

The man who wasn't laughing said, calmly and kindly, "He didn't know what to do, Dick. I'm sure you remember what that's like." Then he did laugh at his friend, and gave him a little dig with his elbow.

Dick tapped the map with his fingernail and said, "California girls would tell him."

Bushwhack swung his head right, then left. "California girls? Which way?"

"You don't need a California girl, mister," said the nicer man. "Stick with the smart Connecticut girl who already did all that math. You could use some help, and she's the girl for you!"

Bushwhack looked like he didn't know whether to turn red or green. He just stood there, blinking *caution.*

"Geez, which problem?" Tink said, glaring at Dick and what's-his-name as she took the book out of Bushwhack's hands.

But the old dudes weren't finished messing with them. "Valentine's Day," said Dick. "Would you be doing math with a girl like that around?" he asked his friend.

The nice friend did not suggest an alternative subject. But he did shake his head firmly. No to pre-algebra.

Tink had heard enough. "Math is perfect for today," she said to Bushwhack. As politely as she could, she waved Dick and friend back toward their map. "Don't you have another state to go to?"

They *loved* her then. "A wise guy!" Dick said. They both got the giggles.

Bushwhack sighed and pulled up a chair. "Number fifteen," he said. "Everyone's a comedian today."

"But not you?" Tink said. She tapped her finger on problem fifteen the way Dick had tapped Los Angeles. "Where do you think they're going in California, the funny farm?"

Bushwhack rolled his eyes.

She leaned closer to him. "I think they're going to hang ten off Malibu," she said. When Bushwhack looked blank, she said, "You know, surfing U.S.A.?"

She couldn't help laughing picturing these two old geezers hunched over on a surfboard, wearing flowered swim trunks. "I think they're going to take a tour of all the Rat Pack movie stars' homes," Bushwhack suggested. "You know, like Sammy Davis Jr."

"Or the Mouseketeers."

"Or Pat Sajak."

"Or Kermit and Miss Piggy."

Bushwhack was warmed up now. "Then they'll go up to San Francisco and ride the little cable cars."

This caused Dick's friend to interrupt, singing, "Rice-A-Roni—"

And Bushwhack (who somehow knew the ending) and Dick both sang, "The San Francisco treat!"

The librarian came all the way across the room to tell them to shut up or get out. After that it was just funny, funny, funny. Bushwhack and Tink were studiously silent, checking each other's math back and forth on their papers, with a third paper passing back and forth with further comments about their two buddies. Beside their map, the buddies seemed to be doing the same, writing out some kind of list on one paper, and folding and drawing on another. Dick's friend began rolling up the California map, and Dick came over to Tink with the folded piece of paper. He put it on the table in front of her, pressing it facedown. "Don't look at it until we're gone!"

"Oh, what now—" Bushwhack began.

The second they were gone, she flipped the paper. They had drawn a big heart with an arrow poking through it.

"Oh, my lord—" said Bushwhack.

"Shh!" Tink opened the paper. Inside it said, in one kind of handwriting, *To a lovely young lady, Happy Valentine's Day.* The other handwriting read, *You're going places, Valentine.*

"What's that supposed to be?" asked Bushwhack, pointing at a small drawing of a sort of crooked rectangle.

"Connecticut," Tink said. "I'm going all over Connecticut. Yee-ha." She shoved the valentine—that's what it was, you know—in the back of her pre-algebra book. She slipped her book into her book bag and pulled her coat on.

"You leaving?" said Bushwhack.

Tink gave him a big windshield-wiper wave. "See you," she said.

She felt weird, leaving. She hadn't gotten what she came for—magazine therapy and solitary misery. She hadn't even finished her lollipop. It was tucked, in its wrapper, back into her book bag, only licked a little. It had quickly become too sweet and sticky, and her mouth had gotten tired of it.

Outside it was still snowing a little. Tink was looking up, her mouth open, catching snowflakes on her tongue to get rid of the strawberry sweetness, when Bushwhack came panting up behind her. "Hundred Percent!" he said. He added, as though he was explaining something, "The library doesn't get *Mad* magazine anymore because it kept getting ripped off."

"So that's what the problem is!" Tink said. "That's why I left, because that's what I was going to read next. And all the time you were just pretending to read *Popular Mechanics*!"

"I did so read *Popular Mechanics*," Bushwhack said righteously. "*And* I did my homework. *And* I deserve my own copy of *Mad* magazine on Valentine's Day. As well as the days I swiped it. But it wasn't even always me."

Tink didn't know what made her say it. "*Everyone* deserves something on Valentine's Day," she said.

"Yeah," said Bushwhack. He stood there helplessly, as if he was not sure where to go next: which state, or which store, or which subject of conversation.

"Forget it," Tink said. "In my opinion Valentine's Day ends when school ends. This is just February fourteenth."

"It is the day when you flirted with some old dudes in the library," said Bushwhack.

Tink thought: flirting? She thought: the slutty side. How could she know where flirting stopped and sluttiness began, even with old guys? "*They* flirted with *me*," she said. "It is the day when you would not get a chance to read *Mad* magazine because of library crime."

"It is the day when you got a valentine from two unknown men," said Bushwhack. "I'm going to tell it all over school."

"It is the day when Mrs. Clampett gave you a big smooch on the kisser," Tink said. "I'm going to tell it all over school."

"You'd better come too, so she *doesn't*," said Bushwhack.

The lion was at Clampett's in the shelf below the register, along with some other animals and ornaments that looked leftover from Christmas. It was made of some kind of plastic or resin covered in a light brown fuzz, with a black nose and eyes and a lion mouth painted on its face. It had a soft mane made out of bunny fur. It was lying on its stomach with its paws together in front of it, and its tail curving along its side. The tail had a little tuft of bunny fur on the end.

Bushwhack picked the lion up and put it on the counter next to the cash register and said to Mrs. Clampett, "We need that." And said to Tink, "Don't you think?", and paid for it.

We?

Mrs. Clampett said, to both of them, "Do you need it or just want it?" Everybody really was a comedian today.

And that gave Tink the idea to say, "We definitely need it."

"You do?" said Bushwhack.

Was she flirting? What would Mitzie and Maggie say about that? And Jackie? Now Tink was all clammed up again. She rolled her eyes and looked away, at some James Bond books that were on a rack sitting there, and saw *Mad* magazine. "We need that, too," she said. Who cared about Jackie?

"Need it or want it?" said Mrs. Clampett.

"Need it," said Bushwhack.

Tink gave Mrs. Clampett the money for it. Mrs. Clampett was wearing a pink blouse, size gigantic, and Tink wondered if she was dressed for Mr. Clampett for Valentine's Day, ew.

And then she and Bushwhack stood there, not picking up the things. "Bag?" said Mrs. Clampett. She slipped the *Mad* magazine into a flat paper bag and placed the lion carefully in a squarish one like a miniature lunch bag. She handed the bags to them the way they'd paid for them: She gave Tink the *Mad* magazine, and gave Bushwhack the lion.

Without looking at each other, they swapped bags.

Tink couldn't look at Bushwhack, so she opened the little square bag, took out the lion, and laid the bag back on the counter. Mrs. Clampett watched her steadily, then watched Bushwhack remove the *Mad* magazine from its bag and return the bag to the counter. He did it elegantly, though, smoothing the flat bag flatter, ironing out the one wrinkle it had developed in its work. And then he took the small bag and folded it neatly along its fold lines and laid it beside the bigger bag.

"Thank you," said Mrs. Clampett. "Now go."

They walked along and Tink petted the fur on the lion's neck while Bushwhack opened up *Mad* and began to read. It was still flurrying, and spots of snow made little wet marks on the new magazine. Bushwhack flicked them off with his fingernail. "Look at this," he said, and Tink had to lean over to read "Spy vs. Spy." They read the whole thing, walking slowly, and laughed their heads off. At last Bushwhack turned to the last page, the one where you have to fold the page that special way to read the jokey picture. "Aha," Tink said, when he had folded it.

"Bushwah," said Bushwhack. Those things were never that funny, but they were a good trick.

"This is where I turn," Tink said. They were at her corner, and she thought about how long Bushwhack still had to walk to get home. He must have thought about it, too, because he rolled up his *Mad* and stuck it in his pocket.

"Happy fourteenth day of the second month, Tink," he said.

It was the first time in eons that he had called her anything but Hundred Percent. "Don't call me that," she said.

"What should I call you? Chris?"

She couldn't say Hundred Percent. The nickname wouldn't work the same way if she wasn't being a good sport about it. A good sport. A flirt. A slut. Who made up these ideas?

"What's your real name, anyway? Tinker Bell?" He knew better.

"Christine. Bernadette. Gouda."

"Christine B. Goode!" He pretended to play the guitar.

She shook her head and laughed. Trust Bushwhack. She liked him. Liked him enough to lose her head and say something stupid like "Happy Whatever yourself, Matthew."

★ ★ ★

TINK:  Hello?

JACKIE:  Help me, Auntie Em.

She sounded breathless, somewhere between laughing and crying, as if she were whispering a scream. It had been a week since Jackie had called.

TINK:  What's the matter?

JACKIE:  Bess and James are downstairs having a candlelight dinner.

Tink wanted to ask where Maggie was. Or Mitzie. But she thought of something her mom had said about Jackie—something about being yourself and taking the high road and being patient—and also she heard the catch in Jackie's voice, so instead she acted sympathetic, not sure if she actually *felt* sympathetic or just needed to pretend to be.

TINK:  Oh, poor Larry Lobster. Are you imprisoned there like a damsel in a dress?

JACKIE:  Yes. It's just a matter of time before they come upstairs and send me down.

TINK:   Then you'll be distressed downstairs?

But she was thinking about what Jackie was saying and—whoo-whoo!—it was kind of weird.

TINK:   You mean they're going to Sleep Together?

Now Tink really was sympathetic. Right now Jackie needed a little sister or brother, someone you could laugh at the grown-ups with.

TINK:   Do you want to come over here?
JACKIE: No, I can't interrupt them.
TINK:   Not even to ask if you can leave?
JACKIE: It's not even the worst part.
TINK:   What is?
JACKIE (starts crying): I was just sure, I was absolutely sure!
TINK:   Of what?
JACKIE: Of James bringing ME something. He comes waltzing in here with the most ginormous bouquet of roses.
TINK:   Really?

She didn't have any idea if her father had brought her mother flowers. She hadn't seen any roses. Maybe, because

Mom had made a heart-shaped cake with pink icing and little red cinnamon candies on top. But they had all pretty much scarfed it for dinner, figuring anything Mom baked was just as much for them as Dad. But had it been?

JACKIE: A dozen red, and a dozen yellow. Passion AND friendship.
TINK:  So what? James is Bess's boyfriend, not yours.

She would never dream of her father bringing *her* flowers as well as her mother—and, presumably, as well as Kitty and Jessie. He would go broke!

JACKIE: Are you insane? What do I care? I just thought maybe he was going to bring me something from Bobby.
TINK:  But Jack, didn't you get a bunch of valentines?
JACKIE: At SCHOOL. (very sarcastically)
TINK:  Sounds good to me.

She said this lightly, so very lightly, but inside she was furious.

JACKIE: So what do I care about THEM? They're not real valentines, anyway. They're just like . . . like brothers or something. It doesn't even count. They only

do it because they always do it. Their moms probably still make them.

TINK: Not to all the girls.

JACKIE: They're not real valentines anyway.

TINK: Define real. Like a card? With a heart on it? In an
envelope with your name on it?

JACKIE: No! Not if they come twenty-four to a box!

Enough to have some left over, in other words.

TINK: Well, what are they supposed to do? They're sixth
graders! They can't afford to go buy cards one by
one at Hallmark!

JACKIE: They could buy ONE. For someone special, the way
I thought I was to Bobby. The way I AM to Bobby.
He's in eighth grade. He knows these things! He
must just be—

TINK: Forgetful? Embarrassed? I mean, to have his dad
bringing it to his girlfriend's daughter.

She felt shivery just describing these relationships. Even
the words sounded too grown-up for her. This happened
sometimes when she talked to Jackie, just the two of them.
Tink got tingly inside. It wasn't ever like that with anyone
else she talked to. Except today, in a different way, with
Bushwhack, which came almost close. Or was it the snow?

Jackie and Bushwhack were the only two people she had ever felt sort of thrilled talking to. Tink couldn't help it if she still felt that way talking to Jackie even when she was ignoring Tink's feelings the way she was right now.

JACKIE: I think he's shy. Bess said sometimes they're the best kind.

TINK:   He's still a total jerk to you. Bringing his sister-whatever with him. Blowing off that party.

JACKIE: Wait. You mean you think maybe Bobby's going to get to me on his own later? And give me something I really want?

Tink didn't see how Jackie could think that was what she had meant.

TINK:   Like what? How is he supposed to know?

JACKIE: Because he's watched me to see what I like. That's what Bess says: they're supposed to pay attention to you, notice the flowers you smell if you go into a flower shop. You give him little hints like that, to help him.

TINK:   I saw something I wanted today in Clampett's . . .

She wouldn't tell Jackie about Bushwhack. She couldn't. She was afraid of what Jackie would say about him.

TINK:   . . . A little lion, with a fur mane and a fur tail, lying with its paws out in front of it and its head up, like he was proud.

JACKIE: I know the ones you mean. They were leftover from Christmas. Does it have a little loop on it? To hang on the tree? They must be on sale. Just buy it for yourself.

TINK:   I got it already.

JACKIE: You did?

Kitty came out of her room with a little box of Valentine candy clutched to her chest, Jessie chasing behind her, grabbing at her arm. They were screaming.

THEM:   AAAAAAGGH!

JACKIE: What's going on over there?

Even though she was laughing, Jackie sounded like the loneliest person in the world. Tink remembered wondering if there was a group that she was in that Jackie might want to be in. Some group this was: screaming sisters and a butt-dancing brother!

TINK:   The usual. Are you coming over?

JACKIE (in a small voice): No. Can't. I wish. Okay, bye.

# 7

# Far Outfield

*(Early Spring)*

For weeks Keith had been annoying Mitzie and Maggie by following Jackie around the way Ms. Cho had said Tink did. It made things chilly between Jackie and Mitzie and Maggie, so Tink wasn't exactly brokenhearted. Also, Jackie and Tink had wondered together whether Keith and Will Wheeler were still friends. "I think they had a lovers' quarrel," said Jackie slyly, and before Tink got to sputter out the question of what she meant by that, she went on, "something like you and Bushwhack." So then Tink had turned her back on her. Jackie peeked around. "You just turned like ten different colors." It had felt like more. That was the power Jackie had over her.

Teasing. Tink was sensitive to teasing, Jackie had said it herself. Or her buttinski mother had, and as usual Jackie had to pass the word. That was what Tink got for having told Jackie about Bushwhack and Valentine's Day. She had *had* to tell her, because Bushwhack's lion was sitting right there on the table next to her bed, so Tink must have inwardly wanted to tell her, because she did.

Jackie's teasing was all in the way she looked at Tink when she heard that Bushwhack had bought Tink the lion. She didn't have to say anything, she just raised her little eyebrow; she just watched when Bushwhack and Tink were passing insulting notes or when he picked her to do a report with, a superior, knowing expression on her face, a little smile. She just noticed. Jackie always noticed.

Once Tink said, "WHAT?"

And Jackie answered, "I'm just happy for you, that's all."

"Well, don't be!" Tink said. "Just shut up!"

When Bushwhack picked her to do the report, she almost choked, but she didn't say no. If Tink ever officially stepped outside the circle, that was the moment. It was a report on satire, which was a big topic in language arts. Ever since they'd read *Brave New World*, Mr. Bergman had put them on the lookout for satire, for any writer or artist or other person making fun of anything or anyone. They got his message that if you had to make fun you should do it in an intelligent way, one that cut deep and sharp, "the laugh that bites," as Mr. Bergman quoted.

It bit, all right: When Bushwhack had said *Mad* magazine was satire, Tink had been observed nodding her head in agreement. Mr. Bergman had just told Bushwhack he could write a comic strip, and Bushwhack had come right out and asked, in front of the whole class, if Tink could draw it. "Whoo-whoo!" went the stupid class, and Tink had turned ten or eleven different colors and looked down at her desk. But of course she said yes, because what could be better than drawing something that Bushwhack had written?

It wasn't like she wanted Bushwhack to be her boyfriend. It wasn't as though after Valentine's Day Bushwhack had started calling her up and talking on the phone or writing her love notes or giving her presents or asking her on dates.

"Did you really expect him to call? What do you think he is, an eighth grader?" asked Jackie.

"Oh, did Bobby call?" Tink was all innocence.

"No," said Jackie. "Not yet." Not since she'd last called him, Tink knew.

"Bushwhack didn't call *yet* either." Tink said. And he wasn't going to. This was Bushwhack, after all. He wouldn't know where to begin. And Tink wouldn't call him, wouldn't flirt that way. That wasn't her style, she thought. Or was it just that she was scared to? She told herself she just didn't want to.

"Lots of boys are like that," Jackie said. "Not aware of girls, like Bobby. It's okay." Jackie acted as if she meant to console Tink, which was awfully nice of her, or maybe was just designed to make herself feel better, Tink couldn't decide which. She was leaning toward the second idea. "Look how shy you are," Jackie went on. "Maybe you just aren't ready for more. I mean, what would you do if Matthew Alva kissed you?"

Tink was dumbfounded. She couldn't picture it. Did she even want him to? How could she know if he wanted to?

"Exactly," said Jackie, puffing up even bigger. "Meanwhile I think I'll die if someone doesn't kiss me soon."

Another division: the ready and the unready.

There was very little Tink could think of to say to Jackie. She just shrugged. Who could say *who* is ready for *what*—themselves or anybody else? She knew for a fact that Maggie had told Jackie she should quit calling Bobby and play hard to get for a while. Were you supposed to be hard to get, as well as not be a slut?

Jackie didn't seem to know either. Although she never admitted it to Tink, Tink knew she regretted having told Mitzie who Bobby was so she could invite him to the New Year's party. She had told everyone all about him, and then he hadn't come. The circle girls knew they'd been let in on a secret previously shared only with Tink and didn't miss an opportunity to raise the subject of Bobby in front of her and Jackie.

It seemed to make Jackie's longing for Bobby even stronger. She reasoned to Tink, "I love him for himself, of course. But if he came along with James more often, it would be better for James's relationship with Bess. And if he went out with me, Maggie could stop worrying that I was trying to steal Keith Kallinka. If I had a boyfriend, they'd stop thinking I was flirting with any boy that breathes."

Tink's hair practically stood on end, that made her so mad. "But you don't!" she said. Jackie just flirted with any boy she *liked,* and maybe that was more what Mitzie and Maggie objected to, how many boys she liked. "I don't see why you care at all what *they* think."

Jackie sighed as if to say Tink couldn't possibly understand.

Tink asked, "Is something wrong with James's relationship with Bess?" She copied Jackie's words, and they felt awkward coming out of her own mouth.

Jackie made a TCH of annoyance. "They had a huge fight," she said. "Mom says they both have too much baggage."

"Baggage?" Tink asked. "Like, problems?"

"Like children," said Jackie. "I don't care. Let them break up. It will make things easier for me and Bobby."

From then on, after school, Jackie hung around the middle school close to the boys' locker room door where she would casually bump into Bobby when he came out from basketball practice. Tink knew because she walked there with her on the way to meet Bushwhack. Bushwhack and Tink didn't walk from school together. That would have been too obvious, just asking for commentary. So he took off right at the end of school, and she dawdled along with Jackie, who had either (a) bought Tink's story about being obsessed with doing her homework at the library or (b) of course figured out what was going on.

Jackie didn't just go stand outside the middle school boys' locker room door, either. That would have been too obvious too. She attempted to leave Bobby with doubt by pretending she was going downtown with Tink.

It wasn't like Tink and Jackie to have an unspoken rule, but they had one about this: Tink wasn't going to point out how foolish Jackie was being about Bobby, and Jackie wasn't going to say she knew Tink was crushing on Bushwhack.

All that week, Jackie had been calling Bobby to ask him for advice on, of all things, pre-algebra. "Why don't you just ask me?" Tink said. They had left the middle school and were walking over the railroad bridge toward the library.

Jackie shook her head. "Bobby's been all the way through it already, in seventh grade," she said. When Tink just stared, Jackie rolled her eyes. What could Tink say? Bushwhack was still using math as an excuse to talk to *her*.

"Is he helping?" Tink asked.

A train went by with a roar, and Jackie watched it go. Then she answered, "No, but Amy did once."

"What?!"

"She answers the phone. She says he's not home yet. But I know he's there. I think he just doesn't like me that way."

Tink felt it like a punch in the stomach—this moment when Jackie let go of her pride and finally admitted reality. She said, "Oh." It seemed the only way to match Jackie's flat statement. Then they were at the library and Tink said, "Are you coming in?" and was relieved when Jackie said no.

"Okay, well see you tomorrow," she said, pretending to be a nice friend. She didn't know what she would have done if Jackie had said yes and come in.

As for Bushwhack, he acted as though it was accidental each time they found themselves at the same library table where they'd sat on Valentine's Day, four times before their project was done. After that they didn't have any more excuse. They didn't see Dick and his friend again. "They must be in California," Bushwhack said.

They got an A. "A to the twelfth power," said Mr. Bergman, who wasn't even their math teacher, but still knew something about exponents. He was correct: it was an exponential comic, including the president and Alfred E. Neuman and a kazoo and a sea turtle and some farmers and even some cows, and a talking lion that commented on what was going on in the story. That part was written by Tink. They had out-satired the satirists with their comic, which used her best cartoon animals and, from Bushwhack, the kind of insults animals would give, that is, calling each other people names. *You fashion model. You short-order cook. You wide receiver.*

After they presented their satirical comic strip to the class everyone clapped. Bushwhack and Tink smiled, looking away from each other, and Will Wheeler made a snorting noise. Mr. B unfortunately had to make the statement that they made a great partnership. Then *everybody* snorted. Tink practically died of embarrassment and couldn't talk to Bushwhack for about four days, just couldn't deal with the whispers and the *whoo-whoo*s. Then it was Friday and they went home for the weekend, and when they came in on

Monday morning, there was this new boy, Stanley Shelton, with a name like a movie star and dark, shiny, thick hair.

Stanley Shelton didn't look like someone in the movies, but there was something about him all the same. He was destined for the circle, but he didn't seem to know it. He had long jeans that hung over soft suede shoes, several navy blue sweatshirts, and a head of hair so shiny and dark that Tink couldn't look at him enough. At first he was quiet and didn't meet anyone's eyes much and blushed if you tried to talk to him. More girls tried than boys. But from flirts and non-flirts, ready and unready, Stanley didn't seem to mind the attention. He had a way of looking up after the girl had gone away, to see who she was.

While they were lining up for recess, Stanley was looking at the bulletin board where the satire projects hung. Tink walked past, and he said, "You drew this?" with his finger pointing to (but not touching, more careful than most) the lion with her fancy signature on it. She stopped, but didn't answer, and he said, "You're really good."

She said, "Thank you."

When she got to her seat she had a coughing fit and covered her face with her hands, turning at least thirteen different colors. Jackie turned, first to see if she was okay, and then to just observe.

Jackie always knew. Tink didn't know how she always knew. But she knew. Was there more space for an extra girl now that Meghan was out with strep throat and Stanley

Shelton had arrived? Jonas + Will + Keith + Stanley + Mitzie + Maggie + Jackie + Tink equaled a round number. Somehow shy Stanley Shelton had been magnetized into the circle group. For a brief time that spring their number blossomed.

The teachers had sent the class down to the far lower field because they were big sixth graders who could kick the ball over the outfield fence in the upper field. Mr. Parisi didn't want any little kids getting clobbered by their long kicks, or corrupted by the bad language that sometimes sprayed from their mouths when they missed the ball or got too far behind in the score. Mr. Bergman had said it: "At this point in the year you people are better suited for middle school than grade school. And this class, I don't know where you get your maturity." Tink figured that was because a lot of them had vocabularies, and all of them laughed when they heard anything as rude as *Two words*.

Now Bushwhack was in the outfield, where he was hunched over waiting for the ball to come his way, calling trash-talk at Will Wheeler, who was kicking. "Come on, Big Wheels, peel out! Burn rubber! Get in your car and drive. You flat tire. You brake pedal. You gas cap." Bushwhack was bored.

Eddie wasn't bored. She was pitching, and she was as fierce as usual, whipping the ball in, rolling it straight and fast at the kicker's feet. Eddie and Tink had long since stopped trying to be friends at all. Having gone up against her pitching on her first ups, Tink was nervous about the second one. She stood toward the back of the line of kickers, getting angrier, wishing Eddie would give her her hardest, straightest pitch and Tink would nail it, send it whistling past Eddie's ear right over her shoulder into the far outfield.

But she didn't get to be up again. When it was Tink's team's turn in the field, Eddie got up first and murdered the ball, which flew down the path to Herbie's. There were too many people playing the outfield to begin with, because nobody wanted to sit on the bench.

"I'm going to find the ball," said Jackie, and Stanley got up and followed her. When Jackie waved Tink along, she was bored enough, or curious enough, to trail behind Jackie and Stanley, with—how odd!—Keith Kallinka at her heels. She didn't look at Bushwhack. She walked past him, out of centerfield, through the gap in the fence.

It made Tink's heart beat faster to follow the others. They were being bad. Not that Bushwhack was any angel. Not that he'd never done anything bad. But now she— *they*—were leaving school property and going to Herbie's, which was a body of water, not Long Island Sound maybe, but still a place where you could fall in and drown, or at least get wet. It was a place they'd probably never go if they weren't in school, because it wasn't that interesting, didn't have that much to offer, was really just a puddle in the woods. But now, it was school hours. Now, they were off the property. Now, Jackie and Tink were in the woods. Alone, without supervision. Alone, with someone cute like Keith Kallinka, even if he was a fool. Alone, with Stanley Shelton.

Stanley had followed Jackie, but he liked *Tink*'s drawings. He had followed Jackie, but Jackie knew—somehow, again—that Tink liked him—or his hair, at least.

Tink hadn't told Jackie how she'd drawn a little comic about him and herself. She had hidden it behind the electric baseboard radiator, the part that ran behind her bed, a place where nobody would ever find it, and it showed them kissing, her hand in his beautiful hair. It embarrassed Tink so much that she would not even allow herself to find it again, would leave it behind the radiator until summer. But all that spring she knew it was there, and she could make herself turn twenty-five different colors just by thinking about it.

It was nothing to do with Bushwhack. What was there about him that she could think about as she fell asleep? His hair? Please. Grease was the word. His eyes? Hardly. Like rain clouds: watery. The way he wore his clothes? Let's not get started. He was in a whole different ballpark, so to speak.

The far outfield was almost the edge of the school property. The four sixth graders—predictably, the less-interested kickball players—were fishing around in the damp, tangled prickers and matted weeds far beyond the outfield fence, not caring if they found the ball or not. Herbie's Pond was over there beyond the fence in the woods, a mysterious pond with a mysterious name.

"Who's Herbie?" asked Stanley.

"This guy who owned the pond," said Keith Kallinka.

Jackie and Tink laughed silently to each other: Kallinka, such a fool. Everybody acted like they knew who Herbie was, but Tink had never heard anybody say it. For all she knew, Herbie was a name made up by Jackie, or more likely by Bushwhack. It was the kind of thing he might do.

Farther into the woods. Jackie turned back and asked, "How far do you want to go?" Passing the buck. Tink shrugged. She was tingling. Stanley looked from Jackie's face to hers. None of them turned back to check with Kallinka. They walked on a few steps, then Jackie stopped and said, "Come on, Keith. Come walk with me." She held out her hand to him like he was Alvin, and they went on ahead of Tink and Stanley, hand in hand.

What that did was make Tink walk with Stanley, make Stanley walk with Tink. "Want to hold my hand?" Stanley said. Oh, Jackie. How could Tink not love her? How could she not love everybody?

"Okay," said Tink.

If you looked up at the sky, things looked pink, there were so many low-hanging maple buds, little pale green leaves starting to come out as well, tinier than squirrels' ears. The mud was brown and shiny, and the sun made penny water of the surface of the pond, and Stanley Shelton was holding Tink's hand.

"I like to draw, too," said Stanley Shelton.

"What kind of drawings?" Tink said.

"Naked girls," said Stanley.

A chill ran through Tink's body, but she did not turn even one different color. "Stanley," she said.

"You'd look good naked," said Stanley.

What a punk! She didn't take away her hand. She stared straight ahead at the pond and said, "That's right, I do." It seemed like a good idea to agree with something like that, better than acting mad. Mature, Mr. Bergman had said.

Stanley took away his hand. He stopped and stood still, looking back up the path toward the kickball game. "My sister would kill me if she knew I had said that," he said.

Tink said nothing. She stood there.

"Some girls would punch me out for saying that," he said.

"It's none of your business, that's all," Tink said. "It's just rude."

"I just think you'd be sexy."

"Stanley," she said. "Cut it out."

"Call me Stan," he said. "My name is Stan."

"Okay, *Stan*," Tink said loudly, feeling annoyed. Sexy!

She didn't have the least idea what it meant to look good naked. Maybe just needing to wear a bra? She knew she should have been mad, and maybe she would be later when she'd had time to think about it, but now she was really just more surprised than anything else. Now she knew what it felt like to be whistled at, she figured. Then again, no. Being whistled at was a compliment, even if it was a rude compliment. This, what Stanley was saying, felt creepy and embarrassing. Not barged-in-on-in-the-bathroom embarrassing, but—ugh! Tink didn't know! She guessed it was better than barking.

"Hold my hand again," said Stanley.

She did. They walked around the pond, and didn't say very much. Stanley—no, *Stan*—was as tall as Tink, and his hair shone so dark and shiny against the maples and above the mud.

Now that he'd shut up about the naked stuff, something changed. He seemed sweeter. Tink began to feel the way she did when she'd learned all the words of a new and great song, and could sing along whenever it came on the radio, better every time.

This past weekend in the car, her father had noticed that she knew most of the words of the songs, and when they got home, he put on his favorite old record for her. He showed her how to put the arm with the needle very gently down and how to make it lift off when it got to the end of the record. It was the Rolling Stones, of course. What was it with this band and the grown-ups? But the record was good, and she listened to it ten or fifteen times, all afternoon, until it occurred to her to flip it to the other side, and then she memorized the other side, too. It was great. This, with Stan, was very new song–like. She held his hand, and they walked around.

In the faraway distance they heard the bell. Jackie and Keith—way ahead now—turned to see if Stanley and Tink had heard. And saw that they were holding hands too. The moment was great, the opposite of the moments when Tink knew she'd be embarrassed if anybody saw her holding hands with Bushwhack—not that he'd ever tried! She hated herself for those moments. She loved herself in this moment.

They kept holding hands as they walked up. So did Jackie and Keith. When Tink and Stanley got to them, Jackie said, "So, are you two going out?"

Stanley—no, *Stan*—squeezed Tink's hand and said, "Sure. Right?"

Everyone looked at Tink. She said, "Sure!"

"Are you two?" asked Stanley.

"Sure," said Keith Kallinka.

Jackie didn't say yes, but she didn't say no.

Then came an even bigger moment, but this one was awful, not great. They caught up with the bunch of sixth graders climbing up the hill from the kickball field. Mitzie and Maggie turned first, then they all glanced back and almost stopped. Eddie, Will, then Bushwhack turned to absorb the sight of Jackie, Keith, Stanley, and Tink. Their faces said first that they knew the four had taken off and abandoned them to the game of kickball, and second they saw that something had happened to those four that hadn't happened to any of them. It was no surprise to some of them that it was Jackie and Keith Kallinka holding hands all the way up the hill. But Stanley and Tink—that had to be a shocker. Mitzie asked them, "Where were you guys?"

Her voice whined. Mitzie was feeling left out while Tink was left in?

"Down at Herbie's," said Kallinka. And proudly he added, "We're going out."

Again, Jackie did not agree or disagree. Instead, she added, "So are Chris and Stanley." Tink felt protected, loved, drawn back into the circle by two strong hands: Jackie's and Stanley's. She did not say anything to Jackie about calling her Chris. She did not even mind. It almost fit her.

Maggie's face! She had let Mitzie ask the question. Now that she'd heard the answer, she laughed, nervously at first, and then stopped herself. Then her face got a confused, angry expression. She and Mitzie dissolved back into the crowd, and you knew, you just knew, that they were telling Will and Donna and all the rest as fast as they could. And what were they telling them? That Jackie was a slut. And what did that make Tink?

As for Bushwhack's face? Tink didn't, couldn't, wouldn't look at Bushwhack's face. But she heard him speak up, because he just would, he had to. She heard his voice say: "You're going out with Stanley, Hundred Percent?" Who would just come out and say that? Tink was so embarrassed, swear to God she thought she'd barf.

She said quickly, "It's Stan. He wants to be called Stan." She didn't look up. She did not say anything to Bushwhack about calling her Hundred Percent. And she didn't know if she turned fifteen different colors or any colors at all. She

didn't remember. It was a blur, except that she remembered, afterward, how clear her voice was. And his. Oh
Bushwhack, she thought in some closed-up tiny squashed
part of her.

But also, was it fair if they were calling her a slut? Did
Mitzie or Maggie or anyone in the class know anything
about her and Bushwhack? What was there to know? She
hadn't held his hand or said she was going out with him
or danced with him at any party. And when Maggie and
Keith were together at the party, nobody called Maggie a
slut. Maybe the only real slut was Keith Kallinka. But he
was so clueless, what could you say about him? What could
you say about Jackie, deciding to go out with him? It wasn't
like *she'd* been given a valentine lion or met anybody at the
library. Tink *knew* she herself wasn't a slut but panicked all
the same. She was a mess, with no idea what to think about
any of it, least of all herself.

That afternoon, in social studies, when the class got a
new project—something about a foreign country—a note
fell into Tink's lap as soon as Ms. Cho told them about it,
before she even started assigning countries. From Keith
Kallinka: *Do Iceland with me.*

Tink couldn't help it: she turned and showed Jackie.
Jackie just rolled her eyes and shrugged her shoulders, as
if to say, "Go ahead, better you than me."

Last fall Tink would have been thrilled beyond thrills
if Keith Kallinka had asked her to lend him a pencil, never

mind share a project. Now she wondered why he hadn't asked Jackie to work with him; they were the ones who were supposed to be going out! Maybe he was just scared. She looked at him, saw his nervous expression as he waited for her answer, and nodded, because it solved a problem for her, too: if Bushwhack were watching, he knew without asking not to ask her to do Tasmania or Tonga or Lower Slobbovia with him. But she didn't know if that was why he didn't ask, or if it was because now she was going out with Stanley.

After that, the circle girls acted like they thought it was cool that Keith Kallinka and Tink were working together. Tink didn't. It turned out Kallinka just wanted to ask her stuff about Jackie, and he did, to the point of being nauseating. He came over to Tink's house the next afternoon to begin drilling her about Jackie, while she tried to read a book about Iceland.

"She doesn't have a dad, right?" he asked.

"So?" Tink thought that was a stupid subject to start with.

"Does her mom have boyfriends?"

This made Tink give him the stink-eye. She thought, afterward, that this was the moment when Keith Kallinka finally stopped seeming even a little bit cool to her. Maybe he really never had been cool, despite being so cute that everyone had a crush on him. Now his cute face was just: a face. Why would Keith assume Jackie's mom had plural boyfriends unless he had heard somebody talking about her? Tink could guess whom.

"Does he have any kids?"

"What?" Tink turned the pages of the Iceland book. The skies in Iceland were blue. The land was green, very green, with red and white houses. It looked like a very clean, cold country, and Tink would have liked to go there and get away from everyone.

"So the boyfriend has kids?"

Was Tink actually *telling* Kallinka anything? She had said only two words and somehow he knew everything. But she had to give him some credit for trying to figure things out for himself and not just jumping to conclusions about Jackie's mother. And why? Because he actually liked Jackie, she reasoned, which allowed her to warm toward him.

He went on, "Is one of them that guy Jackie liked? The older guy?"

Tink didn't say, How do you know about that? She didn't say, What do you know about him? She didn't tell him anything.

"She told me herself," said Keith. "On New Year's."

Tink studied Kallinka. He was so cute and small, like Jackie but not like Jackie. He was still a little boy, with thick blond hair like Walter Warner the Third, just taller. And it wouldn't occur to him not to mention that party to her, like none of the girls had, because they knew the rules of how to talk to someone who didn't get an invitation. She pictured Jackie at the party, confiding in Keith Kallinka about Bobby.

She said, "Ms. Cho says that in Iceland they believe in elves. I think you should dress up as an elf when we give this report, if we ever quit talking about Jackie's mom's boyfriend and write the dumb thing."

"Jackie's mom's boyfriend's son," he said.

The phone rang. Kitty yelled from upstairs, "Tink!"

Tink shoved the book toward Keith. "Do some work, will you? I'm not doing the whole country of Iceland all by myself."

"I dibs the volcanoes," said Keith, without even looking at the books.

★ ★ ★

TINK:    Hello?

JACKIE:  What are you doing?

TINK:    I'm arguing with Kallinka about volcanoes.

KEITH:   There's no argument. Who's that? Jackie?

Tink turned her back toward Keith.

TINK:    What are you doing?

Jackie whispered to let Tink know that Bess was nearby.

JACKIE:  I'm writing a letter to Bobby. I'm telling him how I was swept off my feet by another boy.

TINK:    Swept into Herbie's Pond, more like.

Keith grabbed for the phone. Tink shrieked. They wrestled for the phone. Bushwhack, for one, would never wrestle her for anything. She wasn't sure she wanted him to. But she wouldn't have minded wrestling with Stanley—*Stan*. And she felt certain that she could beat up Keith Kallinka if it was a matter of life and death, or even if it wasn't.

KEITH (sounding threatening): Hundred Percent.

He had never called her that before. It surprised her, and he nabbed the phone and cooed into it.

KEITH:  Jacqueline, come over!
TINK:  She's not coming over so I can be the third wheel.

Tink's mother came into the kitchen and noticed the many colors in Tink's face from phone-wrestling and Jackie-talking and Stanley-thinking. She asked, "What's this you're studying?"

TINK:  Iceland.
KEITH (holding his hand over the phone): Hello, Mrs. Gouda.
MOM:  Keith, I'm so glad to see you. Who's on the phone?
TINK:  Jacqueline Q. MacGillicuddy.
MOM:  I have to go downtown. I can drop Keith off, if you two are almost finished. I want to go to the library.

TINK:    I'll get some more books on Iceland. Keith can take his home and read it. (into the phone) Jack, Keith has to go now.

JACKIE: Oh, put my little sweet-cheeks back on the phone.

TINK:    No, little sweet-cheeks has to go home.


Keith looked shocked. Tink's mother did, too.

★ ★ ★

In the car coming home from the library, just Tink and her mother because the other kids were home with Dad, Mom asked, "Do you have something going with little Keith Kallinka?"

"'Something going'?" Tink spat back her mother's words as if they tasted bad.

"I mean, do you have a crush on him?"

"He's going out with Jackie," Tink said. "And it's not his fault he's short! What if people called me big Christine Gouda?"

"Going out? Where?" Mom ignored the name comment; Tink couldn't deflect her that easily.

"Nowhere! Just going out," Tink protested. "No more questions about this!"

"Just a few," said her mother evenly. "Are other people in your class 'going out'?" You could hear the quotation marks in the way she said *going out*.

"Yes," Tink said.

"Is Jackie always the first to do anything?" Mom said, with a tone of irritation.

"Jackie's my best friend," Tink said.

"Yes. And it can't be easy."

"Mom," Tink said.

"I mean it! You're only twelve years old, not sixteen!"

"I plead the Fifth," Tink said, quoting something Bushwhack was always saying. "I refuse to say anything on the grounds that my words may be used to incriminate me."

Mom looked exasperated. "Why Keith Kallinka? Why would Jackie go out with Keith Kallinka?"

"He's cute!" Tink said. "I mean, Jackie's got eyes."

Mom clicked her turn signal on and glanced to the side, but Tink thought she was smiling as she turned away, which was annoying. Mom said, "She's also very smart. So are you, Tink. You're both too smart to be so boy-crazy."

"That again!" Tink said sarcastically. She said, "If I like ice cream, does that make me ice cream–crazy? How about dogs? Dog-crazy? Are you Dad-crazy, because you like Dad?" Jackie *was* smart. Tink thought of Bobby and the letter Jackie was writing about her little sweet-cheeks Keith Kallinka. What would Bobby think when he read it? What was he supposed to think? He was supposed to think he was missing out on something by not going out with Jackie. So, what if Bobby decided he *was* missing out? Then what? Jackie wouldn't go out with two people at the same time. Would she?

Her mother said, "Besides, do smart girls only go out with cute guys? How about smart guys? How about smart uncute guys? Don't they need love too?" It made Tink think of Bushwhack. She didn't want to think of Bushwhack.

"Can you go out with two people at the same time?" Tink asked. They were getting close to home, turning into the street before the street before their street. Tink wrapped her fingers around the two Iceland books in her lap, which she had passed by the magazine shelves to get. *Mad* magazine was there on the shelf, the same issue that she had bought for Bushwhack. So he mustn't have had to steal this one, because he had one of his own. She wondered if the charm had gone out of the magazine for him, because of not having had to swipe it. This thought was the one that put a smile on her face.

"Why would anyone go out with two people?" her mother said, looking ahead to drive and not noticing Tink's smile. "A woman has to know her own mind better than that."

A woman! Her own mind! Funny she didn't say heart. Was this about smartness, then? Jackie's smartness? Or Tink's? What about the heart? Tink's seemed to be beating extra hard. "But I'm a girl," she said.

"Tinker Bell," her mother said. "You are a lovely girl, and you are going to be a fantastic woman. And you should go out with the whole world before you choose the one. I don't mean to make it sound so serious."

But it was. It was dead serious to Tink, and maybe her mother realized that because she followed up by asking, "How do you know you're going out with anyone?" And, when Tink sat silently, thinking about it, she added, "Did Keith ask Jackie out on a date?"

"Where would they go?" Tink asked, not exactly answering.

"To the movies?" suggested Mom. "Or bowling?"

"Bowling?" Tink echoed.

It was a good idea. She gave it considerable thought as she sat on her bed a little later, thinking of Stan, staring at the lion on her bedside table and trying not to think of Bushwhack. Then she made sure Jackie was the one who suggested it to the circle.

On Saturday, she arrived at the bowling alley with Stan and Jackie and Keith. (Keith's mother had driven them so he could drop off a pile of note cards about Icelandic volcanoes. Tink guessed she really had gotten stuck with covering everything else going on in the country, but she'd be darned if she wouldn't make him dress as an elf.) It didn't take her five seconds to realize that the eight boys bowling three lanes over from them—at the end of the alley—were all Farmers, and that Bushwhack was among them.

Tink was startled. Had he maybe heard the circle people talking about bowling and gotten up a bowling group of his own? She wondered. Bushwhack was smart enough to be that tricky. But that he should care enough to do it, well who knew?

The Farmers were fooling around and being funny, and some of them could bowl, but the bowling alley lady kept going over to make sure only four of them were bowling, and making the others—including Bushwhack—sit down. He sat next to the ramp where the balls came up, spun each ball as it arrived, and stared into the ramp's tunnel, as if he were figuring out how the thing worked. He also made up a lot of new insults, including "you bendy straw," "you marbleized bowling ball," and—a personal best as far as the Farmers were concerned—"you thumb hole."

"Not that you're paying any attention to anything they say," Jackie said in Tink's ear as Tink sat down after yet another gutter ball, her back to Bushwhack. "Not any of those Farmers." Tink shook her head. "Quit looking mopey!" Jackie said.

"I don't feel mopey, I feel guilty," said Tink.

"You really do? How *bizarre*." Jackie looked at Tink with the same expression she got when she told Tink something admiring Bess had said about her (Tink), as if she (Jackie) were wishing Bess would say that about *her*.

"I'm not guilty at all," said Keith Kallinka frankly. "I think they're very humorous, those Farmers."

Stanley looked over at Bushwhack and his gang as though they were complete strangers, shrugged, and turned back toward Tink. Sometimes, she thought, he looked smarter than he acted.

When he turned to pick up his ball, Jackie whispered in Tink's ear. "Look at it this way. It's good for him to see you out with other boys."

"You *would* say that," said Tink snottily.

"He wasn't ever going to ask you out himself, was he? Why should you wait around?"

Tink secretly scrutinized the Farmers. Bushwhack was keeping score and doodling on the score sheet, right in the middle of everything, but he didn't have a bowling ball.

"He doesn't even have any money," Tink said, amazed that Bushwhack would be here under such circumstances. "Look. He's not even really bowling."

"Neither are you," said Keith Kallinka, coming over. "So don't talk about me that way."

"Nobody's talking about you, lava boy," Tink said. Except it sounded like *lover boy,* and Kallinka and Tink both gulped. Then they burst out in hysterical cackles, while Jackie and Stanley stared at them. Tink was beginning to think Kallinka was as—what was that word Jackie had used?—*bizarre* as she was. The whole world was absurd and mixed up.

"Look, people," Jackie said. "None of you know how to bowl. I will assist you." Bess's last boyfriend before James had liked to take them bowling, including Tink sometimes, so Tink knew what she was doing, even if she couldn't always execute it, and Jackie had become a pretty good bowler. She handed Stanley a ball and made him put his fingers into the holes. (The finger holes *and* the thumb hole.) Then she demonstrated her moves, bending her knees and swinging her right hand back, then aiming at the center pin. "When you finish you should be pointing the way you want the ball to go," she said. So when Stanley started bowling wrong, Jackie grabbed him by the arms from the back, guided him as he walked backward to the starting point again, and manhandled him into the position she wanted. "This isn't that hard, Stanley."

"Call me Stan," he said.

"I'm never calling him Stan," said Kallinka to Tink so the others couldn't hear. "He will forever be Stanley to me."

"Chris calls me Stan," said Stanley. And he smiled at Tink in a way that made her remember he thought she would look good naked. Why had she ever asked anyone to call her Chris?

Stan bowled a gutter ball, and Jackie threw her hands up in the air. "What's a mother to do?" she said.

It was no surprise to Tink when the Farmers began bowling the way Jackie had tried to get Stan to—by walking behind each other and bowling together, with lots of cooing sounds and comments about thumb holes. Not Bushwhack so much, but he was laughing, she saw him.

At long last they got out of there. Bess picked the four of them up, and dropped the boys off at their houses first.

Keith Kallinka lived way out of town in a big swanky house, near Bushwhack's house where he only ate pudding, but Stanley lived not far from Jackie, near the highway bridge. After Kallinka got out, Stan and Tink were alone together in the back seat. He held her hand, even though her elbow got twisted from the angle.

"Well, Stan, what did you bowl?" Bess had taken one look at him and, even though Jackie had introduced him as Stanley, knew what he wanted to be called.

"A ball," said Stan, puzzled.

"Doofus," said Jackie from the front seat. "She means what was your score?"

"Well," Stan said, tickling the palm of Tink's hand with his pinky. "I scored higher than those plumbers down at the end."

Tink turned a few different colors and said, "Farmers, you mean?" He was still new in their class, and he mustn't have known everybody yet.

"Oh, is that what they were? I thought from the way they kept talking about holes, they must be plumbers."

An amazing thing happened. Jackie turned a few different colors herself, a most unusual occurrence brought on by her mother in the driver's seat.

"What kind of holes were they talking about?" Bess asked.

"Which holes you put your fingers in on the bowling ball," Tink said. "It was just some boys from our class." She took her hand away from Stan as if she really needed it to lean forward and point. "Didn't you say you lived on Ringo Street?"

"No, it's Starr Lane," said Stan blankly. Bess turned the car, and they waited for Stanley to say more.

"Oh, Stanley," said Jackie, when he didn't.

"It's number four," said Stanley, as if he was wondering what he'd said wrong.

"Of course it is," said Bess.

"Fabulous," Tink said, and the three of them cracked up.

"What?" Stan said.

"The Fab Four," Tink said. "The Beatles? Ringo Starr? Starr Lane?"

"Oh! I get it! Starr Lane! Thanks for the ride," he said. "See you Monday." And he leaned toward Tink and said, "Unless I see you sooner."

"You won't," Tink said, and looked him right in the eyes.

He had hardly closed the car door when Bess began talking about him. "Isn't he a sweetheart," she told them, not asking. "And that pretty shiny hair. I'm glad the boys are finally wising up about you, Tink," she said.

"I think they're all morons," Tink said. She felt that Bess thought she would be silly to like Stanley.

Bess laughed. "Trust you to hit the nail precisely on the head," she said. That made Tink wonder again what was happening with James: nice big old James with his arms around her . . . with his too much baggage . . . with his two dumb kids.

All Sunday afternoon, Tink worked on the Iceland report. Around three o'clock, Keith called. "I'm in charge of special effects," he said. He had a model volcano all ready to go. Tink didn't think he was very interested in Iceland at all, just the volcanoes. Fair enough. She would talk about the whales, and geysers, and hot springs and sheep. And, "I'm in charge of costumes," she said. Kitty had just the thing, and Tink went down into the basement to dig through the Halloween bins and find it. Then, before dinner, she asked Dad to take her to Target for pink face paint, and when she saw *Mad* magazine as they were checking out, he let her get it.

The next morning in school, when the country reports were about to start happening, a number of deliveries were made. Tink had gotten to school early enough to slide the new *Mad* magazine into Bushwhack's desk. Kallinka was there on time, dropped off by his father, who helped him carry a big clay volcano into the room, and was campaigning in writing and in person to Ms. Cho to let his team go first. He was distracted enough that Tink could put the brown paper bag with his costume on his chair.

Then a note appeared on Tink's desk that said nothing more than *I still say you'd look good nakid.* Stan seemed to have forgotten about liking her cartoons and had not really shown any interest in or even repeated the compliment about her drawings that had made her like him in the first place.

She turned thirty different colors and looked around the room. Bushwhack was sitting in his chair holding up the *New York Times* that Ms. Cho got every day and encouraged the class to read at least the headlines of. He had it open in front of him; standing up on the inside of the *Times* was *Mad* magazine, and Bushwhack was reading it undercover. Everyone sitting behind him could see it.

Tink looked away to hide the expression on her face and got up and walked to the front of the room to sharpen her pencil, the note from Stan*ley* (never again would she call him Stan) still in her hand. When she turned to go back to her chair, there was Keith Kallinka staring at her, wearing the two big foam elf ears from Kitty's second grade Halloween costume.

Everyone else was looking at Keith, too, which made it easy for Tink to make one last delivery: She dropped Stanley's note into Jackie's lap.

"Okay, let's get started," said Ms. Cho. "Iceland is up first."

"You want to say anything?" Tink asked Keith. He shook his head, a nervous wreck in front of the class. That's why he'd given her all his note cards. That's why he was standing behind her, posing with his volcano. Keith Kallinka was too embarrassed to do anything more than blow up the volcano and wear ears.

So Tink got on with it. She began by stating that fifty percent of people who lived in Iceland said they believed in elves. "In honor of them," she said, "fifty percent of our group is an elf today." Kallinka took a bow. "Many people think that Iceland is covered in ice and the nearby island of Greenland is covered in . . . grass. But actually the opposite is true. The names were mixed up on purpose by explorers who didn't want to tell other people about the good green land they'd found, which was Iceland."

"Wait." It was Bushwhack, interrupting. "You mean they called the icy place Greenland to fool other explorers into going there instead of Iceland, which was green?" He had folded up the *Times* and hidden *Mad* away. Tink nodded. "That's deception . . . " Bushwhack was thinking. "That's genius. It's like . . ." The class was waiting. "Sabotage . . . camouflage . . . bon voyage!"

He was grinning. Tink grinned back and couldn't stop.

Keith began his volcano demonstration. He could at least talk about volcanoes, if he kept his eyes on his materials. It was predictable enough: vinegar, baking soda, food coloring. But a volcano is always a good thing to have erupting in your classroom along with new kids and boyfriends and vocabulary and naked notes. And by the time it was done erupting Tink had calmed down and was ready to start over.

Jackie called her to discuss all this, of course. Imagine that.

JACKIE: I think . . . that you've been right all along about
Keith Kallinka. He's a fool AND a pal.

TINK:     I'm right about everything.

JACKIE:  Oh yeah? All right, oh wise woman, what do you think about Bobby?

Tink couldn't stop a little moan from escaping from her.

JACKIE:  That bad, huh?

TINK:     What do you want from him, anyway?

JACKIE:  I just want to continue our relationship.

TINK:     Relationship?

JACKIE:  Yes. As in, he comes and visits and we talk and hang out and—

TINK:     Tell me this. Say your mom and James break up for good. What's Bobby going to do? Keep coming over to hang out?

JACKIE:

TINK:     Okay, and maybe this is never going to happen, but what really WOULD happen if your mother and James got married? Then he'd be your brother.

JACKIE:  The worse horror: Amy would be my sister.

TINK:     You could get very good at High Pops very fast.

JACKIE:  Amy and I are never going to be best buds, or any kind of buds.

TINK:     Then why would she come?

JACKIE:  Oh, try to stop her, the stupid jerk!

TINK:     She must like YOU a little. She's not a jerk or stupid.

JACKIE:  I guess I know who you think IS.

TINK:     You didn't used to be.

JACKIE: You didn't used to be, either!

TINK:   Go ahead, Jacqueline, tell me. What am I being a stupid jerk about now?

JACKIE: School. People. Friends. Boys.

TINK:   Well, that seems to cover everything.

JACKIE: Can I give you some advice about Stan?

TINK:   Not to call him Stanley? I'll call him whatever I want to.

She was blustering, bluffing, because she knew Jackie was going to tell her to tell Ms. Cho about the *nakid* note, and she would refuse to.

JACKIE: You shouldn't have broken up with him.

Is that what she had done? Tink wondered whether that was what Stanley had told people. Breaking up seemed such a grown-up thing to do.

TINK:   I was mean to Bushwhack by going out with Stan.

JACKIE: BUSHWHACK? Bushwah!

TINK:   Not to me.

JACKIE: You're ridiculous. No, sorry, Tinky, I don't mean that. But Stanley, he's LIKED. He's admired.

So was Bushwhack. But Tink knew the difference. Bushwhack was liked by Farmers. And her.

TINK:     Stan's cool, but he shouldn't be.

JACKIE: Well, going out with him makes you cool, too.

TINK:     For a minute. But if I was really cool it would have lasted longer than a minute.

She tried not to let the tears out, but couldn't stop them.

JACKIE: Tink!

TINK:     Don't worry about it! Just go out with Kallinka. Do whatever you have to do to have the friends you want.

JACKIE: Mom says you're jealous of me. And I'm not going out with Kallinka. Bushwah.

TINK (her heart pounding): What am I jealous of you about?

Well, that was fast. At least Jackie wasn't going out with someone either now.

JACKIE: You know.

TINK:     No, tell me. No, you know what? Don't tell me. My mom needs me, Jackie. I've got to go. See you. Bye.

Tink hung up and went down to the garage to be alone. Her father had a very precise workbench, with a pegboard of tools with outlines drawn around them so you could tell what went where. Tink took all the tools off it, one by one, laying them down on the workbench, her hands shaking, her eyes dripping tears. Then, furious but determined to hold it together, to calm herself, she began to hang them again in their correct spots.

What was going to happen now? Were she and Jackie still even friends, never mind best friends? Could they be, when they disagreed this much about what made someone a friend—or a boyfriend?

She wondered if Dad had ever noticed his socket wrench was new, or if he'd had a use for it since the last bike adjustment. She decided to adjust some bikes to get it used a little bit. She started with her own bike seat, sitting on it first to check the height. She'd grown since that Sunday in October: Her feet were flat on the floor. Taller again. So she undid the nut and raised the seat up to set her on her toes again.

Jealous? Was she jealous of Jackie? She guessed she always had been. It was great to be an only child, to have all the attention and the clothes, and to be the person your mom took to the movies and shopping, just you, not a whole entourage of kids. Jackie got treated like an adult. Was that why she knew what to do with other people?

Was Jackie happy? She had to be happy, with so many people liking her. She had to be happy, whether or not she was still friends with Tink. So why didn't she seem happy?

Was Tink jealous about the circle? Tink knew she wasn't one of them, but Jackie didn't seem to be able to decide. How many more times would she try those people on, like fancy clothes, and come back to Tink, who must have felt to her like cozy pajamas? But pajamas just lived in the drawer waiting for nighttime, when you needed them. That was not the life for Tink.

She hung the socket wrench in its place above the workbench and thought about Bushwhack. She guessed the first socket wrench was still in the sewer outside their classroom, unless some massive winter storm had flooded it into the Sound. She had apologized with the *Mad* magazine, and he had accepted her apology by reading it in front of the class, but what would happen now? At least she knew who she liked for sure.

Poor Jackie, thought Tink, pretending to like Keith Kallinka to be in the circle. Poor Bobby, trying to deal with his dad's girlfriend, and not impressed by Jackie at all. Poor Kallinka, who might rather have been a Farmer if he wasn't so set on impressing Will Wheeler and the circle girls and even, she realized, herself.

She couldn't bring herself to feel sorry for Will Wheeler or Mitzie or Maggie. She actually couldn't stand any of them, she realized with a bang. And as for Stanley, well, he deserved them!

It was awfully warm in the garage, a warm spring day. Tink opened the garage door to look for Kitty and Jessie and Alvin, to see if they wanted the seats on their bikes raised, too.

# Honky Tonk

## (Spring)

The teachers said they had come up with the lip-synch concert for this year's sixth grade because they were so mature.
As usual, the teachers were perceptive, but slightly behind.
Although the kickball games on the lower field continued, the circle kids had abandoned them. They were the
realm of the Farmers and jock girls like Eddie and Donna.
Instead of heading for Herbie's, Maggie, Mitzie, Jackie,
and Meghan (who did gymnastics), and Keith Kallinka took
to perching on the hill above the game, cheerleading. They
did their best to draw all eyes—cartwheeling and yelling—
especially the eyes of Will Wheeler, Jonas, and Stanley,
who shot hoops far too seriously and acted like they were
too cool to notice.

Tink, meanwhile, was keeping to the shade. On a whim
one day, she asked Jennifer if she wanted to join her sister
Kitty and her fifth grade friends, who were having a jacks
fad. After that, they bought their own jacks and balls, and

kept to themselves, although they only talked during recess, saying little besides counting ball bounces or politely inviting, "Your turn" or "Yoursies, Jen" or "Yours now, Tink."

Once Meghan—better at tumbling than Maggie and Mitzie—came and played jacks, too, claiming she'd twisted her ankle. Tink figured someone had said something mean to her, but they must have made up because the next day it was just Tink and Jennifer again.

Jackie and Tink had stayed apart, no talks or visits or phone calls. Now, when the lip-synch concert was announced, they didn't even turn to exchange a glance, although it was the kind of karaoke thing they both liked to play around with (although only Jackie would ever do it in public).

Ms. Cho advised the kids to start with songs from chorus, because everybody knew the words, and Mr. Antenucci, the chorus teacher, had the recordings so they wouldn't have to go look for them anywhere. Apart from that, they could do any kind of "staging" they wanted.

"What do you mean by staging?" Tink asked.

"It means what the audience sees," said Ms. Cho. "So you can interpret the song however you want. You can make it tell a story, act it out, or just pretend to be the performers."

"Massively cool," said Jonas MacDonald. The class laughed.

"Indeed," said Mr. Bergman, smiling his little smile. "You'll work in crews. Everybody's got to be in a group, or if you're in a tech crew you can float. Divide up as you wish, to begin with."

Tink saw Maggie reach out her hands and grab Mitzie's wrist on one side and Jackie's on the other. Fine and good luck, if that's the way you want it, she thought at Jackie.

"You'll need performers, producers—people to handle the lights, costumes, props and things—and a director. So . . . let's see what you all make of this. We'll take a few minutes to think about songs, groups, and so on, then come back together and formalize things at ten of."

"We don't have to do a chorus song, right?" Tink asked. Despite not knowing who she was going to work with, she wanted to make sure she got to do the kind of song she liked.

"It's easier if you do," said Ms. Cho. "Everyone knows the words already."

Yeah, right. The words to "Lemon Tree," or the song about the Cuban man selling peanuts that the boys sang as "penis," or "Puff the Magic Drag Queen." This was the kind of behavior that had the teachers calling them too mature and sending them down to the lower field by Herbie's. Tink wondered whether the teachers knew what they were getting into, letting them choose their own songs—and whether they really would let them.

Ms. Cho started writing the names of all the chorus songs on the board, but nobody paid attention to any of them except this one ancient song, "Leaving on a Jet Plane."

Maggie dashed up to the board and put her initials next to that one as if there were some competition for it, but there wasn't. Then she went and grabbed Will Wheeler's wrist and pulled him over to their group. "Guess who's leaving on a jet plane," Tink said to Bushwhack.

"If wishing could make it come true," he said.

Tink looked around for Keith Kallinka, but he wasn't there. Absent? Nobody had him by the wrist.

Stanley came and stood by her desk blowing his fists as if they were a trumpet, playing them like a kazoo, and his song was that sex song that was on the radio a lot. She heard it every night and wondered about it, but she didn't want anybody air-trumpeting it to her. "Get as far away from me as humanly possible," Tink said to him.

"You know you want me," said Stanley.

Bushwhack and Tink both just stared up at him from their desks. "Two words," said Bushwhack.

"Add my two," said Tink. "Make it four." She turned and started writing down songs. She knew all kinds of songs from listening to Dad's old CDs and records and Jackie's iPod, and had her favorites in her own iPod that she played while she lay awake each night before going to sleep. Mr. Bergman came over and handed them a few small vinyl discs from his record collection, and they flipped through the stack to be polite. Bushwhack read them aloud over her shoulder, and some people who seemed to have neither a song nor an act nor a crew wandered over to listen.

"Echo and the Bunnymen?" Bushwhack read. "That's an insane name for a band."

Jennifer looked over his shoulder. "'Lips Like Sugar,'" she read. "That sounds awful."

"'Wagon Wheel'?" said Jonas.

They sat silently, thinking the words, and shook their heads.

"'I Want Candy,'" read Jennifer. But that would depend on great props, and they didn't think they could pull it together.

"We need a story," said Tink.

"Make it a story *and* dance," said Bushwhack. "Then we can light it like a rock show."

Tink started thinking about the Rolling Stones songs on her iPod. "Tumbling Dice." Dice were too small for the stage. "Get Off of My Cloud." How were they going to make clouds, and nothing happened in the song anyway. And then she thought of "Honky Tonk Women."

"How about a guy trying to get over some girl who broke up with him?" she asked. "In this song a guy goes to a bar and dances with all these girls, but he just can't seem to stop thinking—"

"Yeah, or stop drinking," said Jonas. "That's 'Honky Tonk Women,' right?" Tink realized he knew all the songs as well as she did. "He's madly in love and he goes crazy. That's a good song to dance to."

"It's great," Tink said.

"What's so great?" asked Jennifer.

"He's insane!" said Jonas with glee. "He's my hero. Wherever he goes, women hit on him."

Tink said, "But he's so in love with his girlfriend that he pushes all the women away, even when it means getting in a fight."

"Is it supposed to be romantic?" Jennifer asked. Her mouth was hanging open a little.

Jonas said, "It's *supposed* to be hot."

"Please," said Tink. Somewhere between romantic and hot, she thought. "He goes to all the hot spots," she said, with an eye on Jonas, who nodded like a bobble-head doll. "And these gorgeous women are everywhere—one in Memphis."

"Tennessee?"

"Yeah, and New York. They dance with him and flirt with him and so other men get mad at him and all through it he still is singing this song to his girl."

"Sounds cool," Jennifer said. Jonas and Tink waited. "Let's do it!"

"Silly man." Mr. Bergman was listening in on their conversation. "Chris, are you a crew member for this lip-synch or a performer?" he asked.

She certainly wasn't going to dance. She'd rather die. "Not a performer," she said.

"Okay, I'm making you the director of this group," Mr. B said. The director? Yes, she wanted to be that, to her surprise. Jonas and Jennifer looked surprised, too, in a less happy way.

"Want to be in 'Honky Tonk Women?'" Tink asked them.

Jonas said, "If I get to be the guy, the Mick Jagger guy."

Mr. B didn't care if they were happy or surprised or not, as long as they were grouped. "Keith Kallinka's in your group, too. He's absent, so I'm just going to assign him."

Jackie was wandering around, and Tink wondered what was going on with "Leaving on a Jet Plane," but she didn't ask.

"Maybe there's an elf part in this," said Bushwhack.

"Kallinka can be the bartender," Tink said.

"He can manage that," Bushwhack said, miming pouring drinks. "What'll you have?"

"What about the rest of us?" asked Jennifer. "What happens in the verses, anyway?"

"A fight in a bar," said Jonas. "You can be the gin-soaked barroom queen. You have to dress up."

"Somebody has to be the divorcée from New York City." Tink looked over at Jackie, wanting her to see her asserting her directorship firmly.

But Jackie thought she was inviting her in. She came over, although she acted irritated. "Who says I want to be in this one?"

Tink realized that it was either her or Jackie in the part of the divorcée from New York City. "You can if you like," she said.

"Ladies?" interrupted Bushwhack. "Drinks are on me." Was he trying to take over? Or to let Jackie in without making her admit she wanted to be in?

"No, they're on the guy singing the song," Tink said, frustrated.

"That's me," said Jonas.

Tink didn't want to be the divorcée, the way she'd be forced to if Jackie was in Mitzie's group. She took action. She ran over to Ms. Cho. "Can somebody be in two lip-synchs if they want? If they're just performing, they can be in two things, right?"

"Who?" asked Ms. Cho.

"Jackie."

"She'd better choose," said Ms. Cho. "There ought to be enough performers to go around. Only the tech people should float."

Tink walked back across the classroom. Bushwhack took her place conferring with Ms. Cho. Was he bailing out of their group? Did he want a different role? Did he want to direct? Once again Tink felt the calling to be in charge.

Jennifer had a piece of notebook paper out and was sketching a slinky dress for her character.

Jackie, who was still hanging around them, said, "My mom has a dress shaped sort of like that. She'd probably let us borrow it."

Us? Tink said, "Jackie, Ms. Cho says you have to pick which group to be in."

Everybody hushed. Jackie frowned. She looked across the room to where Maggie and Mitzie were singing "Leaving on a Jet Plane" and leaning their heads on Will Wheeler's shoulders.

"Which one is the girlfriend?" Jonas asked.

"Oh, they both are," said Jackie disgustedly. "He's supposed to be flying back and forth between one and the other."

"But *that's* not what that song's about!" Jennifer said. "It's about true love, and sadness, not somebody cheating."

"They're making the song kind of twisted," said Jonas, and everybody laughed, including Jackie.

"Aren't they going to want Kallinka?" Tink said. Why break up the old gang for one lousy lip-synch?

"He's assigned to us, for better or worse," said Jonas, shaking his head.

Bushwhack was just standing there looking awkward. "Ms. Cho said I don't have to perform. So I'm here to offer you technical support."

"How about athletic support, Alva?" said Jonas, and did another kind of mime. Tink knew, from Bushwhack's face, that he would have said, "He's no Farmer of mine" about Jonas.

"Are you a floater?" she asked Bushwhack.

"Just like a turd in the toilet!" said Jonas.

"Shut up, already!" Tink told him. Jonas wanted to work with them because he liked their song, but did he think he could be a jerk to them because they weren't the circle kids? "Anybody who wants to be in a different group better find one right now," she said, crossing her arms and raising her eyebrows, trying to stop herself from glaring. Her voice came out high and tight.

"Who died and made you queen?" asked Jonas. But then he sighed and sat down firmly among them and stopped creating conflict for a few minutes, which was a relief.

Tink challenged Jackie: "How about you? Are you staying with us?"

Jackie glanced over at the "Jet Plane" gang. It wasn't much of a circle today, more of a triangle. Even Stanley had melted away from them, maybe when Jackie had. Now he was sitting with Alex Mott and playing air drums on the desk with his fingers. Jackie said, "If you want me," and crossed her own arms, looking at everyone but Tink. Tink nodded. Jackie stayed.

The next day Keith was back. The groups met in the cafetorium so they could start planning how to stage their lipsynchs. When Jackie, Jennifer, and Tink came in, Keith and Jonas were sitting at one of the lunch tables saying clever things to Bushwhack. "Still floating, Alva?" said Jonas MacDonald. Was he going to go back to calling Bushwhack a turd again, just because Keith Kallinka was here and popular? But lately Keith Kallinka had seemed more like someone you would meow at than someone who would bark at you.

"A floater, you say, MacBonas?" said Bushwhack, scowling. He added darkly, "Old MacDonald did *not* have a farm."

"You're all turds!" said Keith Kallinka, completely missing the farmer joke and laughing so hard he squeaked.

"Turd is in the dictionary," Tink said. "It's not a swear." Tink thought of some things Bushwhack might call Jonas: You reference book. You doorstop. You cutting board. But Bushwhack said nothing, and neither did she. Were things going to fall apart so soon under her direction?

"You looked up turd in the dictionary?" asked Jonas.

Jackie laughed so hard that she screamed, overdoing it so everybody stared. Then she said, "Come on, let's go. Jonas, you're the bully customer, right?"

"Who?" Everybody said.

"The guy singing the song," said Jackie. "Mick Jagger." She was helping, they were getting "on task" now (Mr. B's phrase), but Jackie didn't need to think she was running things.

"He's not a *bully*," Tink said. "He's just some broken-hearted guy. He just can't drink his girlfriend off his mind, that's why he's with all these honky tonk women."

"Like me!" said Jennifer.

"You and Jackie."

Jennifer looked pleased. "And Jonas is the what?"

"The bully customer," Jackie said again.

"*I'm* the director," Tink said, giving Jackie the stink-eye.

"What do we need a director for?" asked Jonas.

"It's her job," said Jennifer.

"Because I'm not an actor," Tink said.

The others must have liked being called actors instead of lip-synchers, so they simmered down about Tink taking the director role. It made her feel a little sneaky, a little smart.

Maggie, Mitzie, and Will came over to their group.

"*Yes?*" said Jonas sarcastically. Did he dislike them, then? Tink thought about the party he'd been invited to, the one she *hadn't* been invited to.

Bushwhack did a little dance move. "Big Wheels keep on turning," he sang. "Rolling! Rolling!"

"Keithy," said Mitzie. "If you come be in our group we can have two pairs of people doing the dance. And, hey Jackie, we need a director."

"You'll be fine on your own," said Jackie lightly. She looked down at the paper in front of her, a copy of the song lyrics Tink had printed up for each of her crew, and did not look up again.

"Yeah, Mitzie, you're bossy enough all by yourself, but with Maggie—man!" This was awfully bold for Keith Kallinka.

"Come on, Kallinka," said Will. He was pleading.

"Hey, Wheeler, suck it up," said Keith.

Then Will turned to Jonas.

Jonas simply said, "I like this song better." Will tried to look at the lyrics. He seemed desperate. Jonas swept the paper behind him and smiled up at Will, blocking his view.

Maggie and Mitzie hustled Will away before things got ugly. Jonas, Keith, and Bushwhack laughed in a way that was a little mean, but mostly sympathetic. "Bummer for Wheeler," said Jonas. "So—"

Tink interrupted. "Okay, Bushwhack is tech. Jennifer is the gin-soaked barroom queen in Memphis. Jackie is the divorcée in New York City. Jonas is the customer, the Mick Jagger singer guy. And then we need a bartender. Keith, that's you." Bushwhack ceremoniously handed him the rag from the day before.

They all climbed the stage steps and stood by Keith. Jackie told him, "Okay, so you mop the bar and hand out drinks. And you can punch out the bully customer when he gets out of hand with the ladies."

Jennifer said, "Wait, but isn't that why you didn't want to be in 'Leaving on a Jet Plane'? Because of two ladies and one guy?"

"No, it's because it's not that kind of a song," said Jonas. "But this one is."

"No it isn't," Tink said. "There's just one lady on the stage at a time."

"Let there be both," said Keith. "Let them all get in a fight. Let the ladies fight over the man." For some reason Tink thought of Amy, wearing Bobby's baseball glove to claim him.

"Me!" said Jonas, puffing out his chest. "I'm the man!"

"A gin-soaked barroom queen," Tink said. "One. Not two."

"What kind of a bar only has one lady in it?" asked Jackie.

"There's *got* to be at least two," said Jennifer. She swished her skirt above her knees.

"I could be a great bully customer to a whole line of girls," said Jonas.

"Sure," said Jennifer.

"All right then," said Jackie.

They were going along with it. But why? Because Jonas was a bigmouth? Because he thought he was a star? Tink hadn't liked Eddie for bossing her, or Stanley for being kind of a slime. But there *was* something about Jonas, who didn't really seem to care what they thought as long as they were willing to hang out with him.

"I'm the director!" Tink yelped. "Aren't I?"

They all said, "All right." "Okay." "Yeah."

Whew. She was a little surprised. "All right, look," she said. "The song has two verses, one in Memphis and one in New York. So there can be two Honky Tonk Women. One bartender. One bully customer. It shows how the guy gets in trouble wherever he goes. I like it. Let's rehearse."

Jackie said, "I like the plan. I like the director. I like the bully customer." She patted Jonas on the head reassuringly. Good thing she didn't pat Tink.

"You mean you *like him* like him?" asked Keith Kallinka from behind the piano.

Jackie pulled her hand away from Jonas's head. "Okay, listen, guys—" she began.

"How's the stage going to look different for two cities?" interrupted Tink. They all just stared. Tink blew out her breath. The frizzy front of her hair flew up.

"I know! Wait!" Bushwhack said. He ran into the wings. There was a humming electrical noise, and suddenly everything glowed red: Jonas MacDonald's white button-down shirt, the gleam of Jennifer's cheeks, the blond of Keith Kallinka's hair, and the white of the rag.

"What'd you do?" Tink followed Bushwhack into the wings. He stood by a little console with levers all over it like in *The Wizard of Oz* when the curtain opens to reveal the Wizard.

"Special effects," said Bushwhack. "See? Look. It's the light board. All together they make white," he said, pushing all the levers far away from him. Everything got very bright. "Then these four alone, they make blue—"

Typical of him to know this, to have been in here messing around with the machinery. But Bushwhack explained, "They let me be stage crew for the concerts this year. Since I'm always at school early, Mr. Joseph showed me how."

"New York!" said Jackie on stage. She shook her arms and danced in a circle.

"No, blue should be for Memphis," Tink said.

"My light!" said Jennifer, the barroom queen. Kallinka stood there, bathed in blue, wiping his bar.

"These make red—" Bushwhack demonstrated, pushing four more levers away from him.

"*That's* New York," Tink yelled onto the stage. Jackie began to dance toward Jonas. Tink reached for the levers, her hands tangling with Bushwhack's, and sent the cast into darkness, with the expected result of noise.

"Oh, Jonas, you shouldn't have!" Jackie said in Bess's deep, sexy voice.

Tink pushed the other four levers—the lights that looked yellow—but the stage under it turned pink. Jonas and Jackie were tangoing—or pretending to—hand in hand, cheek to cheek. It gave Tink the funniest feeling, a little wistful (she'd never dance with a boy like Jackie), a little excited, because even if she could never do that, *Jackie* could, and it was going to make their lip-synch good. As a director, she could appreciate having good talent.

Bushwhack saw them over his shoulder, then glanced up at the rack of lights that hung above the stage. He was looking at Tink and Tink was looking at him and both of them were also seeing the tangoing. Tink felt a pang of wishing she could be so bold. Did he?

Tink stood up straighter. She refused to feel so sidelined. She was the director. She went crazy on the blue light lever, making it go on and off.

"Good idea!" Bushwhack dived on the light panel, jerking the levers up and down one after the other. The lights flashed on and off like a strobe, striping the stage in red-blue-white-purple light.

"Yee-ha!" yelled Jonas MacDonald. He let go of Jackie and did a dance around her, herky-jerky in the striped light.

"Wait!" Tink ran on stage. "You've got to attack her!"

"Huh? Who?" Jonas froze, his arms up over his head.

"Me?" Jackie's hands were on her hips.

"It's in the song!" Tink grabbed their shoulders as she never would have dared if she wasn't the director, and pushed them together. "Jackie tries to put up a fight! The tango has to turn into a big clinch," she said, "and Jackie, you don't want him to."

Keith Kallinka said, "Whoo-whoo!"

"Right!" Tink said. "And the gallant bartender leaps out from behind the bar to rescue you." Tink grabbed the rag out of Keith's hand and showed him what she wanted him to do: She tossed the rag wildly into the air, dashed across the barroom to Jackie, and mimed punching Jonas.

"I'm not doing that!" Keith said.

"You are so," Tink directed. She jumped off the stage and stood looking up at the scene, to see how things appeared.

Jackie came and stood on the edge of the stage looking back. "It's going to look fake," she said uncertainly.

"It won't," Bushwhack said from the wings. "I'll do the lights like this." He beat at the levers, and the lights went crazier than before, darker, making the stage shadowy and confusing like something in a spooky old movie.

In the flickering light Jennifer threw a fake punch at Jonas that seemed to hit him but actually went past his cheek, and he fell to the floor with a solid thud and rolled away, dying. "Nice one," he said to Jennifer.

Bushwhack's lights made a window of the stage, a window through which Tink saw her story as if she was really watching it from the outside. It made her catch her breath. I made that, she thought. Tink experienced a moment of power. She yelled, "Okay, bartender, from the top. Just like that."

"I told you, Hundred Percent, I'm not doing that," said Keith. His arms were crossed over his chest and his voice shook. "If I have to be on stage, I'm standing behind the bar."

"It's a piano, Kallinka," said Jonas MacBonas from flat on the floor. He stood up slowly.

"*I'll* punch you!" volunteered Jackie, hopping around. "Let me at you!" Jonas put up his dukes and she biffed his big hands with her little fists.

"Me too," said Jennifer. "We'll take him down."

"No," Tink said. "There has to be a hero."

"Who?" said Jonas. "You? Hundred Percent? In a man suit?"

The thump in the stomach came again. Tink didn't want to be a barroom queen, and she didn't want to be a barroom king either. "Bushwhack," she said. "Get out here."

"Me?" Bushwhack emerged from the wings, his big hands hanging at his sides. "I'm doing tech. I'm an engineer."

"We need a hero," Tink said.

"I'm a hero!" said Jackie, and batted her eyes.

"Me too," said Jennifer. Maybe a girl could have been the hero—with Jennifer's fake punch technique, she did not really need any guy coming in to save the day. But that was how the song went. Tink didn't know if Bushwhack could act, but Jackie and Jennifer could carry it off.

"I'll do the lights in this part," Tink announced before Bushwhack could say another word. "I'll make them blink so fast nobody will even know it's you." Tink added quickly, "Of course you'll have to be a bar customer in the scene already. You can't just show up."

"You can buy a drink," said Keith Kallinka, calm now that he was off the hook. "You can keep your back to the audience. You won't even have to look at them."

Bushwhack wanted to laugh, Tink could sense that. "Can I wear a mustache?" he asked.

He got his mustache on dress rehearsal day. And after that all the boys in "Honky Tonk Women" decided they were wearing mustaches. Jonas's was the first, made out of two paintbrush tips he'd wired and taped together, a short, thin, elegantly-shaped mustache. "What's the point of it, though?" asked Jackie, getting closer as she practiced fake kissing Jonas and finding that the fake mustache got in the way.

Jonas tried to waggle his mustache at Jackie and one end slipped down over his lip. Jackie pretended to have a fainting spell.

"Okay, ACTION," Tink said. "The show is tomorrow."

That was when Bushwhack turned back toward them with his broom-straw mustache attached.

"Where'd you get *that*?" asked Keith. He rubbed his finger over his own upper lip, wishing.

Bushwhack said, "Easy, Kallinka, you'll get one, too." He already had the bristles for Keith's mustache in his hand and was busy wrapping them around the center with a rubber band.

"What does *he* need a mustache for?" Jennifer demanded. "He's just the stupid bartender! And *you're* the hero! Why should you have a mustache? You should have a bowtie or something."

"To stop them all from kissing the heroine," murmured Jackie.

"I'm not kissing anybody!" said Bushwhack, grinning.

"You're the director," Jackie dared Tink. "You should make him kiss the barroom queens after he rescues them."

"You can't make me," said Bushwhack.

"You would if *Tink* were one of them," Jackie said.

"Shut up, Jackass," Tink said. Neither Bushwhack nor Tink was smiling anymore.

"Zero percent chance," Bushwhack said to Tink. She turned and walked away, and Bushwhack must have, too, because two seconds later he plunged them into darkness on the stage.

But Jackie was at Tink's elbow. "Wait and see what happens now!" she said, giggling, excited. "Now he's *thinking* about kissing you, at least."

Tink pretended to grope around in the dark and crashed into Jackie on purpose. Jackie tripped and Tink grabbed her elbow to save her. "Oops, what was that?" she asked flatly. "Why don't you mind your own business, Jacqueline?"

"After what I just did for you?"

"I don't need that kind of help!" Tink said. "Turn the lights on, will you?" she bellowed into the wings.

"Man, who made you boss of the world?" asked Jonas.

Keith was busy masking-taping the broom mustache under his delicate little nose. As soon as the boys were all equipped with facial hair they began yelling, "Disguises! Disguises!"

"Dastardly disguises," said Jonas MacBonas.

"Nasal support," said Keith Kallinka.

When they got back to their classroom, they saw the programs that had been printed up for the lip-synch concert. Tink had filled out the card for their group, and here were the results. Next to "Honky Tonk Women" it said, *DIRECTOR: Christine B. Gouda.* Wow. Jackie was *NEW YORK WOMAN,* Jennifer was *MEMPHIS WOMAN,* Keith Kallinka was *BAR-TENDER,* Jonas was *THE BULLY CUSTOMER.* Matthew Alva was *TECHNICAL SUPPORT* (not *HERO*).

Ms. Cho came and stood in front of Jonas's desk, regarding the mustaches. She glanced at Tink as she said, "I am compelled to remind you people that with privilege comes responsibility. This class—with such a high maturity level—has earned the privilege of directing its own show. Some of you have included material that has a certain edgy quality. Now listen: It cannot have craziness with it also."

The Honky Tonk Men looked at each other and patted their mustaches.

"Craziness?" asked Jennifer.

"Excessive sexiness," said Ms. Cho. "Vulgar language. If you treat your material with respect, others will too."

"Yep," said Jackie under her breath. "Her job's on the line."

Bushwhack sat at his desk, trimming and clipping his mustache over his desk while it was still stuck on his face, scattering broken broom straws.

Ms. Cho looked away from him and cast her eyes across the rest of the class.

"Some of you will be staying in the wings," Ms. Cho continued, "but rest assured, your contribution will be noted by the audience in a special way." Bushwhack whipped the mustache off his face, and something occurred to Tink: Ms. Cho had wanted him on tech support all along. But while Ms. Cho thought she was keeping Bushwhack off stage, where he could make his valuable contribution while staying busy and not going over the edge, Tink was putting him on stage—where who knew what might happen under the lights, behind a disguise?

Tink's nervous stomach got worse in the night as she half-slept, dreaming that the action stopped long before the song did and she was dragged out of the wings to make some more action happen. In the dream the light did not hide her and she had no disguise—no feather boa or broom-straw mustache—and stood there in her father's army jacket with a basketball under her shirt, bazoomas and pregnant belly bouncing as she did the Mexican hat dance while the Stones played on. She woke herself up long enough to switch off the radio, then she slept.

In "Honky Tonk Women," a guy goes into a bar where there are women trying to get his attention, but he can't forget his real girlfriend. Tink thought it was a good song, but the words were kind of stupid. The whole idea seemed kind of stupid, there in the middle of the night. But in the daytime? Well, it was still kind of stupid. But it had romance, sort of. And violence, even if it was fake violence. So naturally the kids would like it. Tink didn't know about the teachers or the parents. It was either going to be a free-for-all, or it was going to be great, or it was going to be awful.

Tink blacked out the lights, the music started, and she took a deep breath and brought the lights up blue on the bar scene. From where she stood—the wizard spot—she couldn't see the jewel-box window stage as the audience would, but she knew it was there.

The song went by really fast.

In the Memphis verse, Jonas went almost too far by trying to pick up Jennifer as Mick Jagger sang, "She tried to take me upstairs." But Jennifer—who must have spent last night in her room with Kleenex and a stapler—dumped a basket of pink tissue roses over his head to get him to leave her alone, then handed him what was left of the Kleenex box so he could blow his nose at the right place in the song.

During the chorus Tink strobed the lights and everybody ran on stage to dance around. Even Bushwhack shuffled and gallumphed around the stage. When the red New York lights came up, Jackie appeared in her mother's platform heels, fluttering her boa and slinging it around Jonas's neck. He bent her over backwards in a tango dip, pretending to kiss her—Tink *thought* he was pretending—while she thumped his chest in protest.

On went the flickering lights of the chorus and in came Bushwhack to save the day. Some jerk in the sixth grade rows of the audience laughed—Stanley?—and then stopped. No klutzy moves here; Bushwhack strode across the stage and grabbed Jonas, setting Jackie aside although she teetered against the bar and Keith had to hold her upright. She hid her face in Keith's shoulder and he patted her back to console her—drama-queen Jackie—while Bushwhack and Jonas fought all over the stage.

"Blood!" yelled some Farmer, and others took up the cry. "Blood! Blood!" They got their wish: Bushwhack delivered a fake punch to Jonas's nose and knocked him to the floor. A big cheer arose from the Farmers, as hero Bushwhack stood over Jonas threatening more action. (Later Alex Mott told them that Ms. Cho and Mr. Bergman were on their feet, ready to rescue Jonas.) Jonas writhed in the throes of death before getting slowly to his knees, holding his face in his hands. He crawled off the stage, then collapsed face-down, his head behind the curtains, his feet on stage, his face towards Tink. He winked. Tink let the lights go all red and pulled his hands and dragged his limp carcass off the stage. She hadn't planned it, but it was necessary. A huge cheer arose. Jonas said, "Wave!"

"What?" The lights were still all red.

"Wave to your public, Tink!" *Her* public?

She stuck her head out from behind the curtain. She waved. The crowd went wild. Jonas yanked her back. "See?" he said.

Tink couldn't stop smiling. "Strobe!" said Jonas. Tink leaped for the lights just as the chorus came around again and everybody danced on stage—Bushwhack and Jennifer, Jackie and Keith. Jackie got on top of the piano and Keith held her hand, still hiding behind his bar and his mustache. Jonas, beside Tink in the wings, waited for the song to end and all the lights to go on, white, before going to take his bow.

Tink stood in the wings. She needn't take a bow. In the end, she hadn't had to do much as the director during the show. She had just turned on the lights and started the music. It was Bushwhack who had done almost everything, been the actual hero, disguise director and tech support all in one. When he took his bow, Mr. Bergman and Ms. Cho got to their feet, clapping. But then Mr. Bergman began stamping his foot and smacking his hands together. "Director! Director!" Ms. Cho joined in, and then the audience did, too.

It took five seconds, maybe ten, but it seemed longer to Tink. Tink's cast was waiting for her, hurrying her up with their eyes. She stepped out on stage next to Jonas, and the applause grew louder. She was sweating with embarrassment. What to do to make this moment end? Tink bent at the waist, then stood straight, and found herself beaming a smile like sunshine at the audience. The lights went down. It was over.

Afterward people said a lot of things to Ms. Cho and Mr. Bergman about the "adult quality" of the performances and the "sophisticated musical taste" of some of the selections, and Tink knew they weren't talking about "Leaving on a Jet Plane," "Lemon Tree," and "I Got You Babe." At least the teachers didn't get fired, because it clearly wasn't their fault the kids had all gone ape in the performance and done stuff they never thought of in the dress rehearsal. "Next stop, middle school," Mr. Parisi said to all of them, and he seemed relieved to say it.

"Whose idea were the mustaches?" people's parents asked them. "Whose idea was the song?" They asked Jonas where he learned to tango and asked Jackie where she learned to dance on pianos and asked Bushwhack how he learned to fake punch. "From Jennifer," he answered. Nobody asked Tink how she learned to direct, and she felt jealous and wished she had more nerve. But just as she started feeling stomach-achy Bushwhack went by and said "Nice wave." For a second she relived her bow and the applause—*hers.*

"I didn't really do anything," she said honestly.

"Nice try, Hundred Percent, but no cigar," said Bushwhack. "I wouldn't be a hero if you hadn't directed me to be one."

Tink's nose prickled. She refused to get sniffly. "You said I couldn't make you do anything," she said and held her breath, looking down the hall to where Jackie and Bess were having some discussion.

Bushwhack stood completely still, as if frozen. Tink waited to see if he'd remember what he'd said nobody could make him do: kiss her. It was a safe enough place if he said no; nothing was going to happen in this bright, overcrowded hallway.

Which one of them was most terrified?

Finally Bushwhack answered. "Maybe I would," he said. "Sometime."

After the lip-synch concert was over, Jackie pulled up her skirt to show Tink a big scab on her knee, from the scrape she'd gotten when she'd nearly wiped out on stage. "Thanks to you," she said.

"That's from me? I didn't mean to get so violent."

Jackie said, "I didn't mean a lot of things. I'm calling you later."

Tink said, "Okay," and went home smiling.

Tink called Jackie before Jackie could call her.

JACKIE: Hello?

TINK: I was a jerk.

JACKIE: You really like that Matthew Alva, don't you?

TINK: No. He's just Bushwhack. You can't change his name on him, too.

JACKIE: He's too young for you, such a baby, Chris—Tink. What do you want with a dork like him, when you could have someone who looks like Stanley?

Stanley had lip-synched "Can't Take My Eyes Off You" right to Donna, the only other girl in the sixth grade with real bazoomas besides Tink.

TINK:    I don't like Stanley. And I don't have to like him. And it doesn't matter who else DOES.

JACKIE:  Okay, you're right. He's a creep. I still can't believe he wrote you that note. But Bushwhack—

TINK:    Bushwhack is extraordinary.

JACKIE:  Extra . . . ordinary?

TINK:    I mean it.

JACKIE:  You're probably right again. But I wouldn't let anybody else hear you say that.

TINK:    WHAT? Because . . . ?

JACKIE:  Because he's kind of, um.

TINK:    Kind of um. Then maybe so am I. I bet you wouldn't want anybody to think you were friends with me.

JACKIE:  Don't be obnoxious.

TINK:    No, YOU don't be obnoxious!

She hung up on her best friend for the second time.

# Baseball Season

## ( late May )

Tink worried all weekend after she hung up on Jackie. Was it the circle she was worried about? Was it Bushwhack?

She felt sorry for herself because she missed Jackie, and because Jackie was making her feel she had to choose between her and Bushwhack. Well, nobody could make her choose! Nuts to Jackie! It was over! When she got to that thought, sometime midway through Sunday afternoon, Tink went into the bathroom and sat on the toilet, waiting, not sure if she was going to throw up. What was this? Was it dumping Jackie for good, just as middle school was getting ready to start, and just at the beginning of a long, lonely summer? Or was it something in herself, something changing that made her nervous and lost? If you got rid of things, or people, who was to say you wouldn't be left empty, with nobody?

After a while, Mom came and knocked on the door and told her dinner was ready. Tink, a little surprised to realize that she was hungry, opened the door. Usually Mom would have just sent one of the kids to get her, so Tink knew her mom had something to say. Or ask. "You okay?" Mom crossed her arms and leaned against the wall at the top of the stairs. They were alone.

Out with it. "Ma, am I obnoxious?"

Mom cocked her head to one side. "You can be," she said. "So can Jackie. So can a lot of people."

How did Jackie get into this?

Mom asked, "How did you like being a director?"

Tink shrugged. There were too many answers.

"Did you feel obnoxious then?" Mom asked.

She shrugged again. "No, it was good. I liked—*making* something," she managed to say.

Mom said, "Sometimes when you have a good idea you need other people to make it happen, and if people like being part of your idea, what's the problem?"

That was a lot of words. "But what if they *don't* like being part of somebody else's idea?"

"Then let them be the one to walk away."

But on Monday morning, Jackie saved a seat for her on the bus. Tink was surprised how easy it was to simply ignore what had happened and go on as before, as long as Jackie was willing to do so, too. And after school, when Jackie asked her if she wanted to go watch Babe Ruth baseball practice, starring Bobby, Tink went along, and listened, nodding agreeably when Jackie droned on about how much much much she liked Bobby, plus his hair, plus his cheekbones, plus—of all things—the wrinkles at the corners of his eyes when he laughed.

Tink could never tell anybody how much she liked someone. Not anybody. Not even Jackie. Especially not Jackie. Jackie liked cool people, older people, cute people, people with shining hair, with muscles under their shirts.

Tink liked Bushwhack.

How could she, when he had that sweaty smell?

How could she, when he looked a little greasy sometimes?

Plus the way his pants were high-water pants. It was just because he was getting taller, and he wasn't rich or anything, so no new pants yet.

Plus the way she felt sorry for him about his father, especially that time he had to hide under the bed.

But also he had taken the bathroom apart, and she couldn't help being impressed by that. Very impressed.

And also he didn't act like he knew that much more about *Mad* magazine than she did. Even if he really did know more about it, he still talked about it to her. He didn't act all superhero-ish to her even though he had saved their bacon in the lip-synch concert. And he didn't get all snobby to her the way Bobby did when Jackie made her go talk to him after baseball practice was over.

Tink tried to tell Bobby the Yankees were overrated, because of course they were.

"Stop!" Jackie scolded her. "Don't mess with the man's passion!"

"I can't help it if he's wrong," said Tink.

Bobby said, "Ha!" and Tink would have liked to go on, because she and her mother had just had a conversation last night about who the big favorites were this season. But Jackie was looking daggers at her, and Bobby didn't take the bait anyway.

Maybe he thought girls were just less well informed and shouldn't even bother talking about baseball, but should only concern themselves with the kind of stuff like Jackie talked about around him. That was, "What do you like to wear best, Bobby, a crew neck or a turtleneck? Because boys look so sexy and modern in turtlenecks." Sexy. She actually said sexy. And maybe Jackie had already tried talking to Bobby about normal things like baseball.

But Tink had the idea that Jackie thought this stuff was what she was supposed to talk to Bobby about. Maybe it was working, who could say? Bobby hung on the wire fence between them, his fingers laced through the diamond shapes, and smiled at Jackie until James showed up to watch with Amy. Then Bobby went back to the dugout to wait for his ups with his team. Et cetera, as they say at the circus.

You see, that is the kind of talk that popped into Tink's head lately. If she said it to Bushwhack, he would laugh. If she said it to Jackie and Bobby, they would stare at her or, worse, at each other.

But actually she said it to Amy, with an eye-roll toward Jackie and Bobby, tossing her a spare ball. Amy caught it, hesitated, then said, "Calling all cars." "Calling all cars!" was from cop shows, but now Amy was saying it chasing down a loose ball from High Pops. This was an interesting girl!

So many people just said things, habitual things. Jackie didn't used to, but now she did: *Sexy. Sweetie. Hottie.* Tink never had either, and now was making up new, interesting things to say—she and Bushwhack. And now there was Amy, who not only seemed to make up interesting things, but was also listening for more. When the ice cream truck came and James asked if they wanted one, Amy said, "Does the deli have dill pickles?" And when it was time to go home in separate cars, she called over, "Farting is such sweet sorrow," which wasn't that creative but was still funny and controversial enough that James, Bobby, and even Jackie all scolded, "AMY." Tink giggled.

But then Bess got to the game, on her way home from work. Tink wanted to leave, but Amy kept throwing the ball. "Stay busy," she said softly to Tink. "Maybe he'll talk to her."

Shock of Tink's life: Bobby came over and started playing High Pops with them, calling over his shoulder to Jackie, "Want to play catch?" It looked to Tink like he wanted James to talk to Bess, too.

The four of them played High Pops with intense focus, and it seemed to Tink that Amy and Bobby were on purpose using Jackie's lame throws or missed catches to move the game farther from where James and Bess were standing, beside the emptying baseball field, saying things, not touching. High Pops went on. So did the conversation. The kids watched the body language of the grown-ups change from cool to hot and teary to relieved and happy.

Who could blame Tink for getting sucked in when Bess came over and gave her a special hug and kiss and said, "James and I are taking the kids home to hold the fort while we go out for a bite. You're coming, too?"

Jackie said, "Sure she is!" And before Tink could even think, she'd been bundled into the back of James's car with the others and whisked off to Jackie's house.

Reluctantly she phoned home. Dad picked up. "Tinker Bell! Where you at?" he asked, in a jolly mood.

Tink didn't have the energy to ask for Mom. "I'm at Jackie's," she said.

"Sounds like a party over there," he said.

"Bess's boyfriend is back," Tink said softly.

"Where's he been?" asked Dad.

"Somewhere else!"

"Oh? Silly man."

"Tell Mom," she said. She hung up.

Before the grown-ups left Jackie put her arms around Bess from the back, squeezed her and said, "Have fun, Mommy."

Then she squeezed James and said, "Have fun, Jamesy."

He turned to her and looked in her eyes and said, "You have fun too, Jacksy." Maybe this group really was somehow becoming a family?

After the grown-ups left, Jackie started showing off. She put the iPod in its dock and started dancing, then said to Tink, "Remember when your brother said his soul was in his butt?" as if the two of them were in some secret club that Bobby and Amy would know they weren't part of.

Well, Tink understood how that felt, so she said, "My brother Alvin who's six?" Jackie's expression showed that she hadn't mentioned the age of Tink's soulful brother on purpose.

Amy laughed. She said, "Bobby's soul's in his pitching arm."

Bobby said, very seriously, "Not my heart?"

Tink said, "I don't think your soul can be in your heart."

He was annoyed. "Well, where's yours?"

"In my ears," Tink said. Actually, she thought, it was in that box under her bed, well hidden from everybody

she knew, along with the program from the lip-synch concert and a story she'd started writing that had Bushwhack
kissing her in it. Completely unrealistic. *Sometime*, he'd
said. But she couldn't picture him ever doing it unless he
became a different person magically overnight.

Now Jackie switched the music to a slow song and
reached for Bobby, and he shrugged and put his arms
around her. When she put her head on his shoulder, Amy
got up. "Gee, Bob, get a room!" she said, a phrase Tink
thought she could guess the meaning of. She stomped into
the bathroom. Tink disappeared into the kitchen and pretended to get a glass of water. When she heard the flush
she carried her water into the hall outside the bathroom,
hoping she could pull Amy her way. She was being a good
friend, that's what she told herself. She wouldn't break up
Jackie's big slow-dancing moment.

Amy opened the bathroom door, clicked the light off,
and charged right into the living room. She switched the
music and put on a fast song, while Bobby and Jackie
stopped and stared, their arms around each other. Tink
didn't know which of them was going to kill Amy first. She
would have put her money on Bobby, but instead Jackie
leaped over and turned their song back on.

"You shouldn't just change people's own music in their
own house," Jackie said sweetly, and turned back toward
Bobby.

"Amy," Tink said, "there's Oreos in the kitch—"

Amy stared at Tink like she was the problem and said, "He's *my* brother."

"So? You think I want a *brother*?" asked Jackie.

Bobby said stubbornly, "We're just friends anyway, right, Jackie? We've talked about this."

Jackie didn't answer him. She turned her attitude on Amy. "He's not even your real brother," said Jackie.

"Come eat Oreos," Tink said to Amy.

"Thank you, I will," said Bobby, and led the way into the kitchen, glaring at everybody. Who knew what he wanted? The most Oreos, that was what. He was more focused on getting a stack of five into his mouth sideways than getting down or going anywhere or doing anything with either of the girls. Tink felt a little wave of sympathy toward him, and passed him the milk.

It was just as well they all had some Oreo nourishment when Jackie started describing her life plan. "It's like it's a gate opening to the rest of my life after this baby school. Middle school, then high school, then college, then I buy my Jaguar and drive from L.A. to San Francisco, and surf the whole way."

"Surfing's cool," said Bobby. "You can do it in Australia, but they have big barriers across the harbors to keep the sharks out."

"I'm going to Africa," said Amy. "I'm going to run a rehabilitation center for elephant families. Not just orphan babies, but any elephant can come. What about you?"

Tink answered, "I'm going to live in the boathouse down by the beach and I'm going to have four dogs, and a piano and a giant screen TV, and the waves are going to crash on the lower level so I can hear them all night from my bed."

"Who's going to be in the bed with you?" asked Jackie.

Was Jackie trying to make her feel stupid? "Somebody with a guitar," she said.

"Oh, whoo-whoo!" said Jackie. "To play you to sleep with his fingers on the strings."

Tink just looked at her. "I never know what you're talking about half the time," she said.

Amy nodded in agreement. "Well, which is it," she said. "Never? Or half the time?"

"I'm not like you," said Tink simply.

"That's no crime, Tink," said Jackie.

It was not the last surprise Jackie was going to throw at Tink that evening. James and Bess had come home, and James had left with Bobby and Amy. Tink was waiting for her mother to come pick her up, and Bess was on the phone with Jackie's grandmother. Jackie announced, "Maggie and Mitzie want to go shopping for graduation dresses, and they asked us to go, too."

Tink did not believe it for a minute. "They asked *me*?"

"Yep," said Jackie. But she was too matter-of-fact about it, and Tink saw right through her. It was either that

1. Mitzie and Maggie knew that Jackie wouldn't go without Tink, so they asked them both. (This she doubted.)

or

2. Jackie wouldn't go without Tink, so she told Tink that Mitzie and Maggie had asked her. (This made her proud of Jackie, but doubtful about her welcome with Mitzie and Maggie.)

But then also she thought

2b. Mitzie and Maggie did not know she, Tink, was coming yet.

"Nope," said Tink. "Not doing it."

"I'm plain and simple not going without you," said Jackie, with a catch in her voice.

"*Why* aren't you going without me?"

"Because they're mean and horrible."

"Then what are you going for?"

"It'll be worse if I don't. They'll get me back. They'll buy something together and make a fad and you're not cool if you don't have it."

"Who cares?"

"And they'll look at everything and make judgments about stuff, and when they see what I buy they'll make fun of it and say it's cheap or cheesy."

Tink asked, "Why do you care?"

"You can't just let people *talk* about you!"

Did they talk about her? About her clothes and stuff? "I can't help what they talk about," Tink said, and truly did feel helpless. "The only thing to do is forget about them." She knew her position was weak.

Jackie said, "Nope, the only way to deal with them is to be with them. See what they like. Hear what they say. Persuade them things I like are cool."

Tink was dumbfounded. "I think you're just wrong," she said, still feeling helpless. She could see that Jackie meant what she was saying. She realized that Jackie was afraid of Mitzie and Maggie. What was Jackie afraid they'd do if she decided *not* to "be with them"?

There was a brief awful silence while Jackie absorbed Tink's statement and Bess watched her respond. Tink swallowed and said, "My mom's going to make me a dress. We already went to the fabric store and got this red, white, and blue—she called it *seersucker,* it's lumpy in a good way." She babbled on. "Mom says it means hours sweating over the hot sewing machine, but she'd rather that than another trip to some store."

"I wish I still had time to sew," Bess said. "I used to love to. But when you have a job outside the home . . ."

"Mom says it's better than shopping." Tink couldn't seem to stop talking about her dress. "She says at my age you can get what you want without the angst of trying to find it on a rack."

Bess said, "I dream of shopping for a figure like yours."

"Oh, *fine*," said Jackie, insulted, and flounced out of the room and up the stairs. "Good night, *Tink*," she called down. "I hope your mother comes soon."

"Frankly," Bess told Tink quietly, "Jackie will be miserable on that shopping trip without you. She's been dreading it."

Tink said loudly, so Jackie would hear, "She'll be in heaven, shopping with those two. She doesn't want to have to worry about me." Or my figure, she thought.

Bess murmured, "They put too much pressure on her. They make her think she has to act like they do. She prefers to be with you, because you're down to earth."

Bess had it completely wrong. Jackie didn't prefer Tink. Tink knew Bess had always wanted Jackie to hang out with Tink because she had no sisters or brothers, and Bess worried she was lonely. Now Tink wondered if Bess was getting back together with James so Jackie would have a brother and sister. She said, "She thinks I'm a baby. She's even given up calling me Chris."

Bess said, "I thought you didn't like it, that was why."

Interesting. Tink said, "I did like it, at first."

Bess said, "But it didn't feel like you?"

Tink shook her head. "I guess it's better than Tinker Bell. Do I look like a Tinker Bell to you?"

When Bess said nothing, Tink peeked up at her.

"You know what I think?" asked Bess.

"Hmm?"

"I think you should stop feeling sorry for yourself."

"What?" Tink startled, sat up straight and looked at Bess suspiciously.

"And stop that attitude, too. I have your best interests at heart and I like you more than you like yourself. But you *should* like yourself. You're smart and funny and you're braver than Jackie, and that's why—" She paused. "If you don't want to be called something, come up with something you want to be called, and answer only to that. You're in charge, you know."

She was? She could be? "I like you, too," Tink told Bess. It was true. All this wasn't Bess's fault. Bess had always seemed to like Tink, or even love her. She believed Bess when Bess complimented her more than she did her own mother.

"And I like myself," said Bess. "Even if other people say things about me or think things about me. It's what I think of myself that matters most. Remember that, you." She tapped Tink on the nose.

"Do you tell Jackie that?" whispered Tink.

"You think she'd listen?"

Tink said, "Tell her anyway."

It was Bess's turn to look as if she felt sorry for herself. "I hope she knows how much I love her, even if we've been disagreeing so much lately."

Tink felt a bit embarrassed but she stuck her neck out and said, "Tell her that, too. She's proud of you. She cares what you say."

"Wise woman," said Bess. "And you—if I can say one more honest thing?"

"Go for it," said Tink.

"Let your mom make a great dress for you. Don't hide behind your clothes."

Tink admitted, "She wants to make a sundress with a halter top."

"Sounds adorable," said Bess. "Don't make that face. Give it a try."

★ ★ ★

JACKIE: I'm going to kill my mom for talking about me to you. And I'm going to kill you, too. What did you say to her?

TINK: Me?

JACKIE: Yeah, you. Who else? Her favorite child. She won't stop talking about how wise your soul is, growing up to be a swan.

TINK: Please stop.

JACKIE: Well, I'm not YOUR mom's favorite.

This was true, lately. Her mother had gotten protective.

TINK:    Sorry I didn't come shopping. Sorry I didn't wait to show you my dress fabric. Sorry I didn't even wait until you got out of the shower to leave. Sorry—

JACKIE: Shut up. I got the best dress, and you and I are going to be gorgeous.

TINK:    What are Mitzie and Maggie wearing?

JACKIE: Ew. They are wearing dresses from the girls' department. Couple of Flatty Patties. I mean, look who's talking, but at least I'm trying to put up a front. I mean, so to speak.

TINK:    Ew is right. What do their dresses look like?

JACKIE: What I'M wearing is gorgeous. It has a keyhole neckline and a full skirt with tulle under it, and I'm going to borrow Bess's shoes. And (loudly, for Bess's benefit) I KNOW SHE LOVES IT, EVEN THOUGH SHE HAD A FIT ABOUT IT.

TINK:    Why?

JACKIE: Because I had a fight with Mitzie about it. And so I walked home by myself without them. Jerks. When Bess came back to get us it was just them. And they told her, "Don't you think sixth grade is too young to wear black?" JACKASSES. That's what Mom—Bess—said. (whispering) She was so annoyed that she's going to let me wear it. Just to show them.

TINK:   Because you're her favorite child, dope.

BESS (in the background): Jackie! Who are you telling that to? Don't drag Tink into this. She's got enough issues!

Tink had issues? Maybe so, but so did Jackie and Bess.

TINK:   What did they get?

JACKIE: THEIR mothers gave them enough to buy Martha Meadows stuff. They're wearing these little SHIFTS—that's what Bess calls them—in pink and green, and they practically MATCH. Like we used to on the first day of school, when we were younger, remember?

Not that much younger.

In the background, Tink heard Bess say, "Put your hand over the phone, Jacqueline."

JACKIE (muffled): What?

TINK:   I can just hang up if you need?

BESS (muffled): Just because those little twerps have money to burn doesn't mean you have to be a green-eyed monster. There's no point in being jealous of look-alike, act-alike little clones of their mothers. And you don't have to spread your superior attitude all over town. Or theirs. You'll give Tink a complex.

JACKIE (muffled): Just because YOU can't buy YOUR daughter Martha Meadows—

BESS (muffled): You're far too mouthy, little girl.

JACKIE (not so muffled): Where do you think I get it?

BESS (hardly muffled at all): I know exactly where you get it.

JACKIE: I'm going to wear my black dress like you said and make them all look like the babies they are. You're the one who said it was mature—or is that another way of saying sexy? Or slutty? Then—

BESS (not muffled in the least): Tink? Jackie has to go now. She's just lost her phone privileges for a week.

# Class Picture

*( last day of school )*

Tink didn't understand why Bess would say yes about Jackie's black dress if she meant no, or why Jackie wanted to wear something so different anyway. She knew she wouldn't get anywhere by calling back, whether or not she was Bess's favorite child or Jackie's true best friend, but she couldn't stop wondering about the confusion of that argument. In the girls' room at school, Jackie snapped at everyone—Tink and Maggie and Mitzie all in the same breath. When Jennifer asked her what was wrong, Jackie announced, "Everybody?" and when the girls looked up at her she held up her hands in claws at all of them.

Meghan exclaimed, "Some people!" and stomped out, making her own announcement to Eddie and Donna (on their way in), "Stay out of Jackie's way!"

Everyone did. Tink didn't join the circle girls in grumbling behind Jackie's stiff and silent back. She didn't seek Jackie out at school, but didn't turn away from her, either.

Tink was neutral, except for on the bus, where she still sat in the same seat she always had, ever since kindergarten—next to Jackie. Each day of school that June, she boarded after Jackie, sat down beside her, opened the bag of Fritos she'd saved from lunch, and held it out. Then she informed her of the number of days left to the end of school: twelve, nine, seven, three, then one.

"Good," Jackie said to each number.

"How you doing?" asked Tink. Or, "What's cooking?" Or, "What's happening?"

Jackie would say, "Nothing" or "Nada" or "Shut up."

At school Jackie didn't seek Tink out, either. Despite the cold shoulder she was getting from the circle girls, she still went and cheerleaded beside them at kickball games or by the basketball hoop. Maggie and Mitzie and Meghan (and sometimes Keith, but sometimes he played four square with some of the Farmers) didn't tell her to go away, so she stayed.

Tink stayed out of it. She played jacks with Jennifer, then wandered around, walking a circuit from the fifth grade jacks games to four square and basketball, kickball and monkey bars. Jennifer said she was going to try out for summer softball. Tink hadn't decided about softball just yet, even though Amy had gone so far as to call her on the phone and tell her when the tryouts were. "Did you tell Jackie?" Tink asked.

"No, but if you think I should, I will," said Amy. Neither Amy nor Tink thought Jackie was interested in softball. Tink didn't know (couldn't tell) *what* Jackie was interested in right now, apart from being with certain people or at least not being pushed out by them. But she couldn't reject Jackie when she saw the way her old friend was now, miserable and torn. And maybe, just maybe, summer softball—or the people playing it—could help. So she printed out an extra announcement from the softball association web page, drew exploding stars all over it, and left it on Jackie's desk.

"We'll see," said Jackie.

If Tink could have held back the calendar, would she have? Would she have stayed in the cozy comfort of sixth grade, in the baby school, where at worst you got barked at, and at best you got to direct something?

Before she knew it, the sixth grade class was taking home bags of old work, scrubbing their desks with shaving cream, and collecting money to get the teachers presents. The last day of school was suddenly here: a morning spent at an assembly where they got their school pictures (yes, *those* pictures: the special sixth grade ones), graduation in the afternoon, without the rest of the school, and then the graduation party, off school property in a pavilion.

After assembly, Tink rushed to the girls' room to have a quiet heart attack about the badness of the class picture, and hurried to hide her copy away. She wasn't surprised by how bad it was. She'd known all along, ever since they took the darned thing on one of the worst hair days of her life. Worst clothes days. Worst attitude days. Ack!

It was June now and she felt different. She looked different now too. The girls' room sinks were made for shorter people than her. Tink's hair was long enough now to pull back into a ponytail. It was a fat, bushy, curly ponytail, but at least her hair wasn't sticking out all over her head. Still frizzy, though. Her mom had made her the halter sundress in red, white, and blue stripes. "You look like a million bucks," her dad had said, which is all you ever need to hear, really.

Tink stood over the sink and rolled her class picture into a tight cylinder and wrapped one of her two ponytail holders around it. One wasn't really enough to hold her ponytail, but it was going to have to try, even if she had to keep fixing her hair all day long. There was no way this picture was getting sent around for signing. She didn't mind passing an empty frame.

Ms. Cho and Mr. Bergman had done this totally cool thing and gotten a bus to take the sixth grade to the party, so the kids didn't have to drive with their parents, but could just go at the end of graduation. Same old kind of school bus, but no younger kids, just all of them on one bus together. Tink got on behind Jennifer, thinking they would sit together, but as they passed Meghan she reached out and pulled Jennifer in. Tink just sat down in the next empty seat, and was happy when Jackie plopped down beside her. They were in front of Will Wheeler and Keith Kallinka, behind Alex Mott and Bushwhack. Prime real estate.

Already the school looked old and small, like somewhere they used to go once. They wouldn't ride the bus back to school, they'd go home with their parents. So this was it. The bus pulled out of the driveway. Tink didn't turn and look back. She looked forward, at the back of Bushwhack's head and the road that led down the big hills to the beach.

They were still all signing each other's picture frames, the way they had been doing since their class pictures had been handed out. Later they could each put the picture in a real frame, with glass, and the cardboard frame would be the mat, with everybody's signatures all around the picture.

Ms. Cho wouldn't let them out of their seats on the bus, but she let them pass the frames around. Tink signed a bunch, and after a while she noticed that Jackie was having some trouble. She was trying to get her frame back in between people signing, to see what they'd written, and this was annoying people. Tink kneeled up on the seat next to Jackie. She could see that Maggie and Will Wheeler had set up an assembly line in which people passed them frames and they signed some fancy signature quickly, without stopping to make anything personal or individual.

"You think you're so popular!" Jackie was teasing them, laughing, but there was an edge in her voice: She was mad at what they were doing. Tink turned away to sign Keith Kallinka's frame, which had made its slow way forward to her, and got distracted a moment. For Tink (and Jackie too, Tink knew her well enough to know) signing frames made her stop and think about the person and what the year with him or her had been like. You only had a square inch to write in, so you might as well make it good.

*KKKKKeithK,* she wrote. *Kinda Krazy. Good luck at middle school. Don't blow anything up.* Meanwhile, he kept talking across her to Bushwhack and Alex Mott, babbling some insults, calling them "you leaky ballpoint pens" and ignoring Mitzie, who kept tapping on his arm from across the aisle until she finally slapped him with her cardboard frame.

Before Tink got to sign her name (Christine B. Gouda, with a big beautiful flourish underneath, a curve with two lines crisscrossing it), Jackie piped up.

"I have an announcement to make!" she said in a big stage voice. She kneeled up on the seat so she could see everyone. Her face was red and she was mad, but she was smiling, and she made her voice warm, bubbly, and charming the way that Bess could. "This is our last day of school!" she said. "We may never be together again!"

There was some fake crying from certain boys, including Will Wheeler.

Jackie did some fake smiling. "You laugh," she said, "but this is the end of seven years of school together! This is a big moment we will always want to remember. So if we're going to sign each other's frames, I think we should do it for posterity!"

Keith Kallinka rolled his eyes. "Define?" he said.

"To be remembered!" said Jackie, pumping her fist in the air. "Sixth grade power! So don't just scribble your bibble on the frame! Write something to the person! Be a pal!"

"Hooray!" said Mitzie, sarcastically twirling a finger above her head.

She was the only one who even pretended, but Jackie bowed as if everyone had cheered, so Tink yelled, "Yay!" Bushwhack clapped, to keep Tink company. A few other Farmers joined in, clapping halfheartedly.

Jackie sat down, and the frames kept going around. When Tink's came back to her, she could see that just about everybody had signed it, and plenty had just signed their fabulous signature, ignoring Jackie. Some signatures were so scribbly Tink could barely make out the names of the fools who had written them.

There were some nice ones, though. Jennifer Marx had written, *To the future Oscar winner for Best Director.* Keith Kallinka had written *Lots of Lava, Keith,* which made her shiver a little. He had even drawn a little volcano. Kute.

Whoops! The frame got whipped out of her hands by Bushwhack. "Hey!"

Bushwhack flapped his frame into her hands and waved his pointer finger at her. "Sign!" he said. He was writing like mad, hiding it so she couldn't see. Here's what Tink wrote on his frame:

100% with curly hair around it and the o's made into crossed eyes, and a mouth with a space between the front teeth like Alfred E. Neuman, that guy on *Mad* magazine. Then her beautiful signature. She wanted to write *ROARRR* or *Remember the lion,* but she couldn't write anything like that; she couldn't even think anymore. She just stopped.

She leaned forward to try to see what Bushwhack was taking so long about, but he stuck his head in the way. "Get your earlobe out of my face," Tink said. "I can't see."

"Get your face out of my earlobe," he said. "You're making the writing bump."

The bus was pretty bumpy all right, so bumpy that when Tink stuck her head right between his and Alex's to grab her frame back, his hair brushed against her cheek.

Did you catch that? His hair brushed against her cheek. His hair. Her cheek.

She bounced back into her seat and read what he'd written.

She had seen what he'd written on other people's frames: his trademark signature, a bush (really just a scribbly knot) with a hand sticking out of it holding a baseball bat. Get it?

Below that he had written Bushwhack (Matthew G. Alva).

But on her frame, and her frame only, below his signature, was this:

$$\text{Stay as ▓▓▓▓▓ as you are.}$$

She studied it to see what it said, but it was too scribbled: No word emerged.

*Stay as _____ as you are.* There wasn't anything she wanted to fill into the blank. It didn't matter what the word was, it amounted to saying stay just the way you are. And that was the last thing in the world she wanted.

She leaned forward, her nose next to his cheek again. "What's that word?" she asked Bushwhack.

He peered at his writing closely. "I don't remember," he said, and shrugged.

"How can you not remember? You just wrote it two seconds ago. Has it gone completely out of your head?"

"Why don't you take a look?" He held the side of his head toward her, like she was supposed to look in his ear.

"Oh, forget it," she said, her face hot. She flopped back into her seat, next to the rear end of Jackie, who was kneeling, looking backward, leaning over Keith to sign someone's frame.

"You give up, Hundred Percent?"

"What's the point? I can't read it, and you can't remember what you wrote."

"It's not my memory that's the problem," said Bushwhack.

"Oh." He meant, he could write it all right. But he didn't want her to read it. But he wanted her to know it was there.

"Pretend I haven't thought of it yet," he said. "Or ask again."

"Why, when you won't even tell me now, and you wouldn't just write it in the first place?"

He mumbled into his lap, "I did so write it."

"What?"

He said slowly, "You traffic light. You SLOW CHILDREN sign. You punctured eardrum. I said, 'I did so write it.'"

"Then there is a definite word under there!"

"Yes, definitely a definite word, with definitions and everything."

"All the definitions are under that cross-out?" Tink crossed her arms and looked at him, and he laughed.

"I'm not telling," he said. "Ask me again sometime."

"How many times do you expect me to ask you?"

He mumbled into his lap again, "Until I tell you."

Then the bus arrived at the beach. Their parents were there, funny-looking the way parents are when you see them when your whole class is near. It was four o'clock, and the graduation party was really, finally happening.

They weren't ever going back to school, and it hit Tink all over again. They had to take their stuff off the bus and give it to their parents, except for the picture frames, which got laid down on the tables at the back of the party so people could sign them more and look at them and so they could be out of the way during the party and not get food and lemonade or other crud on them.

It was strange, because Ms. Cho brought her husband, Mr. Cho, and Mr. Bergman brought his girlfriend, Sal. It was weird to see them dancing in each other's arms, the way old people did, the way the parents did, and the way some of them were trying to get the kids to do with them. Tink's father grabbed her and pushed her around, and even she had enough soul to know that wasn't the way to dance to "I Want Candy."

"Oh, just relax and dance," said her father, and she did, but her mind was somewhere else. She was looking to see where Jackie was, and whether she knew where Tink was, and what she was doing now, without a dad. Tink didn't see her at first, but then the music changed. They'd gotten somebody to put the Rolling Stones on, and Jonas was in the middle getting his groove thing on, dancing like a sex machine, and pointing at Jackie to come join him. "Who's *this* kid?" Tink's father asked, finally standing back, and— oh no—shaking *his* groove thing a little.

"Dad, STOP," Tink said.

"Oh, all right. Go find your friends," said Dad, waving.

Tink walked behind Maggie, Mitzie, and Meghan to go get a drink (and get away from her father) and heard the tone in their voices and some of their words as they watched Jackie and Jonas. They didn't exactly say, "Ew," not with that word, but that's what they were saying.

After a few moments Tink turned to see Jackie dancing with someone else. James! With Bess off to one side smiling at them, and Bobby and Amy nowhere in view.

Tink experienced a blast of teary gratitude for her own parents, went over to them and let her father dance with her for a few minutes until embarrassment took over again and she said, "I think I need to go tell Ms. Cho something." Dad went off to find Mom, and Tink crossed the party toward the table where Ms. Cho and Mr. Bergman sat together, looking ready for summer vacation.

She passed the table where Bushwhack and the Farmers were pretending to drink lemonade up their noses through straws, and another where Maggie and Mitzie whispered about slumber parties everyone wasn't invited to. Keith Kallinka wasn't sitting with either group; he sat off to one side on a bench with his boring parents, where he'd been for the whole party.

Tink went and told the teachers that she was going to miss them. It was true. Ms. Cho said, "Another year, another dollar."

"Do you mean you're glad it's over?" Tink said.

"I have your sister next year, don't I?" Ms. Cho said, and right away Tink got jealous.

"Are you going to miss us even a little?"

The teachers rolled their eyes in response. Stung, Tink turned away.

Ms. Cho grabbed her arm and pulled her close. "You are a brave, good girl," she said.

Tink sniffed. "That's what you think."

"Oh," said Mr. Bergman. "You mean your life of anarchy?"

Tink wasn't sure about that word.

He said, "Hmm. You didn't intend it to be anarchy?"

"What's anarchy?"

"It's civil disobedience," said Ms. Cho. "That's a better description for Chris. She's peaceable, really. But fierce."

Tink was astonished by her teachers' assessment, and confused. She wondered if she was in trouble, even though she had already graduated.

Ms. Cho said, "Listen, kiddo. Middle school is no fun sometimes, and part of that is because some kids write their own rules about who counts. All I'm saying is I have a feeling you won't let their rules apply to you."

Tink nodded. That much seemed true.

"Would you do it over again, Chris?" asked Mr. Bergman.

"Definitely no do-overs," Tink said, laughing. "Seventh grade has *got* to be better. I don't want to be in sixth grade anymore."

"Come back and visit," said Ms. Cho. "The halls will be echoing from your class for years to come. Meanwhile, do what you have to do at your new school. And consider running for something, some sort of leadership role."

Tink tried to imagine herself in seventh grade, leading. Just the idea of the new school gave her a shiver, but she pushed that thought away for later. Still, she stood taller.

"I will," she answered.

★  ★  ★

JACKIE: You said to call as soon as I was alone, so—

TINK:　　"Stay as _____ as you are," that's what he wrote.

JACKIE: Who?

TINK:　　Doesn't matter. What did he mean?

JACKIE: Of course it matters! Name a boy and I'll tell you what he meant.

TINK:　　Keithy.

JACKIE: Is that who wrote that?

TINK:   Not telling. You said name a boy.

JACKIE (sighing): He'd say genius. He said you were a genius, you know, after "Honky Tonk Women."

TINK:   Genius doesn't fit. What would . . . Alex Mott say?

JACKIE: Alex Mott! It was him?

TINK:   Are you going to keep on with this?

JACKIE: Alex Mott would say "Stay as tall as you are."


Hysterical laughter. She was right. Alex was short.


TINK:   Will Wheeler?

JACKIE: VIOLENT. No, wait—


She erupted into giggles.


TINK:   Gorgeous? Stupid? Ignore-able?

JACKIE: Pushy!

TINK:   Are you finished?

JACKIE: No. Give me another one.

TINK (as though exhausted and exasperated): Okay. Bushwhack.

JACKIE: It was him, wasn't it?

TINK:   Nope.

JACKIE: Come on.

TINK:   Jack, tell me.

JACKIE: Friendly. Because you're always nice to him.

TINK: Snore.

JACKIE: That's not enough? Interesting. Very interesting. Stay as funny as you are. He thinks you're very humorous.

TINK: He's right.

JACKIE: And fuzzy. Because you are kind of fuzzy.

TINK: Takes one to know one.

JACKIE: Cute, then. Stay as cute as you are. How about that?

TINK: I'm cute? Not pretty? Not beautiful? (and she quoted her mother here) Baby ducks are cute. But I'm going to be a beautiful swan.

JACKIE: My mom says you have a beautiful soul.

TINK: Geez. But not a beautiful bod? Not a beautiful face.

JACKIE: You're cute. It's true.

TINK: Never mention it again. Promise?

JACKIE: And original. And opinionated. And cranky.

TINK: CRANKY? Well, wouldn't YOU be?

JACKIE: Me? I am charming and precious at all times.

TINK: Did someone tell you that?

JACKIE: You mean on my frame?

She got really serious.

JACKIE: What difference does it make what anyone says? It's not like they get the final word on your personality. You'll probably never have to see any of them when you get to middle school, that's what Ms. Cho told me. So who cares?

Interesting what Ms. Cho had opted to tell different people as they left her class, thought Tink. Also, this seemed like a long speech, for someone who didn't care.

TINK:     What did they write on your frame, Jack?

JACKIE:

TINK:     Was it bad?

JACKIE (crying): They're turds!

TINK (quietly): Why?

JACKIE:  Jonas started it. Although what he wrote was actually nice. He's so smart, you know? And funny—

TINK:     He THINKS he's so smart and so funny.

JACKIE:  I adore him. I mean, not that way. It's just, he's like my best friend ever. Except you. You know what I mean.

Tink didn't.

JACKIE:  He writes (she read off her frame), "Dear Jackie, You're such a good actress you scare me a little. You were the perfect 'barroom queen.'" And he signs it "Bully C."

TINK:     He would.

JACKIE: But then?

She choked up.

TINK:     Jack, what?

JACKIE: So somebody else writes, "Looks like you gave MacBonas a boner, nice work!" Instead of a signature you can read, it's a big scribble. It's gutless. It's piggy.

Even though Tink said nothing, she was thinking how Bushwhack scribbled over his missing word. But no, he would never write such a thing.

JACKIE (sniffing): They wrecked my whole frame, Tink. I can't even show my mom my picture. She'd go into cardiac arrest. And there's more.

She read, loud and angry, "Barroom Queen equals slut."

She read a couple more, crying for real now, until Tink interrupted, yelling.

TINK:     Crunch it up, Jack! Crunch it up and tear it up, right now. Tear it into smithereens and go throw it into the grill.

JACKIE: The whole class has already seen it.

TINK: Your mom hasn't seen it. Don't look at it one more minute. So go right now! Do it! I want to hear the tearing.

JACKIE (with a little, little, little laugh in her voice): Okay. I'm tearing it into tiny pieces. Can you hear it?

TINK: I'm hanging up so you can do it better. And then I'll come over and help you. I'll be there in a flash with the cash.

She didn't know why she said these things. Was it Amy? Or Bushwhack? Or just herself?

JACKIE: You will? What about Bess? She's coming home.

TINK: Burning it is more important than what Bess will say. But wait. Call up Bobby. Tell him to come over and barbecue with you. Tell Amy, too. Party at your house.

Tink hung up the phone and yelled: "MOM!"

Kitty yelled up the stairs, "She went to the store."

Tink called, "By herself?" She meant, did she leave me in charge?

"No," said Kitty. "Dad's home."

Then Tink knew what to do. She went downstairs to her father's little home office, where he sat at his old college drawing desk with the T-square hanging from a little hook underneath. She laid her class picture frame on his drawing desk. "Dad? Can you do me a favor? Can you cut me another one of these? As much like it as you can?"

Dad turned it over and glanced at the signatures. "Nice," he said. "What do you want another one for? You don't want all these goofy autographs?"

Tink realized how much she liked her goofy autographs. The best ones were nice, and the worst weren't bad, just boring. Nothing mean, not like Jackie's.

"It's for Jackie," she said.

"Why, didn't she get one, too?"

"Something happened to hers. She needs a new one."

"What happened to hers?"

It was just Dad curiosity, just plain, not Mom curiosity with all the hidden questions and meanings, so Tink answered, "Some assholes ruined it." It was the first time she'd ever said a swear to her father.

Dad said, "Since when do you use that word?"

"Since they earned it," she said.

"I think better of you than that," said her dad.

"And I think better of Jackie!" she said.

"Was it boys?" said Dad. She shrugged. He said, "If it's boys, then it's not really about Jackie. They're just showing off to each other."

That didn't make any sense. "It could have been some girls, too," she said.

"That's worse, isn't it?" her father asked. He made a little huff, sticking out his bottom lip, like he knew it stunk to be Jackie right now. He reached down between the side of his desk and the wall and came up with some flat, smooth pieces of cardboard. He laid them out on his drawing table in front of Tink, and she pointed to one. And then it was classic Dad: It was magical the way he made things, tender and perfect and glad to be doing it. So carefully, he traced Tink's frame onto the cardboard with a light, sharp mechanical pencil. So perfectly, he cut inside his tracing lines with his sharp, thin X-Acto knife. So gently, he lifted the extra pieces of cardboard away, blew the cutting dust from the edges, and rubbed one finger along them so they were smooth. Then he handed it over.

"Daddy, thank you so much," Tink said.

They wrapped the frame up in some paper and tape.

"Big hugs all around," he said.

"I'll tell her," Tink said, and hugged him herself.

It was not easy to keep the wrapped cardboard frame from turning into a sail as she rode her bike, but she did it. And when she finally got to Jackie's house, Jackie and Bobby stood over the barbecue, stirring the coals.

Amy was sitting on the back steps by herself. Oh, Jackie, that was nice of you, thought Tink. "I'm only here because

I heard you'd be here," Amy said, smiling. Zing. But if Jackie felt it, she didn't show it.

Bobby said, "It's a celebration! You're going to middle school and we're going to high school."

There were some hot dogs thawing on the picnic table, and a loaf of bread for rolls. Tink sidled over and looked into the grill. There were only a few shreds of burned cardboard left in there.

Jackie lied, "I burned that big box of valentines you've been bugging me to get rid of."

Amy said incredulously, "You burned valentines?"

Tink said, "Must be nice, right?" She didn't know why Jackie was still trying to impress Bobby.

Bobby didn't show he'd heard. When he saw Tink watching him, he asked her, "What's in the package?"

"It's for Jackie," Tink said. "It's a present."

Jackie came and took the package and undid the paper carefully. Her face looked like the sun had just come out. "Who—?"

"My dad," Tink said.

"But how did he know?"

"I asked him to make it," said Tink.

"I love your dad!" said Jackie. Then she said, "And I love you, too."

It was the most uncomfortable moment. Tink had heard her mom say that to her friends, sometimes, but she, Tink, had never said it to Jackie. People their age didn't,

Tink didn't think. But she smiled anyway. She understood. She wasn't sophisticated or older, but Jackie needed her. She tried to imagine Jackie telling Tink she loved her in front of Mitzie. It never would happen. Mitzie would say, "Lezzie alert."

Bobby and Amy didn't, but they looked at each other and stuck out their tongues. Tink had to laugh. It was something she and Kitty would do, something brothers and sisters did. But Jackie asked them, "You making fun of me?"

"No more than usual," said Amy.

Jackie made a fist and faked getting ready to punch Amy with it. Amy did the same.

"I'm going to punch you out!" said Jackie.

"I'm going to beat you up!" said Amy.

"Ladies," said Bobby.

Tink blinked. They were all laughing. They were getting along by fighting. They were acting like siblings. "Where are your parents?" she asked all of them.

As a group they rolled their eyes and shuffled their feet. "They're 'shopping for groceries,'" said Jackie. She made her fingers into quotation marks to show Bess and James were using the groceries as a ruse.

"Making out in the grocery store parking lot, more like," said Bobby.

"They didn't think hot dogs were enough to cook out?" asked Tink.

"We told them they had to get out of here," said Amy. "We're taking a stand on public displays of affection."

"It's either that or we have to watch them all the time!" said Jackie.

What they didn't say was what caught Tink's attention: Their parents were staying together, and the kids were together *about it*.

"They always do get around to feeding us sometime," said Amy.

"Hey! We don't have to starve," Bobby said. "We brought—Dad made us bring a celebration offering." He handed Jackie a brown paper bag.

"I'm honored," Jackie said. "What's in it?"

Amy asked, "What would you want to be in it?"

Jackie stood there holding the bag, which was like a lunch bag, but larger, as if it had come from the grocery store. She didn't look inside. She slowly turned and walked toward the grill and Bobby. She paced, thinking. Then she whirled around and pointed at Amy and guessed, "Marshmallows?"

Amy grinned, the first time Tink had ever seen her really, really smile at Jackie. They were just as smart and funny as each other, really, but maybe it was the first time they realized it. "Yup," Amy said. "It's marshmallows. You said you had something on the grill. We didn't know it was just your old valentines."

Tink felt very, very tired, tired and happy. Tired of people. Tired of meanness. Tired of worrying about whether she was mature enough or cool enough or cute enough. She was too tired to be shy and embarrassed at being in the presence of someone adorable. So she decided to just talk to Bobby like he was a normal person, like Bushwhack or somebody. She said to Bobby, "Is it really marshmallows?"

Bobby didn't seem to care or notice that he was in the presence of somebody who wasn't necessarily cute or part of the popular circle at school. "It really is," he said.

Jackie wanted to know, "Whose terrific idea was this?" so much that Tink, who assumed it was Amy's idea, was a little worried that Jackie was going to have to shower approval on Amy, and wouldn't want to.

"Mine, actually," said Bobby. "I wanted to do something you'd really like, and who doesn't like marshmallows?"

It was the first time Tink really liked him. About time, thought Tink, then had to wonder about herself. Was she jealous that Jackie liked him so much? Had it made her be snotty about him? Or had he just not been that likable?

Well, he was likable now. And if Tink hadn't liked him before, he didn't seem to know it. He held out the marshmallow bag to her, and said, "I even found sticks." He had found straightish sticks with short sharp branches just right for holding the marshmallows over the grill.

"Perfect!" she said.

When he smiled at her, she smiled back, and just as quickly realized that she had done so without thinking about it. That was worth a thought in itself. Maybe she could be herself, just Christine B. Gouda, or Tink if she wanted, a hundred percent herself without shredding herself into whoever she had thought she had to be.

All sixth grade, she thought, Jackie had wanted to be in that one circle. Sure, it had been nice of her to have her hand out to Tink to bring her in, too, until Tink was pushed—and pulled herself—away. Because, when had Tink ever liked being in?

Tink glanced up from her marshmallow over the grill at Jackie and Amy and Bobby, then looked down to admire her marshmallow. "Perfect," she said again. It was golden brown and evenly toasted on all its sides. She wondered again which of the kids had written *slut*. She rather suspected Mitzie, although Will Wheeler and stupid Stanley could have done it, too. Now, once and for all, Jackie was out, too, pushed out by whoever was left in there, and Tink didn't think that this time she was going to bother pushing her way back in.

Sixth grade was over, and elementary school was done. Perfect was how things were. Perfect was how she felt. And, if Bushwhack had known, he might even have written that on her class picture frame. Who knew? Maybe he had.

"I need to borrow the phone, Jacqueline," she said.

"Fine, as long as you bring it back," Jackie said. It was her funny joke about the landline in the kitchen.

Nobody laughed. "You said borrow!" Jackie protested.

Tink winked at her.

"Who you calling?" Jackie asked.

"It's a surprise. I'm asking him over."

"But who is it?"

Tink studied Jackie's face, her dark eyes, her hair that had gotten shorter over the spring as she experimented with haircuts. "Who do you think?"

"Matthew Alva," said Jackie. "Matt for short. Bushwhack for long. Technical Support. King of the Farmers."

"You're right," said Tink, looking away. She tried not to let her heart rate increase, but it did.

Bobby said, "Another person with too many names."

"I'm just Christine," said Tink. She stood there with her hands on her hips and watched them all for a reaction.

Amy nodded. "I like it."

Bobby shrugged. "Why not?"

Jackie rolled her eyes. Then she shook her head. "All right, already!" she said. She smiled and shrugged one shoulder. "I wonder what Bushwhack'll think of this group," said Jackie. You could take that two ways.

Tink couldn't help herself. "Is it okay?" she asked.

And Jackie quoted one of Amy's silly phrases, using it in exactly the right place. "Whatever floats your boat," she said.

But Tink didn't just leave it at that. She said, "He does."

★ ★ ★

Tink went in the house and called Bushwhack. "Was it *perfect*?" she asked him.

"Was what perfect?"

"Your hidden word, you walking dictionary."

"No," he said. "You pedestrian crossing. You one-way street. You—"

"Well, it should have been. Simple, everyday words, to go with complicated insults that nobody understands."

"You'll never know," he said. And after a moment he added awkwardly, "So."

She took a breath and went ahead and said it.

"I'm at Jackie's," she said. "We're cooking things on the grill."

"What kind of things?"

"Old valentines. Her picture frame."

"Good idea," said Bushwhack.

"Got anything you need burned? You could come over."

"To Jackie's?" He was incredulous.

"She's going to need some new signatures," Tink said. "She's got mine. If you come, she'll get yours, officially. And tomorrow we can see who else's we can get for her."

"We can—" He stopped. "Okay, that's a cause I can support," he said, sounding formal and uncertain.

She waited, wondering what he would do.

"Are *you* burning anything, Hundred Percent?" he asked.

"Marshmallows," she said. "And my name, in case you weren't sure, is Christine."

"Whatever you say," Bushwhack said. "It's your name. You know what they say."

"You know—Bushwah," she said. "Bushwah to Tink. Bushwah to Chris. Bushwah to Two Words. Do you know where Jackie lives?"

She knew what she was asking. She was asking Bushwhack inside her circle. What gave *her* the right to invite anyone? Well, that was a ridiculous thought, since the circle was now just a diamond or a square or something else small and angular, now that Jackie and Keith Kallinka and Tink—and everyone else in the whole wide world besides Mitzie, Maggie, Meghan, and Will Wheeler were no longer in it. That circle was done, was practically a dot, with those in it facing the empty center, while the rest of them were lines running all over the place, with potential for intersections and new shapes right into infinity.

"Come around back when you get here," she added.

"It's getting late," said Bushwhack. She didn't think his was the kind of house where they would care too much where he went, so she asked herself what he was saying.

"It's not too late," she said. "The sun's still up for hours." She felt him hesitate, and added, "You stopwatch. You second hand. You digital display. You—"

"Okay!" he said, that one word shaded several different colors of realization and gladness. And added, "It is a Hundred Percent still daytime. I'm on my way."

"Don't worry, you haven't missed anything," said Christine. "Just get here as soon as you can."

### THE END

# Acknowledgments

Without BJ, Phil, Lora, and Anne, I would not have had the friendships to write about here. Without BJ's mom Deborah, I might not have had the perspective on being yourself and being a friend.

Without my parents and grandmother and sisters and brother, I might not have understood Tink's solid base of love and kindness.

Without Gail Carson Levine, I might not have had the courage to write this story.

Without Rebecca Stead and Faye Bender, this book might never have gotten finished or sent out or stood up for.

Without Ginee Seo and Taylor Norman, this book might have been less than it is. Thank you to everyone at Chronicle.

And thanks to Mickey, Bethany, Sam, and Emily for being with me through it all.